Marta

Ohio University Press Polish and Polish-American Studies Series

Series Editor: John J. Bukowczyk

Framing the Polish Home: Postwar Cultural Constructions of Hearth, Nation, and Self, edited by Bożena Shallcross

Traitors and True Poles: Narrating a Polish-American Identity, 1880–1939, by Karen Majewski

Auschwitz, Poland, and the Politics of Commemoration, 1945–1979, by Jonathan Huener

The Exile Mission: The Polish Political Diaspora and Polish Americans, 1939–1956, by Anna D. Jaroszyńska-Kirchmann

The Grasinski Girls: The Choices They Had and the Choices They Made, by Mary Patrice Erdmans

Testaments: Two Novellas of Emigration and Exile, by Danuta Mostwin

The Clash of Moral Nations: Cultural Politics in Piłsudski's Poland, 1926–1935, by Eva Plach

Holy Week: A Novel of the Warsaw Ghetto Uprising, by Jerzy Andrzejewski

The Law of the Looking Glass: Cinema in Poland, 1896–1939, by Sheila Skaff

Rome's Most Faithful Daughter: The Catholic Church and Independent Poland, 1914–1939, by Neal Pease

The Origins of Modern Polish Democracy, edited by M. B. B. Biskupski, James S. Pula, and Piotr J. Wróbel

The Borders of Integration: Polish Migrants in Germany and the United States, 1870–1924, by Brian McCook

Between the Brown and the Red: Nationalism, Catholicism, and Communism in Twentieth-Century Poland—The Politics of Bolesław Piasecki, by Mikołaj Stanisław Kunicki

Taking Liberties: Gender, Transgressive Patriotism, and Polish Drama, 1786–1989, by Halina Filipowicz

The Politics of Morality: The Church, the State, and Reproductive Rights in Postsocialist Poland, by Joanna Mishtal

Marta, by Eliza Orzeszkowa, translated by Anna Gąsienica Byrcyn and Stephanie Kraft, with an introduction by Grażyna J. Kozaczka

Writing the Polish American Woman in Postwar Ethnic Fiction, by Grażyna J. Kozaczka

Series Advisory Board

Marta

A Novel

Eliza Orzeszkowa

Translated from the Polish by
Anna Gąsienica Byrcyn and Stephanie Kraft

Introduction by Grażyna J. Kozaczka

OHIO UNIVERSITY PRESS

ATHENS

Ohio University Press, Athens, Ohio 45701
ohioswallow.com
© 2018 by Ohio University Press

To contact the translators: Anna Gąsienica Byrcyn agbyrcyn@gmail.com
Stephanie Kraft dkraft@external.umass.edu

Printed in the United States of America
Ohio University Press books are printed on acid-free paper ⊛ ™

28 27 26 25 24 23 22 21 20 19 18   5 4 3 2 1

Library of Congress Cataloging-in-Publication Data
Names: Orzeszkowa, Eliza, 1842-1910, author. | Gąsienica Byrcyn, Anna,
  translator. | Kraft, Stephanie, translator. | Kozaczka, Grażyna J., author
  of introduction.
Title: Marta : a novel / Eliza Orzeszkowa ; translated from the Polish by
  Anna Gąsienica Byrcyn and Stephanie Kraft ; introduction by Grażyna J.
  Kozaczka.
Other titles: Marta. English
Description: Athens : Ohio University Press, 2018. | Series: Ohio University
  press Polish and Polish-American studies series | Includes bibliographical
  references.
Identifiers: LCCN 2018025200| ISBN 9780821423134 (hc : alk. paper) | ISBN
  9780821446294 (pdf)
Subjects: LCSH: Women--Employment--Fiction.
Classification: LCC PG7158.O7 M313 2018 | DDC 891.8/537--dc23
LC record available at https://lccn.loc.gov/2018025200

The Polish and Polish-American Studies Series is made possible by:

The Polish American Historical Association and the Stanley Kulczycki Publication Fund of the Polish American Historical Association, New Britain, Connecticut,

The Stanislaus A. Blejwas Endowed Chair in Polish and Polish American Studies, Central Connecticut State University, New Britain, Connecticut, and

The Frank and Mary Padzieski Endowed Professorship in Polish/Polish American/Eastern European Studies at the University of Michigan, Dearborn.

Support is also provided by the following individuals:

Thomas Duszak (Benefactor)
George Bobinski (Contributor)
Alfred Bialobrzeski (Friend)
William Galush (Friend)
Col. John A. and Pauline A. Garstka (Friend)
Jonathan Huener (Friend)
Grażyna Kozaczka (Friend)
Neal Pease (Friend)
Mary Jane Urbanowicz (Friend)
Maria Swiecicka-Ziemianek (Friend)

Contents

Series Editor's Preface   ix

A Note on Eliza Orzeszkowa   xi

Introduction   xiii

Guide to Pronunciation   xxvii

Marta   1

Series Editor's Preface

Marta by Eliza Orzeszkowa, reputedly one of the most prominent Polish writers, is an engaging period piece in the social realist genre that details the trials and tribulations of its female protagonist, whose life is upended by the sudden death of her husband. The novel follows the unfortunate woman through her heroic efforts to support herself and her child in a harsh patriarchal society during a period of industrialization and urbanization in nineteenth-century Poland. The novel reveals just how constrained life chances were for a single woman in that world.

Written with considerable narrative verve, the story proceeds briskly, through a series of arresting plot twists, to a final denouement that may surprise and certainly will shake empathetic readers. The feminist sensibilities of the author shine brightly throughout this absorbing book. The story and its star-crossed yet resolute heroine should intrigue general readers interested in period fiction but also provide excellent opportunities for classroom discussion of historical and contemporary—and universal—issues involving gender and class.

This original translation by Anna Gąsienica Byrcyn and Stephanie Kraft is illuminated by an incisive introduction to the work and period by Grażyna Kozaczka, Professor of English at Cazenovia College in Cazenovia, New York. Professor Kozaczka usefully sets the book in historical and literary context and provides a list of questions that can inform discussion as they aid critical consideration of the novel.

Publication of the Ohio University Press Polish and Polish-American Studies Series marks a milestone in the maturation of the Polish Studies field and stands as a fitting tribute to the scholars and organizations whose efforts have brought it to fruition. Supported by a series advisory board of accomplished Polonists and Polish-Americanists, the Polish and Polish American Studies Series has been made possible through generous financial assistance from the Polish American Historical Association and that organization's Stanley Kulczycki Publication Fund, the Stanislaus A. Blejwas Endowed Chair in Polish and Polish American Studies at Central Connecticut State University, and the Frank and Mary Padzieski Endowed Professorship in Polish/Polish American/Eastern European Studies at the University of Michigan, Dearborn, and through institutional support from Wayne State University and Ohio University Press. The series meanwhile has benefited from the warm encouragement of a number of other persons, including Gillian Berchowitz, M. B. B. Biskupski, the late Stanislaus A. Blejwas, Thomas Duszak, Mary Erdmans, Martin Hershock, Rick Huard, Anna Jaroszyńska-Kirchmann, Grażyna Kozaczka, Brian McCook, Anna Muller, Thomas Napierkowski, James S. Pula, and Thaddeus Radzilowski, and from the able assistance of the staff of Ohio University Press. The series also has received generous assistance from a growing list of series supporters, including benefactor Thomas Duszak, contributor George Bobinski, and additional friends of the series including Alfred Bialobrzeski, William Galush, John A. and Pauline A. Garstka, Jonathan Huener, Grażyna Kozaczka, Neal Pease, Maria Swiecicka-Ziemianek, and Mary Jane Urbanowicz. The moral and material support from all of these institutions and individuals is gratefully acknowledged.

John J. Bukowczyk

A Note on Eliza Orzeszkowa

Eliza Orzeszkowa (1841–1910) is one of the most prolific and esteemed Polish prose writers of the nineteenth century. She was nominated for the Nobel Prize in Literature in 1905 together with Leo Tolstoy and Henryk Sienkiewicz, who became the recipient of the prestigious award. Orzeszkowa began her writing career with her short story "Obrazek z lat głodnych" (A picture from the hungry years), published by the literary magazine *Tygodnik ilustrowany* (The illustrated weekly) in 1866. She wrote novels, short stories, and a series of articles and commentaries on education, class discrimination, anti-Semitism, and women's emancipation, all within the frame of Polish literary Positivism.

Orzeszkowa achieved widespread fame at home and abroad with her famous roman-fleuve *Nad Niemnem* (*On the banks of the Niemen*, 1888), which dealt with traditional values of the Polish gentry, issues centering around marriage between members of different classes, and the effects of the January Uprising in Russian-occupied Poland. Throughout her lifetime Orzeszkowa fought for her personal independence by working as a writer, as a teacher at her house in Grodno, which she made available for girls who wanted to pursue their studies under her guidance; and as manager of her own bookstore, which was transformed into a publishing house in Wilno. Her novel *Marta* (1873) presents a widowed heroine facing a grim battle to earn a living in a time when employment opportunities for women were severely restricted; the book is representative of Orzeszkowa's depiction of women and her skill at creating moving and powerful scenes in her fiction. *Marta* explores matters that were vital and close to its author's heart, namely women's education and women's emancipation, which she also discussed in her earlier article "Kilka słów o kobietach" (A few words about women, 1870) and her later novella *Panna Antonina* (*Miss Antonina*, 1891). Orzeszkowa's writings deal with crucial topics that are still at the centers of controversies in many corners of the world today.

Grażyna J. Kozaczka

In her 1898 treatise, *Women and Economics: A Study of the Economic Relation between Men and Women as a Factor in Social Evolution,* Charlotte Perkins Gilman (1860–1935), an American feminist writer and lecturer, clearly identified the differences between opportunities available to either young men or women entering adulthood:

> To the young man confronting life the world lies wide. . . . What he wants to be, he may strive to be. What he wants to get, he may strive to get. . . .
>
> To the young woman confronting life there is the same world beyond, there are the same human energies and human desires and ambition within. But all that she may wish to have, all that she may wish to do, must come through a single channel and a single choice. Wealth, power, social distinction, fame,—not only these, but home and happiness, reputation, ease and pleasure, her bread and butter,—all, must come to her through a small gold ring. This is a heavy pressure.[1]

A quarter century earlier than Perkins Gilman, a Polish author and social reformer, Eliza Orzeszkowa (1841–1910), placed the same issue at the center of her early novel, *Marta* (1873), which tells a story of a twenty-four-year-old widow and mother who gradually learns that the lack of the "small gold ring" makes her economic situation untenable. Orzeszkowa's assessment of the condition of women in late-nineteenth-century patriarchal Poland is just as powerful as are the views expressed by Perkins Gilman. Orzeszkowa writes:

> [A] woman is not a human being, a woman is an object. . . . A woman is a zero if a man does not stand next to her as a completive number. . . . If she does not find someone to buy her, or if she loses him, she is covered with the rust of

perpetual suffering and the taint of misery without remedy. She becomes a zero again, but a zero gaunt from hunger, trembling with cold, tearing at rags in a useless attempt to carry on and improve her lot. . . . There is no happiness for her or bread without a man.[2]

In her novel, Orzeszkowa argues for women's right to economic freedom, to successful and productive lives, to useful and serious education, and to equal employment opportunities. She extols the value of work not only as a means of financial support but also as a means of developing and strengthening character. *Marta* becomes Orzeszkowa's social manifesto. It is a novel of purpose that advances the author's worldview and illustrates it pointedly both with direct authorial commentary and with the story of her eponymous protagonist. This authorial commentary could seem heavy handed at times if it did not testify to the young author's deep engagement in and her passion for the topic. Even before the publication of *Marta*, Orzeszkowa came out with a pamphlet, "Kilka słów o kobietach" (A few words about women) (1870), in which she advocated for sensible education of girls that would prepare them not only for a domestic role as a wife and mother but also for a possible career in the public sphere. Edmund Jankowski in his monograph about Eliza Orzeszkowa argues convincingly that this pamphlet together with *Marta* placed the author in the forefront of the feminist movement in Poland and won her fame.[3]

Orzeszkowa's early life gave little indication of her later espousal of feminist views, fairly radical for traditional Polish society of the early 1870s. She spent her childhood on her father's estate in Milikowszczyzna near Grodno in eastern Poland.[4] Even though her father died when she was only a toddler, his death did not substantively change the family's lifestyle, which was typical of a landed gentry home at the time. Both she and her older sister were educated at home by Polish and foreign-born live-in tutors. In her memoirs, she remembered fondly a Polish teacher who instilled in her and her sister great love for Polish literature and history, but also recalled their intense dislike for a German nanny. Eliza, obviously a precocious child, could not remember a time when she was not able to read both in Polish and in French. She entertained her frequently ailing sister with her own original tales and at the age of seven, she wrote her first novel—a melodrama of crime and guilt. But soon everything changed. By the time she turned ten, her sister died and she was sent to a boarding school in Warsaw where she would spend the next five years. Soon after finishing her formal education, seventeen-year-old Eliza married Piotr Orzeszko, a man twice her age, who owned a neighboring estate. Her own assessment of this period in her life was quite harsh. She wrote, "I was thoughtless and irresponsible. . . . I was nothing but vanity. I was delighted with my beautifully furnished and decorated home, with my clothes, servants, constant visits from friends and young neighbors."[5] Yet it was also then that under the tutelage of several well-educated acquaintances, she began a slow process of self-education by reading voraciously. Her favorite books included classic works of French and Polish literature as well as English Romantics in French translation. She also rediscovered her passion for writing. However, this intense project of self-improvement had for Orzeszkowa some unanticipated results. Within only a couple of years of her marriage, even before she turned twenty, she realized that the lack of any intellectual or emotional connection to her husband made her deeply unhappy. Even though she understood very well that marriage protected her from financial concerns and secured for her a solid social position, she began to consider filing for divorce. What she possibly did not anticipate was that freeing herself from this failed relationship would take many years, would cost her a fortune in high legal expenses, and would expose her to considerable social censure.

Marta, one of Orzeszkowa's early works, is certainly a novel of its times as well as an indirect reflection of the author's life. She chose her protagonist carefully from the ranks of the landed gentry. She understood this class well and knew that many, like herself, were struggling at this difficult time in Polish national and social history. In 1795, almost eighty years before Orzeszkowa published her novel, Poland ceased to exist as an independent country and was partitioned by and absorbed into the three neighboring empires: Russia, Prussia, and Austria.[6] Yet Polish patriots, many of whom hailed from the landed gentry, never accepted the status quo. They continued to fight for the country's independence militarily through armed uprisings as well as culturally through numerous efforts to preserve Polish national identity when language and culture were threatened by the anti-Polish policies of the occupying powers. Orzeszkowa herself became actively involved in the tragic January Uprising of 1863/64 that erupted in the Russian-controlled territory of Poland.

The mid-nineteenth-century political crisis in the Russian empire rekindled Polish hopes for regaining independence. Polish patriots organized numerous clandestine networks in the Russian-controlled Congress

Kingdom of Poland (1815–67)[7] with its capital in Warsaw. The sole purpose of such organizations was to fight for freedom and liberate Poland from foreign domination. Beginning in 1860, a series of patriotic street demonstrations erupted in Warsaw and continued into the following year, when in February marchers were attacked and shot at by Russian troops. The funerals of the five fatally shot demonstrators became a spark for further patriotic actions. The Russian-appointed governor of the Congress Kingdom, concerned about the volatility of the situation, planned to preempt any organized Polish insurrection by announcing conscription to the tsarist army. Such forced military service would cripple the conspirators by removing all able-bodied Polish young men from their ranks. This decision achieved the opposite effect, forcing Polish underground organizations to call Poles to arms and announce on January 22, 1863, the commencement of a Polish armed uprising against Russia.

For more than a year and a half, Polish insurrectionists fought the Russian army.[8] Unfortunately, even with the support of their compatriots from the other two partitions as well as help from Polish émigrés abroad, they were not able to construct a regular Polish army and defeat the Russians. Polish volunteer forces were outnumbered approximately two to one by the regular Russian army. The January Uprising was a valiant patriotic effort that mobilized the entire society, as both men and women of all classes bore arms. The Jewish population also joined in this military effort. In addition, the revolutionaries were supported by an even larger number of Poles in noncombatant roles who helped by supplying food and clothing for the soldiers, caring for the wounded, and burying the dead. Unfortunately, in the end Polish volunteer forces succumbed to the regular Russian army. In addition to the casualties incurred during the heroic but often hopeless battles, the Russian reprisals after the defeat of the uprising further devastated the country and exposed its population to redoubled Russification efforts. This led many Poles to reconsider the value of armed resistance in the existing geopolitical situation and to shift their goals. Rebuilding Poland's economy, strengthening its social structures, and preserving Polish culture became their premier objectives.

In her memoirs published posthumously in book form as *O sobie* (About myself, 1970), Orzeszkowa considered the effects of the trauma of the failed January Uprising on her and her generation. She described herself as a twenty-year-old witness to a national and social catastrophe:

I saw houses, which until recently brimmed with energy and activity, become swept clean of all signs of life as if during some deadly medieval plague. Deep in the woods, I saw mass graves hiding corpses of young men with whom I had so recently danced. I saw gallows, fear in the faces of the condemned . . . and the long lines of shackled prisoners on their way to Siberian exile being followed by their despairing families.[9]

Orzeszkowa understood very well that this national tragedy shook Polish social structure as well as gender balance. Thousands of women—wives, mothers, daughters, sisters, and fiancées of the fallen or imprisoned heroes whose estates were confiscated by the occupying government—were reduced to poverty and left without means of support. The women, who had been trained exclusively for the domestic sphere, suddenly found themselves forced to seek employment for which they were sadly unprepared. In Orzeszkowa's novel, even though Marta loses her husband to an illness and not to the armed struggle, she shares the fate of these desperate genteel women whom she encounters in employment agencies and in garment sweatshops.

The immediate aftermath of the January Uprising marked also a personal turning point for Orzeszkowa and contributed to the development of her writing career. She invested heavily in this patriotic enterprise of Polish independence. She served the military cause by taking up the important and very dangerous job of a courier responsible for securing lines of communication between different clandestine cells. Understandably, after the failure of the uprising, her despair at the scope of the national tragedy and the realization of the hopelessness of the political situation led her to reassess her own life and mission in society. Even though she was spared punitive measures for her active participation in the uprising, her husband was sentenced to exile to a penal colony in Siberia. In a rash decision that she would regret for the rest of her life, she refused to follow him into exile and would eventually divorce him. She did not love Piotr, and as she explained later, she did not know then that she should have sacrificed her own happiness in order to support the man who suffered for Poland.

With her husband in exile, Orzeszkowa quickly learned about financial difficulties. The expensive and lengthy divorce proceedings cost her the estate she inherited from her parents. Even the personal happiness she dreamt of appeared elusive. Her romantic relationship with Dr. Zbigniew Święcicki became impossible due to social pressure. Such a complicated personal life increased her sensitivity to the situation of single women in a society that neither respected nor provided a safety net for them. Likewise, she gained awareness of the constraints placed specifically on women of her social class and learned of the price women paid for breaking social rules and taboos. She, like her protagonist Marta, desired to work in order to support herself. She wrote in her memoirs that she dreamt of becoming a teacher or possibly a telegraph operator in Warsaw, the capital of Poland then under Russian occupation. Her fluency in several languages qualified her for a job at the telegraph office, yet her application was rejected because she was Polish. She recorded in her memoir, "After I returned home, every memory of this humiliation caused me to shake with anger. How was it possible that in Warsaw, we Polish women had no right to work."[10] She explained that at the time her attempts to find employment were not particularly rooted in the emancipation ideology, but instead were necessitated by economic reality. As a divorced woman without a steady income from a landed estate, she needed to work just to survive.

The ideological awareness came a little later, especially after the publication of *Marta*, when the reaction of her female readers made her realize that she had hit a nerve. The fictional situation of her protagonist was a reality for thousands of Polish genteel women, whose lives had been changed by the loss of estates due to punitive confiscation or poor management in the changing economy and who suddenly found themselves, like Marta, needing to earn a living. Orzeszkowa wrote,

> For the first time I began receiving letters from women who were strangers, belonged to different social circles, were of different ages and talents, but they were all thanking me for this book and asking me for practical advice. Many readers told me that they reacted emotionally to this novel and became extremely fearful about their own future. Many began to seek education and work.[11]

Orzeszkowa's novel about a young Polish widow resonated with many women all across Europe. Shortly after its publication, *Marta* was translated into several languages including Russian, German, Czech, Swedish, Dutch, and even Esperanto.[12]

Eliza Orzeszkowa selected the city of Warsaw[13] as the setting of her novel probably as a response to the social changes she observed, and especially to the growth of middle-class culture. She knew the city from the time she attended boarding school there. However, since the school was run by a women's religious order exclusively for the daughters of the landed gentry, students probably had limited opportunities to explore the entire city and very few occasions to interact with its inhabitants. Yet it was in Warsaw that Orzeszkowa solidified her devotion to Polish freedom and her involvement with the issues of social justice. The early 1860s marked significant political, social, and economic upheaval in Warsaw and in the entire Congress Kingdom, which became completely absorbed into the Russian empire after the failure of the January Uprising. Norman Davies argues that changes including population growth, urbanization, and industrialization in parts of the Russian partition were stimulated by the decree issued by the Tsar in 1864 granting emancipation to Polish peasants. Now free of serfdom and for the first time owners of the land they worked on, peasants became more prosperous, increased in number, and started migrating to urban centers, mainly to Warsaw, or abroad in search of employment, thus fueling the growth of the urban working class. In addition, because of the elimination of tariffs, "the products of Polish industry could penetrate the vast Russian market."[14] Warsaw grew in population and became a fairly important center of industry, and even though it could not compete with the economies of the Polish western cities under Prussian rule, Davies contends that the progress achieved by Polish urban economies far surpassed the development of Ukraine and central Russia.[15] This modest progress notwithstanding, the Polish population remained generally resentful of the foreign rule.

Like many fiction writers of her time, Eliza Orzeszkowa saw herself as both a student of the society and its mentor. It is not surprising, then, that in *Marta* she brings her protagonist into contact with several distinct strata of Polish society while at the same time Marta's own social standing undergoes an important evolution. Like Orzeszkowa, she is born into the landed gentry. But both of them, Marta through her marriage and Orzeszkowa through her divorce, migrate to the Polish intelligentsia, an educated class for the most part descended from the gentry. However, while Orzeszkowa's literary talent and the commercial success of her novels kept her well positioned within the intelligentsia, Marta eventually descends into the working class only to end up among the destitute. In her search for employment and in her daily struggles to survive, Marta's encounters might point to the author's sympathies and preferences. While the young woman meets many kind and generous representatives of her own class, the intelligentsia, and receives some support from a few sympathetic working-class characters, Orzeszkowa focuses her social critique on the bourgeoisie, represented in the novel by the rapacious, and even cruel, owners of the garment shops and workrooms. Marta never interacts with any representatives of the Russian occupying forces, and readers might be hard pressed to realize that Warsaw at the time was not a free capital of a free country. It is possible that this was a deliberate decision on Orzeszkowa's part not only because of her single-minded focus on women's issues but also in an attempt to ensure the novel's open and legal circulation without any interference from Russian censors.

In general, Orzeszkowa pays very little attention to the uniqueness of her novel's setting. The city exists as a vague background to her protagonist's lonely struggle for survival. The reader's perception of urban spaces becomes limited to Marta's unhappy experiences. When the city is not mediated by her husband, it takes on a menacing quality. Its ever-present disquieting din intensifies Marta's yearning for the past by bringing back her memories of the idyllic childhood on her father's country estate and the blissful and carefree years of her marriage. At present, the streets of Warsaw seem to Marta at best indifferent, if not openly hostile. They are populated by servants, landlords, shop owners, sweatshop operators, shop assistants, artisans, men-about-town, intellectuals, and even high-class prostitutes who both individually and collectively fail Marta. To authenticate her novel's setting, Orzeszkowa names a few well-known Warsaw streets and some churches, but she takes care not to turn Marta's story into an exotic and uniquely Warsovian or even Polish plot. In this novel of purpose, Orzeszkowa's primary focus is to illuminate women's economic and sexual vulnerability and the failure of society to allow women equal participation in the economy.

Eliza Orzeszkowa introduces her protagonist at Marta's most vulnerable moment, soon after her husband's funeral, when she must move out of her comfortable upper-middle-class home to a substandard lodging in a poor neighborhood, and when she comes to a realization of her complete financial ruin. She is destitute. This young woman who must support both herself and her small daughter has absolutely no assets left after her husband's illness and death, she has no living relatives or friends who could offer help, and her father's estate has been lost to bankruptcy. Orzeszkowa uses this initial situation to highlight several social issues that stem from women's disempowerment. As a woman of her class, Marta has not been educated but rather has been groomed to fulfill the role of a wife and mother and thus perpetuate the patriarchal power structure. Her search for employment reveals her total lack of any marketable skills and qualifications. Even though she is a natural artist and an intuitive writer, her skills were never developed through rigorous education. She can speak French, but not very well; she can draw, but not very well; and she can write, but not very well. She is not able to compete in a tight job market because she has not been prepared for an eventuality of not achieving her success through, as Perkins Gilman put it, "a small gold ring." Even though she meets many kind individuals who are willing to provide charity, nobody can offer practical solutions to her situation because the problem is not unique to Marta but systemic.

Marta's job search teaches her also about gender and class discrimination, social norms that women cannot transgress with impunity, prejudice against working mothers, the lack of good-quality child care, abominable working conditions and worker exploitation in sweatshops, cruelty in relationships with other women, and the double standard. She learns about the victimization of women by sexual predators who prey on the weak and vulnerable and shirk their responsibility for destroyed lives. She is shocked to realize that a young man will be admired for having numerous affairs or even keeping an expensive mistress, but a young woman's reputation will be irreparably damaged by nothing more than being seen engaged in a conversation with a man in a public space.

Through Marta's story and a detailed analysis of her changing emotional states and responses, Eliza Orzeszkowa traces a young woman's journey of self-discovery from her carefree childlike persona controlled by her father and later her husband to independent, responsible adulthood. It is also a process that allows Marta to move beyond self and develop social consciousness. At first, she understands failure exclusively in personal terms—if only she had gained the skills required, she could have kept the job. But facing repeated disappointments leads her to recognize the restrictive power of social norms placed on women, especially on women of her class. Through this heart-wrenching process, Marta, originally so clearly identified with the upper classes of Polish society, begins to appreciate and understand the suffering of the economically dispossessed. She rages against the society that prevents her and many other women from fulfilling their sacred responsibility to themselves as well as to their children, from realizing their dreams of a fulfilled life and motherhood, and even from sustaining physical survival. How much more powerful this realization is than the awakening Edna Pontellier experiences in Kate Chopin's feminist novel *The Awakening* (1899).[16] After all, Edna's journey of self-discovery, no matter how emotionally draining, is not hindered by the real existential issues that Marta faces. Edna, who is financially secure, whose children are cared for by a doting grandmother, and whose friends offer her emotional support, has the luxury to focus exclusively on her own psychological growth. Marta, a single and isolated mother, must find a job and earn a living to save her seriously ill child, for whom she cannot provide nutritious food, medicine, or even a warm bed. Orzeszkowa's message is driven home over and over again: Marta succeeds in gaining psychological and social maturity, but society destroys her. The tragic resolution of the novel suggests that Orzeszkowa cannot identify a safe social space for this changed Marta. She appears to pose too much of a threat to the patriarchal status quo.

During her lifetime, Eliza Orzeszkowa was a popular writer and a contender for the Nobel Prize in literature, and her literary legacy earned her a prominent place in the history of Polish literature. Together with such writers as Aleksander Świętochowski, Maria Konopnicka, and Bolesław Prus, she represents the Polish Positivist movement. Tracing their ideological roots back to the philosophy of Auguste Comte and Herbert Spencer, Positivists asserted that by the mid-nineteenth century, the world entered a period of systematic and continuous growth evidenced by numerous scientific discoveries grounded in experiment and reason. They perceived societies as living organisms to be described and analyzed using the language of natural sciences. In Poland, such theories fell on fertile ground after yet another failure of armed struggle, the January Uprising, to regain independence. The Polish intellectual elite, the intelligentsia, found Positivist ideas very attractive as they justified the rejection of military actions in favor of refocusing attention on rebuilding Polish society and ensuring that cultural connections persisted in the nation split among three separate foreign empires. Positivists set their goal on organic work that involved using only legal means to achieve the cultural and economic growth of Polish society.

Positivist ideals permeate Orzeszkowa's literary output. In addition to women's issues, Eliza Orzeszkowa focused on social improvement, education, and promoting self-fulfillment through hard work. Her interest in problems of her times led her to study the Jewish minority and resulted in two novels, *Eli Makower* (1875) and *Meir Ezofowicz* (1878). *Meir Ezofowicz* is especially interesting. Its title character, a young and sensitive Jew, rebels against his narrow-minded community. Undoubtedly, her greatest literary achievement was the publication in 1888 of her masterpiece *Nad Niemnem* (*On the Banks of the Niemen*), a beautifully written family novel that outlined Orzeszkowa's Positivist social plans. The novel's heroine, a young but impoverished genteel woman, has the courage to break social barriers by marrying an uneducated yet naturally intelligent and patriotic farmer. Through this marriage, she will bring education and progress to the whole village community, thus building a strong Polish society, which will be ready for independence when the time comes. Published almost twenty-five years after the disastrous end of the January Uprising in 1864, this novel suggests ways of coming to terms with a national tragedy of such magnitude.

In her personal life, Eliza Orzeszkowa continued to search for love and happiness, with mixed results. After being rebuffed by a much younger man for whom she formed a decidedly one-sided attachment, she finally found fulfillment in a relationship with Stanisław Nahorski, a well-known lawyer. Yet even this relationship was not without heartache. Nahorski was already married when he met Orzeszkowa, and he was unwilling to divorce his seriously ill wife. Orzeszkowa and Nahorski married only after his wife's death. He was sixty-eight and she was fifty-three. Orzeszkowa continued writing and lecturing on social issues until her death in 1910. She devoted her entire life to the work for public good.[17]

Taking up a novel of social reform written almost 150 years ago, in a far-away country and in very different sociopolitical circumstances, we might be tempted to dismiss it as a quaint historical document replete with nineteenth-century melodrama. Yet the typical melodramatic tropes—the unambiguously drawn conflict between good and evil set on the stage of a "modern metropolis";[18] the effusive expressions of feelings; and the presence of stock characters who may not have deep "psychological complexity,"[19] such as wealthy villains and beleaguered heroines whose virtue is constantly tested—should not to be discounted altogether. As argued eloquently by Kelleter and Mayer, "the melodramatic mode has always lent itself to stories of power struggles and to enactments of socio-cultural processes of marginalization and stratification."[20] Thus, it is hardly surprising that in *Marta*, Eliza Orzeszkowa successfully links the realistic with the melodramatic[21] and employs this strategy to critique patriarchal power relations that marginalize women. She does not allow us to easily file away her ideas and concerns. While reading *Marta*, we are repeatedly struck by the author's approach to women's issues, which is decidedly contemporary— so much so, that we still struggle with many issues she outlined so long ago: the inequality in earnings between men and women, the lack of affordable child care, the educational difficulties that girls face in many countries, and the existence of the glass ceiling women still have not managed to shatter. Eliza Orzeszkowa's *Marta* still has a message for us and still calls us to action.

Notes

1. Charlotte Perkins Gilman, *Women and Economics: A Study of the Economic Relation between Men and Women as a Factor in Social Evolution* (Boston: Small, Maynard & Company, 1898), 71.

2. Eliza Orzeszkowa, *Marta*, transl. Anna Gąsienica Byrcyn and Stephanie Kraft, intro. by Grażyna J. Kozaczka (Athens: Ohio University Press, 2018), 000.

3. Edmund Jankowski, *Eliza Orzeszkowa* (Warsaw: Państwowy Instytut Wydawniczy, 1964), 150–51.

4. Now in Belarus.

5. Eliza Orzeszkowa, *O sobie* (Warsaw: Czytelnik, 1974), 43–44. All translations from Polish-language publications are provided by the author of this introduction.

6. Poland regained independence in 1918.

7. The date of the dissolution of the Congress Kingdom of Poland has been disputed.

8. The tragedy of the January Uprising was captured by the Polish painter Artur Grottger (1837–1867) in a series of nine black-and-white drawings titled "Polonia." These illustrations are housed in the Museum of Fine Arts in Budapest, Hungary, and can be easily viewed online (http://www.pinakoteka.zascianek.pl/Grottger /Grottger_Pol.htm).

9. Orzeszkowa, *O sobie*, 102.

10. Ibid., 107.

11. Ibid., 110.

12. Jankowski, 154.

13. Ignacy Aleksander Gierymski (1850–1901), also known as Aleksander Gierymski, a Polish artist of the late nineteenth century, painted contemporary urban views of Warsaw.

14. Norman Davies, *Heart of Europe: A Short History of Poland* (Oxford: Oxford University Press, 1984), 170.

15. Ibid., 171.

16. Both Kate Chopin's novel *The Awakening* and Charlotte Perkins Gilman's short story "The Yellow Wall-Paper" can be useful companion texts to *Marta,* as all three illuminate powerful social forces restricting a woman's ability to construct an autonomous and fulfilled self. Each uses different narrative techniques to achieve a similar goal and to reach a strikingly similar conclusion. Perkins Gilman in her book *Women in Economics* suggests some solutions to the problem of women's economic disempowerment that could also provide interesting material for a comparison with Orzeszkowa's proposed solutions.

17. Further information about Orzeszkowa's life and work can be found in Józef Bachórz, introduction to Eliza Orzeszkowa, *Nad Niemnem* (Wrocław: Zakład Narodowy im. Ossolińskich, 1996); Grażyna Borkowska, *Pozytywiści i inni* (Warsaw: PWN, 1996); Grażyna Borkowska, *Alienated Women: A Study on Polish Women's Fiction, 1845–1918,* transl. Ursula Phillips (Budapest: Central European University Press, 2001); Jan Detko, *Orzeszkowa wobec tradycji narodowo-wyzwoleńczych* (Warsaw: Czytelnik, 1965).

18. Peter Brooks, *The Melodramatic Imagination: Balzac, Henry James, Melodrama, and the Mode of Excess* (New York: Columbia University Press, 1985), 13.

19. Ibid., 16.

20. Frank Kelleter and Ruth Mayer, "The Melodramatic Mode Revisited: An Introduction," in *Melodrama! The Mode of Excess from Early America to Hollywood,* ed. Frank Kelleter, Barbara Krah, and Ruth Mayer (Heidelberg: Universitatsverlag Winter, 2007), 9.

21. More information about the connections between realism and melodrama can be found in Neil Hultgren, *Melodramatic Imperial Writing: From the Sepoy Rebellion to Cecil Rhodes* (Athens: Ohio University Press, 2014).

Questions for Further Discussion and Writing

1. What social, political, and familial forces shape Marta's character and life? Are they responsible for her tragic end?

2. How do some of the novel's episodic female characters manage to subvert male power and achieve substantial financial success? What do they sacrifice in pursuit of their success?

3. Orzeszkowa's *Marta* illustrates the oppressive power of patriarchy that is detrimental to a healthy development of all members of society. How does the author present the system of power relations between men and women and the disempowerment of women? What attitudes toward patriarchal oppression do her female characters represent?

4. Marta has a very keen moral sense, and the necessity to transgress her moral code causes her great anguish. What is the source of Marta's moral code, given that Orzeszkowa does not characterize her as a religious person?

5. Is Marta's tragic fate at the end of the novel a predictable and logical outcome of her story? What is the root cause of Marta's tragedy, and could it have been averted?

6. In her search for employment, Marta meets several kind men and women who attempt to help her, yet each time their efforts are in vain. Why? What prevents them from solving Marta's problem?

7. Marta's childhood friend Karolina uses men to secure a comfortable lifestyle for herself. What is Marta's view of such an arrangement, and does she pass a moral judgment on Karolina? What does the novel suggest about the sexual vulnerability of women?

8. What are Orzeszkowa's views on motherhood?

9. Orzeszkowa's passion for her topic influenced her narrative technique. She repeatedly interrupts the flow of her narrative by including authorial commentary and analysis. Does this technique still appeal to contemporary readers?

10. How does Orzeszkowa connect gender and class as two powerful forces oppressing Polish women in the late nineteenth century? Was this a specifically Polish intersection of oppression or a broader problem highlighted in other literatures?

11. What does Orzeszkowa's *Marta* contribute to the feminist conversation of the late nineteenth and early twentieth centuries?

12. Some literary critics analyze the tragic outcomes of such feminist texts as Kate Chopin's *The Awakening* and Charlotte Perkins Gilman's "The Yellow Wall-Paper" in terms of the character's personal triumph. Could the ending of Orzeszkowa's *Marta* be described as Marta's victory? Why or why not?

Guide to Pronunciation

The following key provides a guide to the pronunciation of Polish words and names.

a is pronounced as in *father*

c as ts, as in *cats*

ch as guttural h, as in German BACH

cz as hard ch, as in *church*

g (always hard), as in *get*

i as ee, as in *meet*

j as y, as in *yellow*

rz as hard zh, as in French *jardin*

sz as hard sh, as in *ship*

szcz as hard shch, as in *fresh cheese*

u as oo, as in *boot*

w as v, as in *vat*

ć as soft ch, as in *cheap*

ś as soft sh, as in *sheep*

ż as hard zh, as in French *jardin*

ź as soft zh, as in *seizure*

ó as oo, as in *boot*

ą as a nasal, as in French *bon*

ę as a nasal, as in French *vin* or *fin*

ł as w, as in *way*

ń as ny, as in *canyon*

The accent in Polish words almost always falls on the penultimate syllable.

Marta

A woman's life is an eternal burning flame of love, some people say.

A woman's life is renunciation, others claim.

A woman's life is motherhood, cry those who take that view.

A woman's life is pleasure and amusement, still others joke.

A woman's chief virtue is blind trust, all agree, speaking in chorus.

Women believe blindly, love, devote themselves to others, raise children, amuse themselves . . . hence they live up to everything the world demands of them. Yet the world looks at them awry and responds to them now and then with reproaches or admonitions:

"Things are not well with you!"

The more knowing, intelligent, or unhappy women look inside themselves or at the world around them and repeat:

"Things are not well with us!"

For every ill there must be a remedy. Some see it in one thing and some in another, but no prescription cures the sickness.

Not long ago, one of the most justly respected writers in our country (Mr. Zachariasiewicz in his novel *Albina*) stated publicly that women are morally and physically ill because there is a lack of great love among them (for men, naturally).

Heavens! What a great injustice!

May the rosy god Eros fly to our aid and affirm that our entire life is nothing more than incense burned incessantly in his honor!

Since we were knee-high, we have heard that our destiny is to love one of these lords of creation. As young girls we dream of this lord and master every evening when the moon shines or the stars twinkle; and every morning when snowy lilies open their fragrant goblets to the sun, we dream and sigh.

We sigh until the moment when we are free to turn, like lilies to the sun, toward the one who, in our imaginations, emerges from the misty morning clouds or the flood of moonlight as the figure of Adonis sleeping in secrecy. Then . . . what then? Adonis steps down from the clouds, he becomes a man, we exchange rings with him and we marry. This is also an act of love, although the author mentioned above, in his nonetheless beautiful novels, insists that it is always and unalterably a mere act of calculation.

We do not entirely agree with him. It may be an act of calculation in exceptional circles and circumstances, but it is most commonly an act of love. What kind of love? This is a different and very delicate matter requiring much discussion, but it is enough to say that when we go to the altar, veiling our diffident faces in white muslin and coils of tulle, the charming Eros flies before us, brandishing a torch with rosy flames above our heads.

And then? What then? We love again . . . if not the lord of creation who revealed himself in a dream to a young girl and put a wedding ring on a virgin's finger, then a different one, and if we do not love anyone, then we long to love. We dry up, we develop consumption, we become termagants because of our desire to love.

And what comes of all that? Some of us indeed fly through our whole lives enfolded in the wings of the god of love, honest, virtuous, and happy. But others more numerous, by far more numerous, walk on earth with bleeding feet, struggling for bread, peace, and virtue, weeping copiously, suffering greatly, sinning sorely, falling into the abyss of shame, dying from hunger.

The remedy embodied in the word "l o v e," then, does not cure all illnesses.

It may be that one more ingredient should be added for the remedy to be effective.

What ingredient?

Perhaps a page from a woman's life will tell.

||I

On a beautiful autumn day not many years ago, Graniczna Street, a lively street in Warsaw, was filled with people. They were walking and riding, hurrying as business or pleasure dictated, without glancing to the left or to the right—without paying any attention at all to what was happening in one of the adjacent courtyards.

The courtyard was clean and quite large, surrounded by high brick buildings on all four sides. The building farthest from the street was the smallest, yet its large windows and wide entrance, set off by a handsome porch, suggested that the dwelling inside was comfortable and attractively decorated.

A young woman with a very pale face, dressed in mourning, stood on the porch. She was not wringing her hands, but they dangled helplessly, as if she were profoundly sad and distressed. A four-year-old girl, equally pale and also in mourning, clung to them.

Over the wide, clean stairs leading from the upper floor of the building, people in heavy clothes and heavy, dusty shoes descended continuously. They were porters carrying furnishings from a residence that was not large and elegant, but had been pleasant and tastefully appointed. There were mahogany beds, couches and armchairs covered in crimson woolen damask, graceful wardrobes and chests, even several consoles inlaid with marble, a few large mirrors, two enormous oleander trees in pots, and a datura on whose branches a few white blossoms still hung like chalices. The porters carried all these things down the stairs, passing the woman on the porch. They arranged them on the pavement of the courtyard, placed them on two wagons standing near the gate, or carried them out to the street.

The woman stood motionless, glancing at every piece of furniture that was being taken from her. It was clear that the objects she was leaving behind had not only material value for her; she was parting with them as with the still-visible signs of the vanished and irretrievable past, the mute witnesses of lost happiness. The pale, dark-eyed child pulled harder at her mother's dress.

"Mama!" she whispered. "Look! Papa's desk!"

The porters carried a large, masculine desk down the stairs and put it on a wagon. It was handsomely carved, adorned with a gallery back, and covered in green cloth. The woman in mourning looked at it for a long time and the child pointed to it with a thin finger.

"Mama!" whispered the girl. "Do you see that big black stain on Papa's desk? I remember how it got there. Papa was sitting in front of the desk holding me on his knees, and you, Mama, came in and wanted to take me away from him. He laughed and did not hand me to you. I was playing and spilled the ink. Papa was not angry. He was good. He was never angry at me or at you . . ."

The child whispered these words with her little face hidden in the folds of her mother's mourning dress and her tiny body huddling up to the woman's knees. It was evident that memories were exerting their power over her childish heart, wrenching it with pain of which she was not fully aware.

Two large tears fell from the woman's eyes, which had been dry until now; her child's words had evoked the memory of a moment once lost among millions of similar everyday moments. Now she smiled at the unhappy child—smiled with a mixture of delight and bitterness at the thought of that lost paradise. It may even have occurred to her that the freedom and joy of that moment were being paid for today with the last bites of bread that were left for her and her child, and would be paid for tomorrow with hunger; the ink stain that had appeared amid the laughter of the child and the kisses of her parents would lower the value of the desk by more than a dozen złotys.

After the desk, a Krall piano appeared in the courtyard, but the woman in mourning looked at it indifferently. Probably she was not a musician, and the instrument awakened the fewest regrets and memories. But when a small mahogany bed with a colorful yarn quilt was taken out of the house and put on a wagon, her eyes were riveted to it, and the child burst into tears.

"My bed, Mama!" she cried. "Those people are taking my bed and the coverlet you made for me! I do not want them to take it! Mama, take my bed and my coverlet back from them!"

The woman's only reply was to press the head of the crying child more firmly to her knees. Her beautiful black, deep-set eyes were dry again and her pale, delicate lips were pursed and silent.

The child's pretty bed was the last piece of furniture to be taken out. The gate was open wide; the wagons filled with furniture were driven out into the pleasant street, followed by porters carrying the remaining items on their shoulders. Behind the windows of the neighboring houses, the heads of people who had been looking curiously at the courtyard vanished.

A young woman in a coat and hat came down the stairs and stood in front of the person in mourning.

"Madam," she said, "I have taken care of everything. I paid those who were supposed to be paid. Here is the rest of the money." And she handed the woman a small roll of banknotes.

The woman slowly turned her head toward her.

"Thank you, Zofia," she said quietly. "You have been very good to me."

"Madame, you were always good to me!" the girl cried. "I have worked for you for four years and no place was ever better, or ever will be better, than with you."

She rubbed her wet eyes with a hand on which the marks of the needle and the iron were visible, but the woman seized her rough hand and pressed it firmly between her own small white ones.

"And now, Zofia," she said, "be well."

"Madame, I will go with you to the new apartment," the girl exclaimed. "I will call a cab."

A quarter of an hour later the two women and the child got out of the cab in front of a building on Piwna Street. The four-story tenement was narrow in front, but tall. It looked old and sad. Little Jasia stared at its walls and windows with wide eyes.

"Mama, will we live here?"

"Here, my child," the woman in mourning replied in a voice that was always quiet. She turned to the concierge who was standing in the gateway.

"Please give me the key to the apartment that I rented two days ago."

"Ah! In the attic, surely," the concierge replied. "Please follow me upstairs, madame. I will open it right away."

The small, square courtyard was surrounded by a blind wall of brick red on two sides and, on the other two, by old woodsheds and granaries. The women and the child went into the building and started up the narrow, dark, dirty stairs. The younger woman took the child in her arms and went ahead; the woman in mourning followed her.

The room whose door the concierge opened was quite large, but low and dark, and poorly lit by one small window that opened onto the roof. The walls, which smelled of dampness from a fresh covering of whitewash, seemed to contract under the slanted ceiling.

In the corner next to the simple brick cooking stove was a small hearth. Across the room a wardrobe of modest size stood in front of one wall. There was a bed without a frame, a couch covered with torn calico, and a table painted black. There were several yellow chairs with sagging rush seats that were partly ripped away.

The woman in mourning stopped for a moment on the threshold, surveyed the room with a long, slow glance, then took a few steps forward and sank down on the couch. The child stood still and pale next to her mother and gazed around with surprise and fear in her eyes.

The younger woman dismissed the driver, who had brought two small leather bags from the carriage. She bustled about, taking things out of the bags and arranging them. There were not many things, and it took only a short time to put them in order. Without taking off her coat and hat, she put a few very small dresses and some underclothing in one of the bags, then moved the other one, which was empty, to the corner of the room. She made the bed with two pillows and a woolen coverlet and hung a white curtain in the window. She put several plates and cups, a clay water pitcher and a large bowl, a brass candleholder and a small samovar into a cupboard. Then she took a bundle of wood from behind the stove and made a cheerful fire in the fireplace.

"Ah, yes," she said, rising from her knees and turning her face, which was rosy from blowing on the fire, to the motionless woman. "I have made the fire and you will soon have warmth and light in here. Behind the stove you will find enough wood for about two weeks. The dresses and underclothes are in the bag. The kitchen crockery and dining dishes are in the cupboard, and a candle in a holder is there as well."

The honest servant forced herself to speak cheerfully, but the smile was vanishing from her lips and her eyes were filling with tears.

"And now"—she said more quietly, folding her hands—"and now, my dear lady, I must go!"

The woman in mourning lifted her head.

"You must go, Zofia," she repeated. "Indeed you must." Glancing through the window, she added, "It is growing dark. You will be afraid to walk through the city at night."

"Oh, no, my dear lady!" the girl exclaimed. "I would walk to the end of the world in the darkest night for you. But my new employers leave Warsaw very early in the morning, and they have ordered me to return before nightfall. I have to go because they will need me this evening."

With those words the young servant bent down, took the woman's pale hand and would have raised it to her lips. But the woman suddenly rose and threw both her arms around the girl's neck. They wept. The child also burst into tears and seized the servant's linen coat.

"Do not go, Zofia!" she wailed. "Do not go! It is so horrible here! It is so dreary!"

The girl kissed her former employer's hands and pressed the child to her bosom.

"I must go. I must!" she repeated, sobbing. "My mother is poor and I have little sisters. I have to work for them . . ."

The woman in mourning raised her white face and held her thin figure erect.

"Zofia, I will also work," she said in a more assured voice than before. "I have a child and I should work for her."

"May God not abandon you, and may He bless you, my dear, kind lady!" the servant girl cried, once again kissing the hands of the mother and the tearful face of the child. She ran out of the room without looking back.

After the girl's departure, a deep silence filled the room. It was interrupted only by the crackling of the fire and the dull, indistinct street noise that reached the attic. The woman in mourning sat on the couch. The child cried at first, then nestled quietly on the mother's bosom and fell asleep. The woman rested her head on her hand; her arm embraced the tiny figure sleeping on her knees and her eyes stared unswervingly at the flickering firelight.

Now that her faithful, devoted servant was gone, she would not see again the face of the last human being who had been a witness to her past—the last support that had remained for her after the disappearance of everything that had helped and sustained her. Now she was alone, subject to the power of fate and the hardships of a lonely destiny, dependent on the strength of her own hands and brain. Her only companion was this small, weak being who found rest on no bosom but hers, demanded kisses from her lips, and expected nourishment from her hand. Her house, which her loving husband had once provided for her and which she had now been forced to abandon, was welcoming new residents within its walls. The kind, beloved man who had surrounded her with love and prosperity was resting in his grave.

Everything had passed: love, prosperity, peace, the joy of life. The only traces of this unhappy woman's past, now vanishing like a dream, were her painful memories and this pale, thin child who now opened her eyes after a short sleep, threw her arms around the woman's neck and, touching her face with her little lips, whispered:

"Mama! Give me something to eat!"

Her request did not yet arouse fear or sadness in the mother's heart. The widow reached into her pocket and took out a purse containing several banknotes—the only fortune left to her and her daughter. She threw a shawl around her shoulders, told the child to wait calmly for her return, and left the room.

Halfway down the stairs she met the concierge, who was carrying a bundle of wood to one of the apartments on the second floor.

"Dear sir," the widow said politely and timidly, "could you bring some milk and rolls for my child from a nearby shop?"

The concierge listened without stopping, then turned his head and replied with barely concealed unwillingness:

"And who has the time now to go for milk and rolls? It's not my job here to bring food to the tenants."

He vanished behind the curve of the wall. The widow made her way down the stairs.

"He did not want to help me," she thought, "because he thinks I am poor. He was carrying a heavy load of wood to those he expected to pay him for it."

She went to the courtyard and glanced around.

"And why is madame looking around?" someone said in a hoarse, unpleasant voice very near her.

The widow saw a woman standing before a low door near the gate. She could not recognize her in the darkness. A short skirt, a large linen cap, and a thick scarf thrown askew on her back, together with the sound of her voice and the tone of her speech, showed that she was a woman from the countryside. The widow guessed that she was the concierge's wife.

"My good lady," she said, "will I find anyone here who would bring me milk and rolls?"

The woman thought for a moment.

"Which floor do you live on?" she asked. "Somehow I do not know you."

"I moved to the attic today."

"To the attic! Then why is my ladybird babbling about bringing her something? Can you not go to town yourself?"

"I would pay someone for the trouble," whispered the widow, but the concierge's wife did not hear, or pretended not to. She wrapped her scarf more snugly around her and vanished behind the small door.

The widow stood motionless for a moment, not knowing what to do or whom to turn to. She sighed and let her hands fall helplessly. After a while, however, she raised her head, approached the gateway, and opened the wicket leading to the street.

It was not late evening yet, but it was quite dark. The narrow thoroughfare, filled with crowds of people, was poorly lit by a few streetlamps. Wide spaces on the sidewalks lay in total darkness.

A wave of chilly autumn wind blew into the gateway through the open wicket, flying into the widow's face and rippling the ends of her black shawl.

The rumble of carriages and the clamor of mingled conversations deafened her; the shadows filling the sidewalks frightened her. She took a few steps back in through the gate and stood there for a while with her head down.

Suddenly she stood up straight and walked forward. Perhaps she remembered her child, who was waiting for the food; perhaps she was conscious that she must now muster her will and courage to obtain what previously had been freely available to her every day and hour. She threw her scarf over her head and walked through the gate. She did not know which direction to take to find a grocer's shop. She walked a long way, looking carefully at window displays; she passed a few cigar stores, a café, and a fabric store, and then turned back, not daring to go further or ask for information.

She turned and went in a different direction. After a quarter of an hour she returned, carrying several rolls in a white handkerchief. She brought no milk, for there was none at the store where she found the rolls. She did not want to go on searching; she could not look for a shop any longer. She was worried about her child. She returned quickly, almost running. She was a few steps from the gate when she heard a man's voice behind her, singing a song:

"Stop, wait, my dear—from where have you marched on your pretty little feet?"

She tried to convince herself that he was not singing to her. She walked faster and her hand was on the gate when the singing changed to speaking:

"Where are you going so quickly? Where to? The evening is so lovely! Perhaps we could go for a stroll!"

Breathless and shaking with fear and indignation, the young widow darted through the gate and slammed the wicket behind her. A few minutes later Jasia saw her entering the room. She ran toward her and nestled in her embrace.

"You did not return for so long, Mama!" she cried. Suddenly she went quiet and looked at her mother. "Mama," she said, "you are crying again, and you look the way you looked when they carried Papa out of our house in the coffin."

Indeed the young woman was trembling all over, and large tears were running down her flushed cheeks. She was shaken deeply by her fifteen-minute excursion into town—by her struggle with her own fear, her rapid walk over slippery streets amid crowds and cold winds, and, above all, the insult of being accosted by an unknown man for the first time in her life.

But she evidently made up her mind to overcome her feelings, for she quickly calmed down, wiped away her tears, and kissed the child. As she stirred up the fire, she said:

"I have brought you some rolls, Jasia, and now I will set out the samovar and make some tea."

She took the clay pitcher from the cabinet and, ordering the child to be careful of the fire, went down to the well in the courtyard. Soon she returned, breathless and exhausted, with one arm bent from the weight of the pitcher filled with water. But without resting even for a moment, she began to set out the samovar.

She was doing this for the first time in her life, and with difficulty. In less than an hour, however, the tea was drunk and Jasia was undressed and asleep. Her quiet, even breathing showed that she was sleeping peacefully. The traces of tears shed abundantly all day had vanished from her pale little face.

But the young mother did not sleep. She sat in front of the fading fire in her mourning dress, still as a statue, her hair falling in loose black braids. She was resting her head on her hand, thinking.

At first, her white forehead was wrinkled deeply with pain. Her eyes were filled with tears and her chest rose with a heavy sigh. After a while, however, she shook her head as if to push away the sorrows and fears that had overwhelmed her. She rose, stood erect, and said quietly:

"A new life!"

Indeed, this woman, young, beautiful, with white hands and a slender waist, was entering a new life. For her this day was the beginning of a future as yet unknown.

What had her past been like?

||l

Marta Świcka's past had been short because of her age and simple because it was uneventful.

Marta was born in a manor house that was neither splendid nor very affluent, but charming and comfortable.

Her father's estate a few miles from Warsaw comprised several hundred acres of fertile land, large, flowery meadows, a lovely birch grove that furnished wood for the winter and space for romantic strolls during the summer, a large orchard full of fruit trees, and an attractive house with six front windows looking out on a circular lawn. It had cheerful-looking green blinds and a porch with lavender morning glories and beans with scarlet blossoms entwined around its four columns.

Nightingales sang over Marta's cradle, and old lindens waved with dignified gravity. Roses blossomed and ripening wheat formed waves of gold. The lovely face of her mother leaned over her, and her little head, with its black hair, was covered with kisses.

Marta's mother was a beautiful, kind woman and her father was a good man with a fine education. She grew up as an only child among loving, doting people.

The first pain that darkened the cloudless life of the beautiful, cheerful, blooming girl was the loss of her mother. Marta was sixteen years old at that time. She despaired for a while; she yearned for her mother for a long time; but youth placed a healing balm on her heart's first wound, her face regained its rosy color, and joy, hope, and dreams returned.

But other calamities soon followed. Marta's father, partly because of his own imprudence but mainly owing to economic changes that had taken place in the country, found himself in danger of losing his estate. His health weakened; he saw that he was facing both the collapse of his fortune and the rapid approach of death. At that moment, however, Marta's future seemed to be secure: she loved and was loved.

Jan Świcki, a young official occupying a high position in a government office in Warsaw, fell in love with the beautiful dark-eyed girl, and awakened in her similar feelings of respect and love. Marta's wedding took place only a few weeks before her father's death. The ruined aristocrat, who perhaps once dreamed of a grander future for his only daughter, joyfully placed her hand in that of a man with no fortune but with a capacity for hard work. He died peacefully, believing that at the altar Marta's future had been thoroughly safeguarded from the unhappiness of a lonely life and the danger of poverty.

For the second time in her life Marta experienced great pain. But this time it was assuaged not only by her youth but by her affection for her husband and, in time, their child. Her beautiful family estate had been lost forever and passed into the hands of strangers, but her beloved and loving husband created a soft, warm, comfortable nest amid the hubbub of the city. In this home soon sounded the silvery voice of a child.

Five years passed happily and quickly for the young woman amid the comforts and duties of family life.

Jan Świcki was a conscientious, capable worker. He received a good salary, sufficient to surround the wife he loved with everything she had been accustomed to from her childhood, everything that lent charm to every moment and peace to each new day. To each? No, only to the next. Jan Świcki did not have the foresight to think of the distant future at the expense of the present.

Young, strong, hard-working, he counted on his youth, strength, and industriousness, never dreaming that these riches would be depleted. But they were, and too quickly. He was taken with a sudden, serious illness from which neither his doctors' advice nor his frantic wife's efforts could save him. He died. His death not only put an end to Marta's domestic happiness but pulled from under her the base of her material welfare.

So the marriage altar did not render the young woman forever immune to the misery of loneliness and the hazards of poverty. The axiom, old as the world, which states that nothing on earth is permanent proved itself as true in her case as it ever is. For it is not completely true. Everything that comes to a person from the outside passes, changing around him under the influence of thousands of currents that become entangled as they move forward, currents in which social relationships and laws take form. All these are subject to the frequent intervention of what is the most terrible force of all, because it is unpredictable and impossible to figure into one's calculations: blind chance. Yet a man's destiny in this world would indeed be regrettable if all his strength, his inner riches and his truth resided only in those external elements, which are mutable and fleeting as waves governed by wind.

Indeed, there is nothing permanent on earth besides what a man possesses in his heart and head: knowledge that shows him his paths and how to walk in them, work that brightens solitude and keeps poverty at bay, experience that tutors him, and elevated feelings that shelter him from evil. This permanence is only relative; it is broken by the sullen, unyielding power of illness and death. But as long the process of movement, thought, and feeling called life continues, and develops soundly and durably, a man does not lose himself but provides for himself, helps himself, supports himself with what he managed to accumulate in the past. It serves him as a weapon in his struggle with the complications of life, the fickleness of fate, and the cruelty of chance.

All the external forces that had befriended and sheltered Marta until now had failed her, leaving her abandoned. But her fate was not at all exceptional. Her misfortune was not caused by some bizarre adventure or astonishing disaster rare in the annals of human history. Financial ruin and death had destroyed her peace and happiness. What is more common everywhere in our society than the first? What is more inevitable, more frequent and inescapable, than the second?

Marta had found herself face to face with what happens to millions of people, millions of women. Who has not met, many times in life, people weeping by the rivers of Babylon in which the ruins of a lost fortune are floating? Who counts how many times he has seen widows' mourning clothes, pale faces, and orphans' eyes wearied with tears?

Everything that had been part of the young woman's life had been taken from her, had slipped away, but she still had herself. What could she be only for herself? What had she managed to accumulate for herself in the past? What tools of knowledge, willpower, and experience could serve her in the struggle with complicated social issues, poverty, chance, and loneliness? Among these questions lay the enigma of her future, the issue of her life and death—and not only hers, but her child's.

The young mother had no material wealth, or almost none. Her entire fortune consisted of a few hundred złotys from the sale of her furniture after the payment of some small debts and the costs of her husband's funeral, some underlinen, and two dresses. She had never had any expensive jewelry, and what she had had she had sold during her husband's illness to pay for worthless medical advice and equally worthless medicines. Even the cheap furniture that filled her new residence did not belong to her. She had rented it together with the room in the attic, and was obliged to pay for it on the first of each month.

That was the sad, unvarnished reality of the present, but it was clearly defined. The future remained undefined. One had to take possession of it—almost to create it.

Did the young, beautiful woman with the slim waist, white hands, and silky raven hair flowing over her shapely head have the strength for conquest? Had she taken anything from her past that would enable her to create her future? She thought about this as she sat on a low wooden stool by the glowing coals in the fire. Her eyes, filled with a look of unspeakable love, were fixed on the face of her child, who was sleeping peacefully among white pillows.

"For her," she said after a while, "for myself, for bread, peace, and a roof over our heads, I will work!"

She stood in front of the window. The night was dark. She did not see anything: neither the steep roofs bristling below the high attic with all its stairs and landings, nor the dark smoke-stained chimneys above the roofs, nor the streetlamps whose blurred light did not reach her little window. She did not even see the sky because it was covered with clouds and no star was shining. But the noise of the great city reached her ears incessantly; even the nocturnal noise was deafening, though it was muffled by distance. It was not late; on the wide, splendid boulevards as in the narrow, dark alleys, people still walked, drove, and ran about in the pursuit of pleasure or the search for profit—ran where curiosity, some desire of the heart, or the hope of gain called them.

Marta lowered her head onto her clasped hands and closed her eyes. She listened to the thousand voices merged into one enormous voice that was unclear and monotonous and yet full of feverish outbursts, sudden silences, dull shouts, and mysterious murmurs. In her imagination the great city assumed the form of a huge hive in which a multitude of human beings moved, surging with life and joining in a race. Each one had his own place for work and for rest, his own goals to reach, and his own tools to forge a way through the crowd. What sort of place for work and rest would there be for her, a woman who was poor and cast into a boundless sea of loneliness? In which direction should she proceed? Where would tools be found to pave a way for a penniless, abandoned woman?

How would those human beings treat her, those people who chatted endlessly on the streets, who exuded this feverish murmur, rising and falling like a wave, in which she immersed her hearing? Would they be just or cruel to her, compassionate or charitable? Would those tightly closed phalanxes that were crowding toward happiness and wealth open before her? Or would they shut even more tightly, so the newcomer's arrival would not leave less room for others, would not forestall them in this strenuous race?

Which laws and customs would be favorable to her, and which would be adverse? Would there be more of the former or the latter? Above all, would she be able to overcome hostile elements and exploit friendly ones every moment, with every heartbeat, with every passing thought? Would she be able to consolidate every vibrant fiber of her being into wise, persevering, unwearying strength, strength that would ward off poverty, preserve her dignity in the face of humiliation, and shield her from fruitless pain, despair, and starvation?

Marta's entire soul was fixed on these questions. Memories that were both delightful and agonizing, memories of a woman who had once been a carefree, radiant girl walking lightly through the fresh grass and colorful flowers of her family's country home, then spent joyful days, free of worry and sadness, at her beloved husband's side, and now stood in a widow's gown near a small window in this attic with her pale forehead lowered onto her tightly clasped hands—through all this day these memories had been swarming around her like phantoms that lured her, only to leave her torn and bleeding. Now they flew away before the stern, mysterious, but tangible reality of the present.

This reality absorbed her thoughts but did not seem to frighten her. Did she draw courage from the maternal love that filled her heart? Did she have the pride that despises fear? Or was she ignorant of the world and herself?

She was not afraid. When she lifted her face, there were traces of tears shed profusely for several days, and there was a look of sorrow and longing, but there was no fear or doubt.

||||

The day after her move into the attic, Marta was in town at ten in the morning.

It was crucial for her to reach her destination. A burning thought, an anxious hope must have been driving her forward, because she walked quickly and slowed her steps only when she reached Długa Street. Here she walked more and more slowly, a weak blush covered her pale cheeks, and her breath came more quickly, as it usually does when an eagerly anticipated but somewhat frightening moment draws near. Such a moment demands all one's powers of thought and will, while awakening hope, timidity and— who knows?—perhaps a feeling of inadequacy when the habits of one's entire life collide with the daunting strangeness of a new situation.

She stopped in front of the gate of one of the most ostentatious townhouses and looked at the number. It was apparently a number that she remembered, because after taking a long, deep breath she began slowly to approach the wide, sunlit entrance.

She had hardly taken a dozen steps when she saw two women coming down the steps. One was dressed with painstaking care, even a certain elegance. Her bearing was confident and her expression was not merely serene but self-satisfied. The second was younger—very young, and pretty. She wore a dark woolen dress, a threadbare shawl and a little hat that remembered more than one autumn. She walked with her arms down and her eyes fixed on the ground. Her red eyelids, pale complexion, and thin waist gave her entire figure a look of sorrow, weakness, and fatigue. It was clear that the two women knew each other well, for they spoke intimately.

"My God! God!" the younger one said quietly, almost moaning. "What will I do now? The last hope is lost. If I tell my mother that I have still not gotten any work, her illness will get worse. And there is nothing to eat at home . . ."

"Well, well," replied the older woman, in whose voice a note of sympathy sounded above a tone of strongly felt superiority, "do not worry so much! Just work a little on your music."

"Oh! If I could only play as well as you, madame!" the younger one exclaimed. "But I cannot . . ."

"My dear, you do not have the talent!" said the older woman. "What can you do? You do not have the talent!"

As they were speaking, the two women passed Marta. They were so absorbed, the one in her self-satisfaction and the other in her despondency, that they did not notice the woman whose mourning dress brushed past them. But she stopped suddenly and followed them with her eyes. It was clear that they were teachers who had left the place to which she was going, one with a beaming face, the other in tears. In a half an hour, perhaps a quarter of an hour, she would also be descending the stairs she was now mounting. Would her visit end in joy or tears? Her heart pounded when she rang the bell on the door, which bore a gleaming brass plaque with the inscription:

INFORMATION BUREAU FOR TEACHERS
LUDWIKA ŻMIŃSKA

At the sound of the bell the door opened into a small entrance hall. Marta passed through it into a spacious room lit from two large windows that faced the crowded street. The room was adorned with fine furniture, including a new, ornate, and expensive grand piano that would be noticed at once by anyone who entered.

There were three people in this room. One stood up to meet Marta: a middle-aged woman with hair of an uncertain color, smoothly combed under a shapely white cap, and rather stiff posture. Her face, with its regular features, had nothing noticeable about it. Nor did her gray dress, which had no decoration apart from a row of monotonous buttons down the front. Nothing about her either attracted or repelled. She was dressed from head to foot in a style that was businesslike and nothing more. Perhaps at a different time or in another place this woman could smile freely, express tenderness with her eyes, extend her hand in warm greeting. But here in this drawing room, where she received people who called on her for help and counsel, she appeared in the character of a professional intermediary between these visitors and society. She was as she was supposed to be: polite and proper but reserved and cautious.

This room was a drawing room in appearance only; in fact, it was a place of business just like other places of business. Its owner offered advice, guidance, and useful contacts for those who demanded them from her in exchange for mutual services rendered in kind. It was also a purgatory through which human souls passed, ascending to the heaven of a position secured or descending to the hell of involuntary unemployment.

Marta stopped in the doorway for a moment and looked at the face and figure of the woman walking toward her. Her eyes, which yesterday had been full of tears, today were dry and shining, and had taken on an expression that was exceptionally shrewd, almost penetrating. All the young woman's powers of thought were visibly concentrated in them as she tried to look through the outer casing and into the depths of the being whose lips would issue a judgment, for good or ill, concerning her future. Marta was coming to someone on a matter of business for the first time in her life. The matter was one of the utmost importance to poor people: the need to earn a living.

"Madame has come to the information agency?" asked the proprietress.

"Yes, madame," she replied, adding, "I am Marta Świcka."

"Please sit down, madame, and wait a little until I finish my interviews with the ladies who came first."

Marta sat down in the armchair that was pointed out to her. Only then did she turn her attention to the two other persons in the room, who differed immensely as to their age, dress, and bearing.

One was a woman of twenty, very pretty, with a smile on her pink lips and blue eyes that looked around brightly, almost joyfully. She was wearing a light-colored silk dress and a small hat that set off her fair hair exquisitely. Ludwika Żmińska must have been talking with her just before Marta entered, for she turned back to her immediately after greeting the new arrival. She spoke English, and from the first words of her answer one could guess that she was an Englishwoman.

Marta did not understand the women's conversation because she did not know the language they spoke. She only saw that the Englishwoman's easy smile did not vanish and that her face, her posture, and her way of speaking expressed the confidence of a person who was accustomed to being successful—who was sure of herself and the fate that awaited her.

After a brief talk, the proprietress took a sheet of paper and began to write in a flowing hand.

Marta watched every move attentively, for this scene had a bearing on her own situation. She saw that Ludwika Żmińska was writing a letter in French; she saw that it mentioned a figure of 600 rubles, and that on the envelope she was writing the name of a count and of the most beautiful street in Warsaw. Then, with a polite smile, she offered the letter to the Englishwoman, who rose, bowed, and left the room with a light step. She held her head high; her lips curved in a satisfied smile.

"Six hundred rubles a year!" Marta thought. "Good heavens, what wealth! What good fortune to be able to earn so much! If I get even half that sum, I will be easy in my mind about Jasia and myself."

Then she looked at the person with whom the proprietress began speaking after the Englishwoman left—a person who drew her interest and compassion.

She was a woman perhaps sixty years old. She was thin; her withered face, with red eyelids, was covered with a dense network of wrinkles. Her hair was almost completely white; it was parted in the middle and combed back smoothly under her black, rumpled hat, the relic of a fashion long past. A black woolen dress and an old silk stole hung loose on her gaunt body. Her small white hands, with almost transparent skin and bony fingers, rolled and squeezed a linen handkerchief that lay on her lap. A corresponding anxiety was reflected in her once-blue eyes, now faded and without luster, which she lifted to the face of the proprietress. They moved from one object to another, mirroring her apprehension and the painful jerking movement of her exhausted mind as it searched for a point of support, comfort, and peace.

"Have you ever worked as a teacher?" Ludwika Żmińska asked her in French.

The poor woman stirred in her chair, moved her eyes up and down and along the wall, squeezed the handkerchief convulsively, and began quietly:

"*Non, madame, c'est le premier fois que je . . . je . . .*"

She broke off. Obviously she was searching for the foreign words that could express her thought, but they escaped her tired memory.

"*J'avais . . .*" she began after a moment, "*j'avais la fortune . . . mon fils avait le malheur de la perde . . .*"

The proprietress sat cold and upright on the couch. The elderly woman's linguistic errors and grating pronunciation did not bring a smile to her lips, nor did her agitation and painful anxiety awaken any pity.

"That is sad," she said. "Do you have only one son, madame?"

"I do not have him anymore!" the elderly woman said in Polish. But, suddenly recalling her obligation to display her foreign language skills, she added:

"*Il est mourru par désespoir!*"

The elderly lady's faded eyes did not moisten with tears or shine with the slightest gleam when she uttered the last words. But her pale, narrow lips trembled in the labyrinth of wrinkles that surrounded them and her sunken chest shook under the old-fashioned stole.

"Do you know music, madame?" the proprietress asked in Polish, as if she were adequately informed as to the elderly lady's command of French after hearing her few words.

"I used to play, but . . . a very long time ago . . . I do not know, really, if I could now . . ."

"Or perhaps German language. . . ."

The woman shook her head.

"Then what can you teach, madame?"

The tone of the question was polite, but so dry and cold that it amounted to dismissal.

The elderly woman did not understand that, or did not allow herself to understand. She had counted most on her knowledge of French to help her receive a small nest egg that would save her from destitution in the final days of her waning life. Sensing that the ground was giving way under her feet, and that the owner of the agency intended to end the interview without giving her any referrals, she grasped at the only remaining life raft and, squeezing her linen handkerchief still harder in her trembling fingers, quickly began to speak:

"*La géographie, la histoire, les commencements de l'arithmétique . . .*"

All at once she went silent and looked at the opposite wall with flabbergasted eyes, for Ludwika Żmińska had risen from her seat.

"I am very sorry," she began slowly, "but at present I do not have a position that would be appropriate for you, madame."

She finished and stood with her hands folded over the bodice of her plain gray dress, clearly waiting for the other woman to take her leave. But the elderly lady sat as if riveted to her seat. Her restless hands and eyes seemed frozen. Her pale lips opened wide and quivered nervously.

"None!" she whispered after a while. "None!" she repeated. She rose stiffly from her chair as if she were being moved by a force other than her own. But she did not leave. Her eyelids swelled and her pale eyes became glassy. She rested her trembling hand on the frame of the chair and said quietly:

"Perhaps later . . . perhaps sometime . . . there will be a place . . ."

"No, madame, I cannot promise you anything," replied the proprietress, always in the same firm, polite tone.

For a few seconds the room was utterly silent. Suddenly two streams of tears gushed over the old lady's wrinkled cheeks. She made no sound; she did not say a word. She bowed to the proprietress and hastily left the room. Perhaps she was ashamed of her tears and wanted to hide them as quickly as possible; perhaps she was in a hurry to visit another agency with the hope of finding new employment.

Now Marta was alone with the woman who was supposed to decide whether her most ardent hopes and desires would meet with fulfillment or failure. She was not afraid, but she was deeply saddened.

The scenes she had witnessed had made strong impressions, stronger because they were new. She was not accustomed to seeing people looking for work, chasing after a piece of bread. She had never guessed, never been aware that that chase involved so much anxiety, distress, and disappointment. Work had existed in Marta's imagination, whenever she had thought about it, as something one need not lean out far to obtain. Here, at the first stop on this unknown road, she began to understand much that was daunting and saddening.

But she did not give way. She assured herself that she was a young, healthy woman, well brought up by excellent parents, and that she, the wife of a sensible man who had made his living working with his mind, could not meet with the same fate as that poor, sad girl she had met on the stairs, and this elderly woman, a hundred times unhappier, who had just rushed out with two streams of tears coursing down her wrinkled face.

Ludwika Żmińska began with the question she usually asked at the start of her interviews with candidates for teaching positions:

"Madame, have you ever worked as a teacher?"

"No, madame. I am a widow. My husband held a post in a government agency. He passed away a few days ago. This is the first time that I have wished to enter the teaching profession."

"Ah! So you have a diploma from an institution of higher learning?"

"No, madame. I was taught at home."

The women exchanged these words in French. Marta expressed herself in that language well and easily; her pronunciation was not perfect, but it had no peculiarities that offended the ear.

"Which subjects are you able and willing to teach?"

Marta did not respond at once. It was odd: she had come here intending to find work as a teacher, but she was not certain which courses she could actually teach, and wanted to teach. She was not accustomed to evaluate her intellectual assets. She only knew that they were sufficient for a woman in her situation: a gentleman's daughter and a government official's wife. However, she did not have long to think. She recalled the subjects she had studied hardest during her childhood, the subjects that formed the foundation of her education and that of her contemporaries.

"I could give lessons in music and French," she said.

"As to the second," replied the proprietress, "I note that you speak fluently and accurately in French, although that is not all that is required to teach. I am certain, however, that French grammar and spelling and even a little French literature are not foreign to you. But music . . . forgive me, madame, but I must assess the level of your artistic attainment if I am to find the appropriate way to utilize it."

Blushes appeared on Marta's pale cheeks. Having been schooled at home, she had never taken examinations in front of anyone. She had never performed for an audience outside her family circle. Several months after her wedding, she had closed the piano her husband had bought for her, and then opened it only a few times—when only the four walls of her pretty drawing room were listening, and Jasia's little ears as she jumped on her nanny's lap in time to her mother's music.

However, the woman's demand had nothing offensive about it. It was based on the simple and generally accepted law that in order to judge the value and properties of anything, one has to see it, consider it, and apply it in a situation for which it is appropriate and useful. Marta understood that, so she rose from her armchair, took off her gloves, and approached the piano. She stood there for a moment with her eyes on the keyboard. She recalled her girlish repertoire and hesitated, unable to choose among the compositions she had played well enough to earn praise from her teachers and hugs from her parents. She sat down, still debating inwardly, when the door opened with a rattle and a woman's sharp, penetrating voice sounded from the threshold:

"*Eh bien, madame! La comtesse arrive-t-elle à Varsovie?*"

With these words a lively, handsome woman burst rather than walked into the room, a woman of average height with a dark complexion. She wore a somewhat peculiar coat with a scarlet hood that glowed garishly against the deep black of her hair and the olive tone of her skin. Her dark, glittering eyes darted around the room and fixed on the figure of the woman sitting at the grand piano.

"*Ah, vous avez du monde, madame!*" she exclaimed. "*Continuez, continuez, je puis attendre!*"

She threw herself into an armchair, rested her head on the back of it, and crossed her legs, showing very graceful feet in pretty shoes. Then, folding her arms on her chest, she fixed her inquisitive, penetrating gaze on Marta.

The blushes on the young widow's cheeks deepened. The presence of another witness to her performance made the situation no less unnerving. But Ludwika Żmińska turned toward her with heightened interest and an expression that seemed to say, "We are waiting!"

Marta began to play. She played "The Maiden's Prayer." During the time when she had studied music, all young ladies played "The Maiden's Prayer," a sentimental blend of melancholy tones mingling with moonbeams from the windows and sighs rising from girlish bosoms. But the information agency's drawing room was lit by clear, sober daylight. The sighs of the woman playing "The Maiden's Prayer" were not the sighs that fly to the "heavenly realm," or the green field where the black horse gallops. They were sighs which, when stifled, continue to rise, pouring into the ear of the woman and mother the cry that is simple, earthly, trivial, and commonplace and yet tragic, ominous, insistent, and rending:

"Bread! Wages!"

Ludwika Żmińska's narrow eyebrows knit only slightly, but enough to make her face look cooler and more austere than before. Artful smirks flitted over the swarthy face of the Frenchwoman lolling in the armchair. Marta herself felt that she played badly. She no longer had the touch for those garlands of tender notes that long ago had seemed a melody fit for angels. Her fingers had lost their adroitness and floundered, not always striking accurately. She made mistakes in certain passages; she pressed the pedal unnecessarily; she left out entire measures. She lost her way on the keyboard and stopped to search for it.

"Mais c'est une petite horreur qu'elle joue là." The Frenchwoman spoke in an undertone, but Marta heard her.

"Chut! Mademoiselle Delphine!" Ludwika Żmińska whispered.

Marta struck the last chord of the wistfully romantic piece. "I must play better!" she said to herself. At once, without raising her eyes or her hands from the keyboard, she began to play Zientarski's dolorous *Nocturne*.

But she did not play any better; she played even worse. The composition was more difficult. She felt pain and stiffness in her fingers, which were long out of practice. She sensed that her playing was not making a favorable impression on the woman on whom her fervent hopes depended. She felt that her awkward touch on the keyboard was depriving her of one of the few tools that she had so counted on to help her obtain gainful work. Every false note from her fingers was tearing away one of the few threads by which her own and her child's welfare hung.

"Elle touche faux, madame! Hé! Hé! Comme elle touche faux!" the Frenchwoman cried again, glancing around with her laughing eyes and resting her graceful feet on an armchair close by.

"Chut, je vous en prie, Mademoiselle Delphine!" the proprietress repeated, drawing herself up with displeasure.

Marta rose from the grand piano. Her blushes turned to purple blotches; her eyes flashed with chagrin. It had happened! A tool she had relied on had fallen from her hands; a thread she might have followed to find a new profession had been severed irreparably. She knew now that she would be given no employment as a music teacher. She did not lower her eyes, but marched with a steady step to the table where the two other women were sitting.

"I never had any talent for music," she began in a voice that was rather soft but not muffled or trembling. "I studied it for nine years, but what one has no gift for, one forgets easily. And for five years after I was married I did not play at all."

She smiled a little as she spoke. The Frenchwoman's bright eyes were fixed on her and it made her uncomfortable. She was afraid of seeing pity in them, or a sneer. But the Frenchwoman did not understand Marta's Polish. She yawned widely and loudly.

"*Eh bien! Madame!*" She turned to the proprietress. "Finish with me. I have only a few words to add. When will the countess arrive?"

"In a few days."

"Did you write to her about the conditions I laid down?"

"Yes, and she accepted them."

"So my four hundred rubles are certain?"

"Absolutely."

"And my little niece will be able to stay with me?"

"Yes."

"And I will have my own room, a servant of my own, horses for riding whenever I like, and two months' holiday?"

"The countess agreed to all the conditions."

"Very good," said the Frenchwoman, rising. "I will visit you again in a few days to learn if the countess has arrived. But if she does not come or send for me in a week, I will break the contract. I do not want or need to wait any longer. I can get ten such positions. *Bonjour, madame.*"

She nodded to the proprietress and to Marta, and then left. On the threshold she pulled her bright red hood over her head; as she opened the door, she hummed a French song off key. For the first time in her life Marta felt something resembling jealousy. As she listened to the French governess's conversation with the owner of the agency, she thought:

"Four hundred rubles and permission to have a little niece with her! A separate room, a servant, horses, a long vacation! Good heavens! So many conditions! This woman's situation is so fortunate, so wonderful, although she does not seem either well educated or very attractive! If I could get four hundred rubles a year and have Jasia with me. . . ."

"Madame!" she exclaimed. "I would be overjoyed to take such a position."

Żmińska thought for a moment.

"That is not absolutely impossible, but it would not be easy, and that is why I doubt that it would be advisable for you. Surely you acknowledge that in my relations with the people coming to me, it is my duty to be candid. With your French, which is well enough, though not quite Parisian, and your limited training in music—almost none—you could only teach beginners' lessons, madame."

"What does that mean?" Marta asked with a pounding heart.

"That means that you would receive six hundred, eight hundred, or at most a thousand złotys yearly."

Without even a moment's reflection Marta said:

"I would agree to that salary if I could be accepted with my little daughter."

Ludwika Żmińska's eyes, which had expressed the sort of hope that inspires ideas, now grew cold.

"Ah! You are not alone. You have a child . . ."

"A four-year-old girl, calm, gentle. She would never cause trouble for anyone."

"I believe you," Żmińska said. "Nonetheless I cannot give you the smallest hope of getting work with a child."

Marta stared at her in surprise.

"Madame," she said after a moment, "the person who just left was hired with permission to keep a small relative with her, and many, many other benefits. Is she so well educated?"

"No. Her education is no better than average. But she is a foreigner."

The stern proprietress smiled for the first time during their conversation, and her cold eyes looked at Marta's face as if to say:

"What? You did not know this? Where do you come from?"

Marta came from her native village, where roses bloomed and nightingales sang; from a beautiful residence on Graniczna Street, a warm place with four handsome walls that stood between her and the surrounding world. She came from a realm in which first the naïveté and limited awareness of a growing girl prevailed, then the joy and limited awareness of a young married woman. She came from the quarters of society in which a woman lowers her eyes, and so she sees, asks, and knows nothing. She did not know, or she may have heard in passing, something to the effect that what Jove may do, an ox may not. Ludwika Żmińska's cold but comprehending eyes, with irony wandering through them, looked at her at that instant as if to say:

"The woman in that glaring red hood, who spoke sharply, shrieked loudly, and put her feet on the chair, is Jove, and you, poor creature, merely born in this land where all the mothers of our children are born—you are an ox."

What she really said was, "If you could part with your daughter, if you could leave her somewhere, perhaps you could find a post with a salary of a thousand złotys a year."

"Never!" cried Marta, clasping her hands. "I will never part with my child! I will not give her to strangers! She is all I have left on earth."

The cry burst passionately from her, but she quickly understood its irrelevance and uselessness. She mastered herself and began calmly:

"Since I cannot hope for a permanent position, please provide me with work as a private tutor . . ."

"Giving lessons in French?" the proprietress interjected.

"Yes, madame, and in other subjects as well—for example, geography, history, history of Polish literature . . . I studied all that once and afterward I read—not a great deal, to be sure, but I always read. I would work and I would fill in what is lacking in my information—"

"It would be of no use," Żmińska interrupted.

"What do you mean, madame?"

"Neither I nor any other owner of an information agency could in good conscience promise you lessons in the subjects you have mentioned."

Marta stared at the woman with wide-open eyes. Żmińska added after a brief pause:

"Because these courses are taught almost exclusively by men."

"Men?" Marta stammered. "Why exclusively by men?"

Żmińska raised her eyes and fixed the young woman with a look that said again:

"Where have you come from?"

Then she said:

"Because men are men."

Marta had come from the realm of blissful feminine obliviousness. For a moment she reflected on what the owner of the agency had said. For the first time in her life, complicated, enigmatic social issues forced themselves on her consciousness, though their aspect was blurred and indistinct. She saw, dimly, their interconnected contours and reacted instinctively with a troubled feeling, but they did not teach her anything.

"Madame," she said after a moment, "I think I understand why men are more often in demand for teaching positions. They are more highly educated, more thoroughly educated, than women . . . yes. But this consideration only holds if teaching takes on wider dimensions, when the knowledge of a teacher must be both broad and concrete to fulfill the needs of a pupil's maturing mind. I, madame—I do not lay claim to such pretensions. I would like to teach introductions to history, geography, the history of our literature—"

"Usually men teach these introductions," Żmińska interrupted.

"Certainly, when they are giving private lessons to boys," Marta interposed.

"And girls as well," the owner of the agency concluded.

Marta thought again. After a moment she said:

"Then what is left for women in the field of teaching?"

"Languages. Accomplishments . . ."

Marta's eyes shone with hope. Żmińska's last word reminded her of one more tool that she had not thought about.

"Accomplishments," she repeated quickly. "Not only music, then. I studied drawing. My drawings were even praised sometimes."

Żmińska's face again took on an expression of interest.

"Undoubtedly," she said, "a knowledge of drawing might be useful you, but less than skill in music."

"Why, madame?"

"Because a drawing is silent and music can be heard. Anyway," Żmińska added, "bring me some examples of your drawing. If you are very clever at it, if you know how to draw something that indicates that you have a great talent, a highly developed talent, I will be able to find you one or two lessons."

"I am not very clever at drawing," Marta replied. "I do not think I have great talent, and I would not say that it is highly developed. I know just enough about drawing to teach the basic rules."

"Then I cannot promise you drawing lessons for beginners," Żmińska replied, calmly folding her hands on her chest.

Marta clasped her hands more tightly as an unpleasant feeling came over her.

"Why not, madame?" the young woman whispered.

"Because men give those lessons."

Marta lowered her head to her chest and sat lost in thought for about two minutes.

"Forgive me, madame," she said at last, raising her face with an apprehensive expression, "forgive me, madame, for taking up your time. I am an inexperienced woman. Until now perhaps I have paid too little attention to human relations and matters that did not concern me personally. I do not understand everything you have told me. My common sense, and I believe I have it, refuses to accept all those impossibilities that you have pointed out to me because I do not see their causes. Work, as much work as possible, is more than a matter of life and death for me because it is a matter of life and of raising my child. I am confused . . . I want to think justly about these matters, to understand them, but . . . I cannot . . . I do not understand."

As Marta spoke, the owner of the agency looked at her indifferently at first, then keenly and attentively. A warmer light kindled in her cold eyes. She looked down suddenly and was silent for a while. A few wrinkles appeared fleetingly on her stern forehead and a sad smile played for an instant over her usually indifferent lips. The cloak of professionalism behind which the owner of the information agency concealed herself did not fall away altogether, but she became transparent. One could now see a woman who recalled many pages from her own life and many scenes from the lives of other women. She raised her head slowly and met Marta's bright, anxious, searching eyes.

"You are not the first—" she began in a less dry voice than she had used until now—"you are not the first to speak to me in this way. For eight years, since I took over the management of this agency, women differing widely as to age, capability, and status have come here continually to talk with me and have said, 'We do not understand!'

"I understand what they do not understand because I have seen and experienced a great deal. However, I do not undertake to explain dark and incomprehensible things to the inexperienced. They will be explained by the battles that all must fight, by disappointments that no one can escape, and by facts clear as day and gloomy as night."

As she said these words, a bitter irony sounded in the voice of this woman with her face set like steel, a woman who was no longer young. Her eyes still rested on Marta's pale face. In their depths there was a little of the sympathy with which a mature person who knows well the dark sides of life looks at a naïve child who has her future before her.

Marta was silent. A moment ago she had told the truth: thoughts were swirling in her head, and she had no words for what was suddenly presenting itself to her imagination and challenging her judgment. She perceived one thing clearly and distinctly: that work is not something that lies within easy reach of a human being, especially a woman. And she saw one more thing clearly and distinctly: Jasia's white face and her large, dark, childish eyes, whose gaze gored her heart with an enormous, urgent need that could not be pushed back into the distance.

"You struggle with your thoughts in vain," Ludwika Żmińska continued after a moment. "They will not tell you anything because you have not lived in the real world until now. First you had your own world of girlish dreams, then family feeling. What lay beyond that did not concern you. You do not know the world, although you have been living in it for more than twenty years, just as you do not know how to play, although you studied music for nine years. And so the facts that surround you on every side will govern your life and will teach you about the world, people, and society.

"As for me, I only want to say this, and I can and should. In our society, madame, a woman can only earn a good living and save herself from great suffering and poverty if she has perfected some skill or has genuine, vigorous talent. Elementary knowledge and average talent bring their possessors nothing, or at most a dry, hard piece of bread sodden with tears and smeared with humiliation. There is no help for it; a woman must excel in some area and win a name, fame, and popularity. If she stands two degrees lower in skill and talent, she has everything against her and nothing supporting her."

Marta listened avidly to these words, but the longer she listened, the clearer it was that ideas were flowing through her mind and words rising to her lips.

"Madame!" she said. "Do all men have to excel at something to win a life free of great suffering and poverty?"

Żmińska burst into quiet laughter.

"Are clerks copying documents in offices, shopkeepers and sales assistants, or teachers giving instructions in basic geography, history, drawing, and so on, highly accomplished in any field?"

"Then," Marta exclaimed with an exultation unusual for her, "then forgive me, madame, if I repeat: Why, why is the field of work open for one sex without restriction but measured for the other sex by handbreadths, by inches? Why could my brother, if I had one, give drawing lessons if his talent was the same as mine, while I could not? Why could he copy documents in offices while I could not? Why could he use, for his benefit and that of those who depend on him, all his faculties of mind, while I cannot use anything more than the piano, for which I have no talent, and the knowledge of foreign languages, which I do not possess at an advanced level?"

Marta spoke with trembling lips and fiery eyes and cheeks. She was not a great lady on a velvet sofa in a drawing room chatting wittily about equal rights for women, nor a theoretician in an office with four walls weighing and measuring male and female brains to find similarities and differences. The questions that crowded to her lips were questions that tore at her heart because she was a mother, set her cheeks aflame because she was poor, and arranged themselves before her like a shield protecting her from starvation.

Żmińska shrugged her shoulders slightly and said slowly:

"Madame, you have repeated this word: 'Why?' over and over. Without formulating a categorical answer, I will tell you that it is above all because men are heads of households and fathers of families."

Marta stared at the woman as if she were looking at a rainbow. The brilliant gleam in her eyes, evoked a moment ago by her curiosity and the turmoil of her feelings, was hidden by two tears that came from under her eyelids and covered it like a glaze. Her hands seemed to clasp each other involuntarily.

"But, madame," she said, "I am a mother."

Ludwika Żmińska stood up. In the hallway the doorbell sounded, announcing the arrival of a new person. The owner of the agency intended to end her conversation with the young widow.

"I will do everything in my power to find you suitable work. However, do not expect to receive an offer very soon. In general, in the field of teaching, the number of available candidates greatly exceeds the demand. Teachers with high linguistic and artistic skills are needed and they receive rather good positions, but they are the fewest; their numbers do not even meet the demand. As for education at the beginner level, so many women are employed in it, or want to be, that the excessive competition has not only lowered salaries to an unbelievable level but made it difficult—for most, impossible—to obtain that sort of work.

"Nonetheless I repeat that I will do everything in my power to find lessons for you to give. That, after all, is in my best interest as well as yours.

In a few days, in a week, come again, and perhaps I will have some information for you."

After saying this, the owner of the agency was cloaked again from head to foot in her mantle of professional coolness and rigidity, for a new woman had appeared in the room.

Marta left. She walked slowly down the stairs. She was not crying like the young woman who had descended the same stairs an hour ago, but she was deeply preoccupied. Only as she went out into the street did she look up from the pavement and walk faster. She still had much to do that day.

In the building next to the one where her apartment was located, there was a cook shop. Marta entered and asked that dinners be delivered to her apartment. Because of the proximity of the two buildings, it was agreed that for a small fee, dinners would be brought to her attic room by a small boy. An advance payment of ten złotys a week was required. It was a large sum for Marta, whose entire fortune amounted to less than two hundred złotys.

As she opened her purse, which contained all the money she possessed, Marta felt an undefined but painful anxiety. The feeling intensified when she entered the apartment of the supervisor of her building and handed him twenty-five złotys for the month's rental of the room and the furniture. Earlier at the grocery shop she had bought sugar, tea, buns, a small lamp, and some oil. It all took a quarter of her money.

Jasia, who had been shut in the room all morning, gave a joyful cry on hearing a key turn in the lock. She threw herself on her mother and covered her face with kisses.

The impression of the moment is the only power that exercises a strong influence on children's ways of perceiving the world. The future does not exist in their thoughts; the past is quickly erased from their memories. For a child, yesterday is the distant past. The surroundings and events of a few days ago vanish and spill back only in a mist of forgetfulness. Jasia was happy.

The narrow sunbeam entering the attic room through the small window delighted her. The fireplace with its sooty depths aroused her curiosity and occupied her attention. She became acquainted with the new furniture. She laughed at the two chairs that had one leg shorter than the other three, and likened them to the crippled elderly people she had seen on the city streets. The solitude in which she had spent the entire morning had given her a repertoire of thoughts to express to her mother that kept her eager little tongue running loudly and rapidly.

For the first time the child's cheerfulness was disquieting to Marta. Yesterday, when Jasia remembered her dead father more clearly, when she was still saddened by the loss of the home she had lived in and all the beautiful things she was accustomed to see, she had wept and refused to eat. She had raised her large, dark eyes to her mother's face with an expression of painful pleading and unwitting fright. Then Marta would have given everything she still had to bring a smile to her thin lips and a healthy blush to her pale cheeks. But today the child's silvery smile filled her with a vague but oppressive alarm.

How had her situation changed? She was alone, as she had been yesterday; she was poor, as she had been yesterday. But between yesterday and today there had been this morning of reckoning, when, as she entered the unfamiliar world for the first time, she had come to an accounting with herself that was sterner than ever before.

Yesterday she had been certain that in another day she would have work, and be able to calculate her income and see the future in clear outline. But that day had passed and her future remained unknown. She had been asked to wait without being told how long, and to wait for something that would be quite meager.

"How inexperienced I was, thinking I would not have to wait. I was so foolish to expect great things from myself!" So Marta thought that evening, standing by the window behind which a dark autumn sky hung while the din of the great city rose incessantly.

"What a crowd! People of all classes, ages, and nationalities are pressing in where I intended to find a path for myself! Will I be able to make my way among them, and how, for I am so little equipped for that struggle? And if I do not find a way in? If a week . . . two weeks . . . a month passes and I find no work?"

The thought sent a cold shiver through her. She turned quickly and glanced at the head of her sleeping daughter as if she were suddenly afraid— as if she saw danger hanging over the child.

|||

It was an ugly November day, gray, rainy, and muddy. Marta walked very quickly from Długa Street to Piwna Street, from the information bureau to her home. The clouds were weeping, but the young woman's face glowed.

People hid under their umbrellas from the rain and wore coats to protect themselves from the cold, but she did not cover herself at all. She was as indifferent to nature's annoyances as she would have been at that moment to its caresses. She ran lightly over the muddy sidewalks with her head high and her eyes bright.

Never since she had lived in the attic had walking up the three long flights of dark, dirty stairs been so easy. She smiled as she took the heavy, rusty key from her pocket. Still smiling, she crossed the threshold, almost skipping. She knelt, opened her arms, and when the dark-eyed child ran to meet her with a joyful cry, hugged her quietly and tightly. She pressed her lips to the girl's forehead.

"Thank God, thank God, Jasia!" she whispered. She wanted to say something more, but could not. Two tears ran down onto her smiling lips.

"Why are you laughing, Mama? Why are you crying?" Jasia babbled, touching her mother's burning cheeks with her little hands.

Marta did not answer. She rose and looked into the black fireplace. Only now did she feel that she was wet, and that it was cold in the room.

"Today we can light the fire in the fireplace," she said, taking the last bundle of wood from behind the stove.

Jasia jumped for joy.

"A fire! A fire!" she cried. "Mama, I love a fire! You have not lit one in the fireplace for so long!"

When the yellow flames shot up with a warm light that filled the dark hearth and a wave of pleasant heat spread through the room, Marta sat down in front of the fire and took her child on her lap.

"Jasia!" she said, leaning over the small, pale face. "You are still a little girl, but you should understand what I will tell you. Your mama was very, very poor and very sad. She had already spent all her money and in a few days she would not have been able to buy dinner for you or for herself, nor wood to start the fire in the stove. Today your mama got work for which she will be paid. That is why when I came in, I told you to thank God. That is why I lit the beautiful fire, so today we would be warm and happy."

Indeed, Marta had gotten work, after a month of waiting and more than a dozen fruitless trips to the information bureau. At last Ludwika Żmińska had announced that she had French lessons for her. When Marta heard that her wage would be half a ruble per day, it seemed that a gold mine had opened before her. On this wage she could live with her child in this same

room, if she managed her expenses as carefully as she had until now, or perhaps somewhat more carefully. She could live! The three words meant
everything to this woman, who only a day before had been trying to find
out where and to whom she could sell some spare clothes.

In the first glow of success she seemed to see a brighter future.

"If you make a name for yourself as a conscientious and skillful teacher
in the home in which I place you," Żmińska had said, "it is quite possible
that many others will ask you for private lessons. Then you will have the
right to choose and to demand more advantageous conditions than the ones
offered you now."

With that Ludwika Żmińska ended their conversation.

Two words lodged in Marta's mind: "conscientious" and "skillful." The
first did not frighten her at all. The second she pushed from her mind without knowing why. She wanted to forget it and not mar the first moments of
peace she had had in many weeks.

At the hour agreed upon, Marta entered a house on Świętojerska Street.
In the beautiful, tasteful, rather expensively decorated drawing room, a
young woman met her. She was very pretty and nicely dressed, the true
model of a Warsaw woman, with lively, graceful manners, a bright, clever
expression, and quick, animated, elegant speech. She was Maria Rudzińska,
the wife of one of the city's better-known writers. A laughing twelve-year-
old girl with lustrous, intelligent eyes ran into the drawing room close behind her, wearing a short, full, stylish dress with lavish trimmings and
pulling a long, red rope that she been using a moment earlier for gymnastic
exercises in her parents' large, comfortable apartment.

"Surely I have the pleasure of seeing Madame Marta Świcka," said the
lady of the house, offering one hand in greeting and pointing with the other
to an armchair standing near a sofa. "Madame Żmińska told me a great deal
about you yesterday, so I am truly glad to meet you. This is my daughter,
your pupil. Jadwisia! Madame is so kind as to offer you French lessons.
Remember not to cause her any worry, and study as well as you did with
Mademoiselle Dupont!"

The girl, with her lithe, slender figure and serene, intelligent face, bowed
very gracefully and without the least timidity to her future teacher.

At that moment a doorbell sounded in the hallway. No one entered the
drawing room, but after a few seconds the portiere that almost completely
covered the door of the adjoining room moved, and in the opening, between

heavy folds of crimson fabric, a pair of black, fiery eyes appeared. Clearly they belonged to a masculine face, because above them a few inches of swarthy forehead could be seen, with thick, black, closely clipped hair above it and a corner of a black beard thrust out below. But all that was hardly visible among the thick folds of material, and remained unnoticed by the persons talking in the drawing room with their profiles to the door.

The lady of the house continued her conversation with Marta.

"My daughter's last teacher, Mademoiselle Dupont, taught very well, and Jadwisia made significant progress in her studies. Nonetheless my husband believed, and he convinced me, that it was not altogether well done on our part to offer employment to a foreigner when all around us so many worthy women from the city were looking hard for work and only finding it with great difficulty. In any case, my husband and I require one thing of all the teachers who form our daughter's mind: that they offer her a serious, wide, comprehensive education in all areas of a given subject, so that our child will master the subject and have all aspects of it at her command."

Marta bowed silently and stood up.

"If you would be so kind as to begin the lessons today, madame . . ." said her hostess. She also rose and with a polite gesture pointed to the door with the portiere behind which a pair of eyes, a mustache, and a beard had vanished when the women got up. "Here is the room set aside for my daughter's studies."

The room was decorated more modestly than the drawing room, but it was tasteful and comfortable. Beside one wall stood a large table covered with a green cloth; it was full of books, notebooks, and writing materials. Jadwisia felt at home here. She raised her pretty eyes to her new teacher's face and then, with a serious expression, moved a comfortable armchair to the table and placed several books and many thick notebooks in front of it.

Marta did not sit down right away, however. Her face, thinner and paler after a month of waiting, was covered at that moment with a look of deep reflection. She lowered her eyelids and her hands trembled a little as she touched the table. For several minutes she stood with her face and her body quite still. She might have been thinking of what her pupil's mother had said; she might have been asking herself some question and searching for the answer in her mind or her conscience.

When she looked up, she met the eyes of the lady of the house, which were fixed on her. For a moment their gaze wandered from head to foot over the slim, delicate, elegantly beautiful figure of the new teacher. They paused for a little at the sight of the wide white ribbon—the mourning band bordering her black dress—then rested on Marta's pale, pensive face with a look of compassion and a little curiosity.

"Madame, you are in mourning," Maria Rudzińska said in a low, kindly voice. "For your mother, or perhaps your father?"

"For my husband," Marta said quietly, lowering her eyelids again slowly and heavily.

"So you are a widow!" Maria exclaimed. Her voice rang with the sympathy and fear a happily married woman feels when she hears that another woman has been deprived of her happiness, and is reminded that her own is not immune to the vicissitudes of fate. "And perhaps . . . do you have any children?"

This time Marta's eyes sparkled as she looked up.

"I have a daughter, madame!" she said as if the word had suddenly, forcefully reminded her of something. She sat down in the armchair and, with her hands still trembling a little, began to open the books in front of her one by one.

As she examined the books, Marta realized that twelve-year-old Jadwisia had learned a great deal and advanced far in her studies. The fluent annotations sprinkled through the notebooks displayed an easy mastery of the greatest difficulties of the language—a mastery that penetrated its basic elements and its subtle nuances—and proved that the girl's former teacher had been extremely well versed in her subject. Marta moved her hand over her eyes as if to clear her vision or chase away a troublesome thought, and, closing the books and notebooks, asked her pupil several questions. Meanwhile Maria Rudzińska approached the window and took up a small piece of needlework. She was about to sit down by a small table when the portiere was drawn aside a little and a resonant masculine voice spoke from behind it:

"Cousin Maria! Please come here for a moment!"

Maria crossed the room quietly. Her friendly glance settled once more on the face of her daughter's new teacher before she silently closed the door to the drawing room.

In the middle of the room stood a young man perhaps twenty-six years old, slender, graceful, and dressed in the latest fashion. He had an oval face, an olive complexion, dark hair, and eyes black as coal. His appearance was pleasing, even engaging at first sight; there was a striking vivacity about him, an easygoing, cheerful air and an impatience, a rash, capricious exuberance that after a closer look seemed excessive. His eyes smoldered and flashed and around his lips, which were half covered by a black mustache, a swarm of smiles appeared, blandishing and playful. In the twinkling of an eye his face could glitter with a witty, jocular expression. Clearly he was a man of perpetual cheerfulness, always smiling, but it was also clear that he was a happy-go-lucky fellow who cared about nothing in life. That was evident from his weary face, which contrasted noticeably with his youthful figure, ardent, glowing eyes, and childish, almost empty smiles.

At the moment when Maria Rudzińska entered the drawing room, the man's posture was peculiar, to say the least. He stood facing the door to Jadwisia's study, which Maria had just closed, and bending backward a little, with his hands raised and his eyes fixed on the ceiling. This theatrical posture was accompanied by a theatrical and comic expression of delight.

"Olek!" Maria reprimanded him. "What is this nonsense?"

"Goddess!" the young man said in an undertone without changing his posture or the expression on his face. "Goddess!" he repeated and, sighing like the hero of a comedy, lowered his head and hands.

Maria could not keep from smiling. She shrugged her shoulders and sat on the sofa with her needlework, saying in a slightly reproachful tone:

"Olek, you have forgotten to greet me!"

Hearing these words, the young man rushed over and kissed her hand several times.

"Forgive me, Maria, forgive me!" he said in the same pathetic tone as before. "I was so enchanted! Ah!"

He sat on a chair beside the young woman, pressed his hand to his heart, and raised his eyes to the ceiling again. Maria looked at him as one looks at a teasing child.

"What madness has come into your head again?" she asked after a moment, trying to be serious but unable to hide a smile. "Did you meet a new goddess on the way to my home, and has she thrown you into this fit of ecstasy? I really am afraid that she has deprived you of your judgment for the entire day."

"Maria, you are cruel with your rationality," said the young man, sighing again. "It was in your own home that I saw the beauty . . ." and with a melodramatic gesture he pointed to the door of Jadwisia's study.

Maria seemed half astonished and half inclined to burst out laughing.

"Do you mean—" she asked—"are you referring to Jadwisia's new teacher?"

"Yes, cousin," the young man replied, suddenly adopting a sober expression. "I am appointing her queen of all my goddesses."

"But where have you seen her, silly?"

"When I arrived at your home, I found, while I was still in the hallway, that you were engaged in conversation with your daughter's new teacher. I did not want to disturb you, so I entered by the kitchen door and looked through the portiere. All joking aside—what a beautiful person! Her eyes! Her hair! What regal height!"

"Olek!" the hostess interrupted with barely perceptible distaste. "Obviously she is an unhappy woman in mourning for the loss of her husband . . ."

"A young widow!" the young man exclaimed, raising his eyes again. "Perhaps you do not know, cousin, that there are no nicer beings on earth than young widows, when they are pretty, of course. A pale face, sentimental eyes . . . I adore pale faces and sentimental eyes in women."

"You are raving!" Maria said, shrugging again. "If you were not my cousin and I did not know that, despite your hollowness, you were fundamentally a good boy, I could hate you for your strange disregard for women."

"Disregard!" the young man cried. "But, cousin, I love women! They are the goddesses of my heart and my life."

"Goddesses that you count by the dozen."

"The more objects of love one has, cousin, the more one loves . . . These are exercises, and only through these exercises does a heart take on that strength, that fire which . . ."

"Olek, enough of this," his hostess interrupted with strong, visible distaste. "You know very well how I worry about the direction in which your mind and heart are moving."

"Cousin! Cousin! Little cousin! Amen! For God's sake, say amen!" the young man exclaimed, pushing away the chair in which he was sitting and folding his hands as if in prayer. "Nothing is less suited to a sermon than a pair of beautiful female lips."

"If I had truly been a good cousin to you, I would have preached them to you from morning till night."

"And it would have done no good, cousin. A sermon should be short, an exhortation drawing on the rules of morality, philosophy, and art. It would be better if you could tell me something about that dark-eyed nymph who deserves a pleasanter fate than the drudgery of teaching your Jadwisia."

"It would be better," she rejoined spiritedly, "if you told me what you are doing here at this time of day."

"And where should I be if not at your feet, my dear cousin?"

"At the office," she replied curtly.

The young man sighed, wrung his hands, and let his head fall onto his chest.

"At the office!" he whispered. "Oh, Maria! How cruel you are! Am I a herring? Tell me: do I look like a herring?"

As he asked these questions, the man with the perpetual smile raised his head and looked at his hostess with wide-open eyes and such a comic expression of remorse, indignation, and astonishment that Maria could hardly keep from laughing out loud. But after that brief flight of merriment, her face grew sober.

"You are not a herring," she said, looking at the sewing she was holding in her hand to keep from laughing again. "You are not a herring, but you are . . ."

"I am not a herring!" the young man exclaimed as if he were breathing deeply once more after a moment of terror. "Thank God, I am not a herring! And since I am not a herring, it is plain to see that I cannot stew at the office for whole days like a herring in a barrel."

"But you are a man, and you should think seriously of your life and its purpose. Can you do nothing more than idle away your time and pursue your—goddesses? I truly grieve for your good heart and for your talents, which are not lacking. A few more years of such a life and you will become one of those who have no goal, no occupation, no future. We already have too many such people among us."

She broke off with an expression of genuine sadness, and looked down at her needlework. The young man stood erect and said solemnly:

"Amen! The sermon was long, but one cannot deny that it was infused with a certain moral essence. My heart, bathed in that essence like a sponge soaked in tears, falls at your feet, my dear cousin!"

"Olek!" said the lady of the house, rising from her seat. "You are unreasonable today, as usual. I cannot talk with you any longer. Go to your office and I will go to my kitchen!"

"Cousin, dear! Maria! To the kitchen! *Fi donc! c'est mauvais genre!* A writer's wife to the kitchen! Her husband may be writing about a woman's obligation to be poetic, and she goes to the kitchen!"

He stood up and looked after her with outstretched arms. "Cousin!" he called once more. "Maria! Ah, do not leave me!"

Maria did not turn back. When she reached the door to the hall, the young man rushed toward her and seized her hand.

"Maria, are you angry with me? Are you really angry with me? Shame on you! Come, now! Did I intend to offend you? Do you not know that I love you as if you were my own sister? Maria, dear! Look at me! Is it my fault that I am young? I will improve. You will see. Only first let me grow a little older!"

He kissed the young woman's hands, and on his face, expressions mingled with and rapidly succeeded each other: resentment, vacuity, sadness, affection, cajolery. An observer might either laugh or turn away with a shrug, but it was impossible to be angry with this grown-up child. So Maria Rudzińska's resistance to those kisses and his apologies ended in a smile.

"How much I would give to see you change, Olek!"

"I would give much to be able to change, Maria! But nature is not a servant. The wolf is drawn to the forest."

With those words he hunched over like a child timidly expressing its demand and pointed to the door of Jadwisia's study.

"What now?" Maria asked, putting her hand on the doorknob.

"I will not say a word more about the dark-eyed goddess, whom, I see, you shield like a guardian angel with wings of pious care!" Olek exclaimed, grasping her hand again. "But, cousin, you will introduce me to her? Will you?"

"I have not the least intention of doing so," Maria replied.

"My dear! My sweet! My only love! Introduce me to her when she comes in! Say: This is my brother, a model of all the finest qualities, a young man of good heart . . ."

"And a great good-for-nothing as well!"

Maria left the drawing room. Olek stood by the door, uncertain if he should remain there or follow her. Then he turned on his heel, stood in front of the mirror, straightened his tie, and tidied his hair. He hummed a song, then stopped humming and tiptoed to the door of the study. Half-opening the portière, he put his ear to the door. Behind it one could hear little Jadwisia's voice saying:

"*L'imparfait du subjonctif!* I have forgotten how to write in the third person. Which tense is used to form *l'imparfait du subjonctif?*"

The answer did not follow at once. One could hear pages turning in a book. Apparently, the teacher was searching there for the information she had to give her pupil.

"*Du passé défini de l'indicatif,*" Marta said after a moment.

Olek straightened himself, raised his eyes and repeated quietly:

"*De l'in-di-ca-tif!* What an angelic little voice!"

It was quiet in the study. The pupil was busy with her writing. After a while she asked again:

"*Bateau!* I do not know how to write *bateau. Eau* or *au?*"

There was no answer. The teacher said nothing.

"Ah!" whispered Olek. "It is going rather hard for my goddess! Apparently she does not know how to answer the question put to her by that little wiseacre, or maybe she is dreaming . . . ah!"

He left the door on tiptoe and went to the window. He had hardly looked out into the crowded, busy street before he exclaimed:

"What do I see? Miss Malwina in town so early in the morning? I run! I fly! I'm off!"

He rushed to the door and was opening it in a great hurry when he came face to face with Maria, who was returning to the drawing room.

"For Heaven's sake!" she said, stepping back into the hallway. "Where are you rushing to? Your office?"

"I saw Miss Malwina through the window," answered the young man, hastily putting on his coat. "She went toward Krasiński Square, probably to do some shopping at the stores. I must be there . . ."

"Are you afraid that Miss Malwina might spend a great deal of money at the stores if you do not watch over her?"

"Money? Nonsense! But she might lose a piece of her heart on the way. Goodbye, Maria. Give my respects to the dark-eyed goddess," he said from the stairs.

Less than an hour later, Marta entered her room in the attic. When she had left it, she had had a lively face and a light step. She had smiled as she pressed her little daughter to her bosom, kissed her forehead, and explained how she should play with her doll during her absence, using the two crippled chairs as its bed and its cradle. Now she returned, walking slowly with lowered eyes and an expression of sober reflection on her face. To her child's shouts and hugs she responded with a quiet, fleeting kiss. Jasia looked at her mother with large, comprehending eyes.

"Mama!" she said, throwing one little arm around her mother's neck. "Did you not get any work? You are not laughing. You hardly kiss me. You are like you were then . . . when you could not get any work."

These two beings of different ages were thrown so closely together amid poverty and solitude that the child sensed her mother's sadness and anxiety from the woman's look and the limpness of her kiss. But Jasia's question was fruitless. Her mother's head was resting against her hand; she was lost in thought and did not hear it. After a while Marta got up.

"No," she said quietly, "this cannot be. I will learn, I must learn, I must be competent! I need books." After a moment's thought, she opened a small bag and took one object from it, wrapped it in a handkerchief, and went to town. She returned with three books: a French grammar, an anthology of model texts, and a history of French literature for schools.

That evening a small lamp burned in the attic room. Marta sat next to it with an open book. She leaned her forehead on her hands and devoured the text with her eyes. The complex grammatical rules, the thousands of enigmas involved in one of the most challenging spelling systems in the world, became muddled before her eyes like tangled threads—a labyrinth of facts and instructions either completely unknown to her, or as good as unknown, because forgotten. Marta concentrated with all her powers of memory and comprehension, striving in a single night to absorb, understand, and remember everything that could not be mastered except through hard work over many years and a slow, patient, systematic course of study, perfected by degrees. The poor woman thought that strenuous, feverish effort would compensate for years of intellectual stagnation; that the present moment would weigh equally on the scale with all the past; that enormous desire is the same as possibility. She deceived herself.

But she could not deceive herself for long. Her energy was wasted in feverish exertion and her body and spirit were exhausted by the strain, so that progress was impossible. The present moment, full of painful anxiety, imbued her heart with vague but acute bitterness. This woman, deprived of every resource on earth, began to understand that she was disappointed with herself—that she was unsuited to studies which, if they were to bring forth copious fruit, need peace, as a bird developing its wings needs air. The strongest desire, the most fervent aspiration of the soul, the most ferocious burst of willpower could not enable an uninformed mind to grasp all the mysteries of a subject at once—could not enable the untrained powers of comprehension and memory to bend like sensitive strings, make circles as quickly as lightning, and, like wax softened in the refiner's fire, absorb all that was infused into them.

Marta could not deceive herself for long. But, beating back such analytical thoughts, she clung with all her strength of mind and will to the thought: "Learn!" She was like a shipwrecked man struggling with waves and holding on to a plank with both hands, who thinks, as long as he can still hold on, "I am keeping my head above water!"

Now, just as before during the long autumn nights, the mysterious sounds of the city swelled like roaring winds to a massive scale and then subsided, but Marta no longer heard them. She was afraid to listen to them, because they overwhelmed her with the undefined fear that envelops a human being who finds herself falling with no hope of rescue into a powerful, unknown, precipitous element.

At midnight she was pacing around the room, which was lit by the lamp's pale flame, with a bright red flush on her cheeks. Her dark braids hung down her back; her hands were clasped tightly with nervous energy. Her lips continuously whispered foreign words from the book that lay open in the lamplight. To her tired mind, its pages seemed to bristle with barbs—with rows of thousands of endings, marks, numbers indicating rules and parentheses showing exceptions. It was a work written by Chapsal and Noël to explain many of the subtleties of the sophisticated speech of the Franks. The words Marta repeated from dusk to midnight, and often from midnight to dawn, were boring declensions and conjugations over which thousands of children yawn throughout the world.

But Marta did not yawn. The dry, monotonous sounds, the school walls echoing with boredom, had a more tragic meaning for her. She struggled with them and with herself, with her uncertain comprehension, her untrained memory, her scattered thoughts, and her impatience, which filled her body with nervous tremors. She struggled with everything around her and most of all with everything inside her, and from this dogged battle she emerged with nothing, or almost nothing.

She progressed slowly, very slowly. The next day would eat away and often cast into an abyss of forgetfulness what she had achieved with great toil the day before. Knowledge drew nearer and then receded, offering crumbs of benefit but taking vast amounts of strength and time. Marta wrung her hands. She sat as still as a statue over the book for whole hours with her face turned to stone. She got up, crossed the room with a feverish step, drank cold water, dipped her forehead and eyes in it, and studied again, only to wake up the next day and tell herself: "I still know nothing!"

"Time! Time!" the young woman cried inwardly, calculating how many poems she could memorize every day, how many pages every week. "If I had two years, a year, or even a few months!"

But time, which had once so generously allowed her moments of idleness and leisure, hounded her now with the fear of hunger, cold, shame, and poverty. She wanted a year for herself, and not even tomorrow was hers. Tomorrow she was supposed to know everything that one can hardly learn in a year, or many years; she ought to, she had to, if she did not want another means of earning a living to slip through her fingers. The period of her life at which this woman had begun her struggle for her welfare and her child's was not an opportune time for studies. Yet she continued to study.

A month passed from the day the young widow had entered the handsome residence on Świętojerska Street. The lady of the house always greeted her cordially and spoke to her kindly, even warmly, but the warmth was colored by a more and more visible tinge of reserve, uneasiness, and even constraint. Little Jadwisia, like a well-behaved child, was unfailingly polite to her teacher, but a playful beam darted from her lively, dancing eyes from time to time, and a roguish smile ran across her blooming lips. It was quickly stifled, but it betrayed the pupil's inward surprise and satisfaction at penetrating the sad secret of her teacher's lack of knowledge. "Why, I know more than she does!" the girl told herself.

The day came when Marta was supposed to be paid for her entire month's work by her pupil's mother. Maria Rudzińska sat in her drawing room with her sewing, which she had let fall on her knees because she was lost in thought. Her usually serene face, the face of a happy woman, was somewhat clouded today; her beautiful eyes were fixed with a sad expression on the door of the study, which was closed and covered by the portiere.

"May I know why my dear cousin is so gloomy today?" said a male voice by the window.

Maria turned her eyes toward the voice.

"I am really very worried, Olek. Please show some consideration and do not try my patience with your jokes."

"Oh! Oh! Oh!" the young man said, folding the newspaper that had been hiding his face. "What a solemn speech! What happened? Was the article sketched by your talented husband's pen not accepted for publication? Did the tip of Jadwisia's little nose hurt? Did the apple cobbler not bake well? Did . . ."

The young man asked these questions with his usual comic emphasis. But suddenly he stopped talking, rose, approached his cousin, sat next to her and gazed into her face longer and more attentively than one would expect from such an effervescent, flighty person.

"No," he said after a moment. "It is not the article, Jadwisia's nose, or the apple cobbler. Indeed you are worried, Maria, and about something important. What is it?"

He spoke the last words with a note of real tenderness in his voice. He took her hand and pressed it to his lips.

"Well," he said, looking into her eyes, "what is worrying you? Tell me."

At this moment, the man of perpetual laughter looked like a fine young fellow, genuinely attached to his cousin. Maria looked at him kindly.

"I know that you have a good heart, Olek, and that you are genuinely concerned about what is distressing me. I would gladly tell you, but I fear that you would make a joke of it."

Olek sat upright and put his hand on his heart.

"Speak boldly, cousin!" he said. "I will listen to you as seriously as a priest in the confessional, with the feeling of a brother to whom you have often been a good angel and confessor. As I listen to you, I will be ready for anything. If you desire a singing tree or a talking bird, I will cross mountains and seas for it. If Jadwisia has a pain in her leg or her face, I will call all the doctors who eat and sleep in Warsaw. If someone has offended you, I will challenge him to a duel, or . . . or I will give him a beating with a cane, and that I will do and execute all that, I swear on the beautiful eyes of my goddesses, on memories of my childhood passed with you, Maria, on the dusty walls of my office, and on the cells of my heart in which my blood flows with yours!"

As the young man said all that, his chameleon-like nature covered his face and figure with so many rapidly changing colors—looks, tones, postures expressing idle giddiness, sincere feeling, theatrical exaggeration, and true readiness to exert himself for her sake—that Maria wanted to be angry, but also to laugh, and to press the hand of this frivolous man who nonetheless reminded her of childhood years spent with him, and of their common blood.

"The matter is not very important," she said after a moment's hesitation. "It is nothing that could influence my life or the lives of persons dear to me. It is only that I feel terribly sorry for the poor woman who at this moment is there, behind that door—"

"Ah! So this concerns the dark-eyed goddess? Well! Thank God! I breathe more freely. I really thought that some misfortune—"

"In fact, it is a misfortune, though one that affects, not us, but her."

"A misfortune? Really? Well, I will also feel a little sorry for this interesting widow. But what could have happened to her? Did her dead husband appear to her in a dream? Did—"

"Do not make jokes, Olek! She is, I see, a more unfortunate woman than I thought at first . . . poor . . . and apparently she lacks qualifications."

Olek opened his eyes wide.

"Lacks qualifications! And that is her entire misfortune! Ha! Ha! Ha! *Beau malheur, ma foi!* So young and pretty . . ."

Suddenly he went silent: the crimson portiere had moved aside and Marta was entering the drawing room. She came in, took a few steps, and stopped, resting her hand on an armchair. She was very beautiful at this moment. A hard struggle, perhaps the last throe of a long inner conflict, covered her pale cheeks with a bright flush. A minute or two before, in a spasm of painful feeling, she must have plunged her hands into her thick, dark hair because two black, curly strands were falling onto her forehead, contrasting almost gloomily with the deep pallor that her red cheeks accentuated. As she stood there, with her head slightly bent and her eyes down, her posture did not express either hesitation or anguish, only deep, thorough deliberation.

It was enough to glance at her to see that she was contemplating something profoundly serious—a step that she was unable to take without great effort, without concentrating all her powers of will. Finally she raised her head and approached the lady of the house.

"Is the lesson over already?" asked Maria, who had risen when the young widow entered and was trying to adopt an easygoing smile.

"Yes, madame." Marta's voice was slightly lowered, but steady. "I have finished today's lesson with Miss Jadwisia, and I have come to inform you that it is the last. I cannot teach your daughter any longer."

Surprise, sadness, and embarrassment—the latter the strongest—could be seen on Maria Rudzińska's face. In the face of this voluntary renunciation, the good woman did not allow herself to say the word she had thought of saying for a long time.

"You will no longer teach my daughter, madame?" Maria stammered. "But why, madame?"

"Because—" Marta replied slowly and quietly, "because I am incapable of teaching her."

She lowered her eyes and the blush on her cheeks rose to her forehead, covering her entire face, as if she were overcome with shame.

"I was mistaken about myself," she continued. "Being poor, I understood that I should work. I saw and heard that women who were poor, or reduced to poverty . . . in most cases become teachers. So I thought I would also find work and wages in this profession. I was told that I was only capable of teaching French. And I really thought I knew this language because I speak it easily and well. But now I am convinced that that does not constitute a comprehensive knowledge of the language, and that I have never studied it thoroughly. I see that I have even forgotten the knowledge I acquired during my childhood. That knowledge was discontinuous, superficial, and imprecise, so it is no wonder that I do not remember much. The foreign lady who gave lessons to your daughter was an excellent teacher. Miss Jadwisia knows more than I."

She stopped speaking for a moment as if to gather her strength again.

"Indeed, earning a living is very important to me," she said. "Nonetheless, when I realized that I could not learn quickly everything I should know, I thought that I should not act against my conscience. When you made an agreement with me, you said that above all you demand of your daughter's teacher that she offer her a wide, well-grounded education covering all branches of the subject. I cannot even dream of teaching like that. You have been so kind that besides being dishonest, I would be ungrateful if I—"

Maria did not allow the unhappy woman to speak any longer. She grasped both her hands and pressed them tightly in her own.

"My dear, dear lady!" she exclaimed. "I cannot deny what you are saying about yourself, but, believe me, I find it very sad to part with you. Perhaps I could help you in some way. I have acquaintances, connections . . ."

"Madame," said Marta, raising her eyes, "my only desire is to be given an opportunity to work."

"But how? What do you want to do, and what can you do?" the lady of the house asked quickly.

Marta was silent for a long time.

"I do not know," she replied at last, very quietly. "I do not know what I can do, or if I can do anything well." She looked down as she spoke the last words. Her voice quivered with humiliation.

"Perhaps you would like to give music lessons, madame? Just now one of my relatives is looking for someone who could give music lessons to her daughter."

Marta shook her head.

"No, madame," she said. "I am ten times weaker in music than in French."

Maria reflected. She clung to Marta's hands as if she feared that the widow would leave without receiving advice and help.

"Perhaps—" she said after a moment, "perhaps you studied at least a little natural science? My husband is the guardian of a boy who does not do well in school, so to prepare him, to tutor him . . ."

"Madame," Marta interrupted, "my knowledge of natural science is so cursory that it almost amounts to nothing."

She hesitated, then added after a moment:

"I know how to draw a little. If you know someone who would need drawing lessons . . ."

Maria thought for a moment and shook her head.

"This is extremely difficult," she said. "Few people study drawing, and what is more, it is men who usually teach this subject. Such is the custom."

"Then," Marta began, pressing her employer's hand, "it only remains for me to say goodbye and to thank you for your kindness and helpfulness."

Maria reached for an elegant envelope with a lilac edge in which a few banknotes could be seen, but at the same moment someone standing beside her touched her sleeve. It was cheerful Olek, who throughout the entire conversation had stood at a distance, carrying himself demurely and wearing an unhappy expression. He stared at the young widow's face, half enchanted, half moved with genuine compassion.

She had no attention to spare for him. Perhaps she had seen him when she entered the drawing room, but why should she concern herself about this man who was going to be a witness to her humiliating confession when she herself was, inherently and most devastatingly, a witness to it?

Why should she concern herself with an assumption that someone's eyes were on her at the moment when she herself was looking, terrified, into the depth of her own helplessness and the even deeper abyss of hardship that awaited her?

Marta was oblivious to the young man's presence. Maria, who had forgotten about him, felt someone lightly pulling her sleeve and turned around, a little surprised. She was even more surprised at Olek's expression. His darting eyes were sad and his lips, usually wreathed in vacuous smiles, had a gentle, even somewhat serious look.

"Maria!" he said quietly. "Your husband works for one of the illustrated magazines. Perhaps someone who can draw is needed there."

Maria clapped her hands.

"You are right!" she cried. "I will ask him!"

"But it must be done right away!" Olek cried with his usual animation. "There is a meeting at the editorial office today."

"And my husband is at the meeting."

"It would be easy to inquire about this while the meeting is going on."

"I will write to my husband right away—"

"Write? Nothing of the sort! It will take too long. I will go and call Adam out of the meeting."

"Go, go, Olek . . ."

"I run, I fly, I'm off!" he cried. He seized his hat and with unusual alacrity put it on before he reached the threshold. Without remembering to say goodbye to the two women, he rushed out into the hall. There he threw on his coat and cried once again: "I run, I fly, I'm off!"

And indeed he ran, flew, and was off down the stairs as he had been a month ago, when he wanted to catch up with the young beauty he had seen through the window. Maria was not mistaken in attributing a kind heart to her cousin, and her eyes followed him to the threshold with a certain satisfaction. Then she turned to Marta again.

The young widow stood motionless with a hotter flush on her face than before. She could not help seeing that she had awakened pity, not only in the woman who had pressed her hand a moment ago, but also in this young man who was almost unknown to her, whom she had seen only a few times in passing. It was the first time in her life that she had been an object of sympathy. She herself had almost asked for it. She could not avoid it or reject it; her need was too pressing. Yet the compassion these people were showing her, a benevolent enough feeling in itself, seemed to fall on her like a crushing burden, weighing her down.

She was displeased with herself and unhappy about her conversation with Maria, who had induced strangers to pity her. It occurred to her that she should be stronger, more reserved, more aloof. At this moment she felt as if a part of her personal dignity were lost, as if for the first time she had put out a hand for alms. When the cousins had exchanged lively words about her, when the young man had rushed out of the room to go somewhere and make a request concerning her to people she had never seen, she had felt an enormous desire to leave—to leave at once—to repay their sympathy with a word of thanks, but not to accept any charity, and to say:

"I hope to manage on my own."

The desire was powerful. It obstructed her voice and sent a wave of blood rushing to her head, but she did not surrender to it. She did not leave; she stood still with her head down and her hands clasped tightly. From the depths of her being came a gloomy whisper:

"I cannot hope to manage on my own. I cannot trust myself."

It was a sign of an emerging sense of her own incompetence. Under the influence of this feeling, an undefined but painful shame was growing inside her. "If I were alone in the world!" she thought. "If I did not have a child!"

"Tell me, madame," Maria said, "how can I let you know about the results of my own and my husband's efforts to find work for you? Will you leave your address?"

Marta thought for a moment.

"If you will allow me," she said, "I will come myself to get that information."

At first she wanted to give her address. Then the thought occurred to her that this young, happy woman might forget about her. She was ashamed to be an object of pity, but she was frightened at the thought that the hope of gainful employment that gleamed before her eyes would vanish again, leaving her in terrible uncertainty—in a situation in which she would have nothing to count on.

Wages! What a prosaic, trivial, purely mundane expression! readers may exclaim. If in its place there were burning love, longings of the heart, an elevated dream, the young woman's feelings and thoughts would revolve in what they believe to be the proper orbit, and arouse more sympathy, stronger compassion! Perhaps. I do not know. It is certain that Marta thought or felt that the only guarantor of the life and health of the one person she loved in the world—her child, who assuaged the longing that filled the lonely corners of her poor room—was not the loftiness but the purity and honesty of her thoughts and dreams, and work that would bring a wage.

Perhaps she was mistaken. Only her future was to prove the truth or error of her thinking.

After they had exchanged a few more words, Marta said goodbye to the lady of the house. Maria reached for the envelope with the lilac rim.

"Madame," she said a little shyly, "here is a month's payment for teaching my daughter."

Marta did not reach for it.

"I do not deserve anything," she said, "because I did not teach your daughter anything."

Maria wanted to insist, but Marta grasped her hand, pressed it hard and quickly left the room.

Why did she leave so quickly? Could it be that she wanted to escape the first temptation in her life? She felt that the money she was offered did not belong to her, that she had not earned it. She felt—though perhaps her good intentions were misdirected—that if she had accepted it, she would have been acting dishonestly.

So she did not take it. But when at the gray hour of dusk she opened her purse and counted the coins there in the uncertain light of the waning day, because for economy's sake she had not turned the lamp on; when she realized that her money, received from the sale of one of her two dresses, would only be enough for a few days, and then she would have no more; when little Jasia, huddling up to her mother's knees, complained that the room was cold and asked for a fire in the fireplace, and she had to refuse her because the supply of wood had run low and she could not dream of replenishing it now; when at the end of the evening darkness enveloped her, magnifying her sadness, changing her uneasiness to anxiety; some mysterious power of the imagination conjured up before her eyes a handsome envelope with lilac edges and three five-ruble notes inside. Marta rose quickly from her seat and turned on the lamp. The phantom of unearned money vanished with the darkness, but a dull fear lingered in her mind.

"Could it be possible," she exclaimed, "to regret that I did not act dishonestly?"

This deeply humiliating thought roused her spirit, reviving energies that had been dormant for a time.

"It seems to me," she said to herself, "that I worry unnecessarily. Why, they promised me a new occupation. I used to draw well enough; some said that I had quite a talent for drawing. If only the task is given to me, I will fulfill it well! Good heavens! I will try as hard as I can not to let employment slip through my fingers this time. And the fact that strangers will furnish it to me because of their pity and compassion—what of it? I should not feel humiliated by that! I am still too proud for my own good! I have heard many times that poverty can go hand in hand with pride, but that must only be a theory. I am convinced otherwise!"

The last thought recurred the next day, when Marta walked downstairs and knocked shyly at the door behind which the supervisor of the building lived. He received her in a room that was warm and comfortably furnished.

"Sir," Marta said, "in two days the rent is due for my room and its furnishings."

"Yes, madame," he replied in a tone that was suited both to a statement and to a question.

"I have come to tell you that I will not be able to make a payment just now."

A look of distinct displeasure came over the supervisor's face. He was not a hard man, however. His face was honest and kind, and long years of care had left their traces on it. He looked intently at the young woman's face and said after a moment's reflection:

"This is very unpleasant, but what can one do? The apartment that you rent, madame, is not very large, and I believe that the owner of the house will not terminate your tenancy after the first late payment. But if it is repeated—"

"Sir!" Marta interrupted, speaking animatedly. "I have the promise of work which, I believe, will give me a livelihood."

The supervisor bowed in silence. Marta blushed, and with her eyes down, went out to the street. Soon she returned to her room, bringing in her shawl various items that she had bought in town. She could no longer have dinners brought from the cook shop; she even reproached herself for having bought them until now, because she had spent more than she should have. She hardly thought about herself because in the face of the other cares that oppressed her and the goal toward which she was pressing, she could pay little attention to the amount and type of food that was to sustain her. She thought a glass of milk and a few rolls each day would keep up her strength. But little Jasia, shivering from cold in the poorly heated room, needed warm food at least once a day. So the young widow had spent a few of her remaining złotys for butter, groats, and a small pot.

"Instead of heating the stove in the morning, I will do it at noon," she thought, "and I will cook a little hot food every day for Jasia."

She could not reconcile herself to the thought that the child would have to stop eating meat. The little girl was already pale, thin, and worn down by many discomforts to which she was not accustomed. But fresh meat was expensive, and cooking it took a lot of wood. So Marta bought a pound of smoked ham.

While she was doing her errands, she remembered that there were such places as cheap soup kitchens. She had heard about them once when she was still the wife of a clerk who drew a large salary, and she herself had contributed generously to charitable institutions. But apart from the fact that even the soup kitchen might be too expensive for her in her present situation, Marta felt an instinctive, insurmountable disgust at the thought of seeking refuge under the wing of a philanthropic institution.

"Such a thing exists for elderly people," she thought, "for the sick, for the handicapped, for children deprived of care, for people who are chronically ill or morally or mentally disabled. I am young and healthy. I have not yet tried many things that I would perhaps be able to do. Should I run to a public charity just because I could not find a place for myself in one profession?

"Never!" she thought. She opened her purse and counted the coins that remained after her shopping. She still had about three złotys.

"This will be enough to buy milk and rolls for Jasia and me for a week," she thought. "Meanwhile these good people will find work for me."

Marta's acquaintances on Świętojerska Street were genuinely kind people. They were making sincere attempts to help the poor woman who had awakened their compassion and respect. Their goodhearted efforts were helped by the fact that Maria Rudzińska's husband had a fine position with an illustrated magazine, one of the most prosperous in Warsaw and therefore one of those most able to expand its staff. He had held this position for a long time; he did excellent work and was highly respected. His view counted for a great deal with the publisher and at the editorial meetings. If he interceded for someone, his request could not be disregarded.

Moreover, Adam Rudziński was a writer almost entirely devoted to the study of social issues, among them the situation of poor women. He had seen Marta several times in his home when she was giving lessons to his daughter, and the young woman's engaging appearance, her mourning dress, her dignified bearing and magnanimous behavior, about which Maria enthusiastically informed him, reinforced his zeal on her behalf.

The outcome of those efforts was favorable and not long delayed. One more pair of hands was not excessive for a magazine requiring many people to pool their talents. Only the level of the new worker's capability had to be assessed for her request for work to be accepted or rejected.

Although Adam Rudziński's efforts brought a speedy result given the circumstances, however, from Marta's point of view the intervening time was very long. From the day she voluntarily resigned from the teaching profession, a week passed, and her scanty supply of money was almost completely exhausted. Aside from that, the enforced idleness weighed heavily on her, robbing her of sleep and pricking at her conscience. One morning she went out to town, made her way to Długa Street and knocked at the door of the information agency, where Ludwika Żmińska received her with a much colder, more businesslike air than before.

"I have heard," she said, "that you no longer give lessons at the home of Mr. and Mrs. Rudziński. That is a pity—a great pity for me as well as for you, because the reputation of my agency depends in large part on the good opinion of such households."

Marta blushed; she understood the reproach that was couched in those words. She raised her head quickly, however, and said with a sincerely apologetic expression:

"Forgive me, madame, for disappointing you—"

"A disappointment affecting me personally would be of very little importance," Żmińska interrupted. "But if people cannot rely on my word, my agency suffers greatly."

"I misled you," Marta continued, "because I misled myself. Miss Rudzińska was a pupil too far advanced in her studies for me. But I believe that if the lessons had truly been at the beginners' level, I would have been equal to the task. That is why I have come to see you again, madame. Could I not be given beginners' lessons?"

Ludwika Żmińska's bearing was very cold indeed.

"There are far more people looking to teach beginners' lessons than people needing to take them," she said after a moment, in a voice tinged with irony. "The competition is enormous; the pay is very low. Forty pennies, two złotys at most, for an hour."

"I would take any wage," Marta said.

"Indeed, you would have to take it, since it could not be otherwise. However, I do not promise you anything. I will see, I will try . . . In any case, all the places that I know of today are taken, and you will have to wait for a long time."

As the owner of the agency was speaking, Marta was looking at her attentively. Her eyes were sad and thoughtful but calm as she searched the face of this woman, who was no longer young, for the gleam of responsiveness and goodwill that appeared in it when she had come here for the first time. But this time Żmińska was unmoved, cool, and official. Marta recalled her words from two months ago:

"A woman can pave a way for herself, acquire an independent existence and a position inspiring respect, if she has a special talent or has perfected some skill."

Marta did not have either of those qualifications. The owner of the agency, once disappointed by her and familiar with her limited capabilities and slender supply of knowledge, probably considered her an intrusive, compromising client rather than one likely to be beneficial to her agency. Here where perhaps five, perhaps fifteen people appeared every day in the same situation as hers, with the same requests on their lips, with the same insufficient funds of knowledge, the person who received them could not express the long-enduring sympathy that underlay her professional exterior.

Marta understood that her career as a teacher was over. Wherever she would go in search of a teaching position, her store of knowledge would be scrutinized, and when it proved to be second-rate, she would be dismissed or pushed into the ranks of those who were waiting a long time for small earnings. She would be content with a low salary, but she could not wait for long.

As she walked from Długa Street to Świętojerska, Marta had one thought:

"I was so unreasonable. I did not know the world or myself when on that first evening in that miserable room, I thought I only needed to say that

I was willing to work to join the ranks of those who are employed. Now I go from street to street, from one house to another, looking for . . . and yet . . . if I had been able . . ."

ⅠⅠⅠ

Maria Rudzińska smiled as she welcomed her visitor, pressed her hands warmly, and said, anticipating her question:

"The magazine at which my husband is a member of the staff and a coeditor needs a person who knows how to draw. Here is a sketch done by a well-known artist; you are asked to copy it. As to payment, that will all depend on the merits of your work. What you draw now is a sample that will determine further orders."

The pale ray of the December sun, shining through the city's forest of ledges and curtains of walls, gilded the small window of the attic and glided over the black surface of the table at which Marta sat with her eyes fixed on the drawing that lay in front of her. There were only a few spreading trees in it, and several thick bushes. They shaded the beautiful figure of a seated woman, and a pair of children's heads with smiling faces leaned out from garlands of tangled branches. Far in the background, in vague but graceful outlines, appeared a country cottage with an ivy-covered veranda and a misty, winding road behind it that vanished in the distance.

It was a simple composition representing a scene from daily life in the country, but, executed by the dexterous, inspired hand of a talented artist, it was a beautiful though small work of art. From the rural cottage, with its four simple windows staring charmingly at the viewer, and the figure of a slender woman in a delightful, carefree posture sitting in the shade of a tree, to the playful faces of the children appearing from behind the intertwined rose branches, and the winding road that melted into mist and space, everything was felicitously envisioned and well presented, enchanting the eye, awakening the imagination, and inclining the mind to form comparisons and guesses. The exquisite accuracy and exceptional lightness of the drawing went hand in hand with the poetic idea, emphasizing and enhancing its merits. The artist had drawn on inspiration and technical proficiency alike when, with a light and confident hand, he drew the first lines on the paper, creating a composition full of deep feeling, simple charm, and quiet harmony.

The technical qualities of the drawing did not attract Marta's attention at once. Her first thoughts about it were distracted by the power of recollection and tragic contrast. From a country cottage, from shady trees and dense shrubbery, from the face of a young mother watching the wavelike movements of two small childish figures behind a pristine thicket, memories spilled over, flooding the young woman with feelings that were pleasurable and painful at the same time. Once she had also lived in a quiet, flowery, shady retreat; she had trampled fluffy grass with her light feet, picked roses from branches that leaned toward her, and, with her little hands full of fragrant flowers, run toward a veranda shaded by ivy, like the one in the picture—in front of four windows warmed by the heat of the sun, a veranda hung with a green tent, a cool, refreshing shelter ready to receive the beloved child of the house!

And her mother's look of concern had followed her nimble feet, while the solicitous maternal voice called to her not to go too far from the house, on that road full of stones and ravines, obstacles and dangers, that made its twisted way to where it became lost among mysterious hills and unseen spaces. She had called in vain! Her motherly heart had quivered in vain!

The time came when the child from the country cottage took to the road that ran out from behind its walls and followed a winding, stony path. She had traveled into the world of mysterious hills, unknown places, obstacles, and dangers, and arrived here, where at the top of a tall urban building rose four close, bleak walls, cold, stifling, and lonely. This was the contrast between the past and the present. Marta lifted her eyes from the drawing and glanced around the room, resting her gaze on the pale child who shivered from cold though she was covered with her mother's woolen scarf, and huddled with her head to her knees like a bird in distress.

The familiar, vividly remembered song of a little bird tinkled in Marta's ear—the same bird, it seemed, that in the drawing brushed the top of the rose bush with its open wings. Her child's breathing, heavy and trembling from the cold, seemed to blend with this echo from distant memory. Along the paths of recollection came her mother's beautiful face, then her father's gentle countenance, and after that she saw before her the dark eyes of a young man, eyes whose deep gaze declared "I love you" while his lips said: "Be my wife." All those faces, dearer to her than life and veiled forever by the obscurity of death; all the places where the unclouded idyll of her childhood and early youth had unfolded; all the extinguished lights, the vanished charms, the poisoned joys and broken supports, now quivered with life, resumed their former shapes and colors, and were concentrated in one picture suspended before her as if in a frightening, ugly, bare frame: the cold, empty, gray corners of her forlorn room.

Marta no longer stared at the drawing. Her unmoving eyes, fixed on empty space, were covered with a glassy film that did not dissolve in tears. Her breath came quickly and heavily, but she did not sob. A violent spasm of tears wracked her visibly, but she fought it. She struggled to suppress the rapid beating of her heart and to push from her fevered mind the swarm of memories and the wave of dreams. A mysterious voice inside her cried that with each tear from her eye, with every sob that made her chest heave, with every second passed in this enormous torment of the soul as she wept over the graves of her hopes and love, a fraction of her strength and will would be lost and her energy, patience, and endurance would wane. And she needed so much strength, will, and endurance! The noon of her life had become as severe and demanding as its dawn had been caressing and indulgent.

"Mama!" A moaning voice spoke up and Jasia raised her pale little face. "It's cold here today! Light a fire in the fireplace."

As her answer, Marta leaned over, took the girl in her arms, and pressed her slender body tightly to her bosom. She sat still for a while, clinging with her lips to the small forehead. Suddenly she got up, wrapped Jasia snugly in the woolen scarf, and put her on a low stool. Then she knelt before her, smiled, kissed her pale lips, and said in a tone that was almost carefree:

"If Jasia plays nicely with her doll, tomorrow or the day after I will finish my work, buy some wood, and make a fire for Jasia, a lovely, warm fire. Will that be fine, Jasia? Will that be fine, my darling?"

She smiled as she said this and warmed the girl's cold hands in hers. Jasia also smiled, and with two kisses closed her mother's eyes, which were gazing at her. Then she reached for her doll and a few small wooden toys and stopped looking into the bare, chilly, sooty fireplace. There was total silence in the room. Marta sat at the table and looked at the work of the splendid artist.

Now the memories and sorrows that she had conquered and pushed away by force of will lay in the depths of her soul, not dead, but quiet. Her face was calm as she concentrated all her powers of mind on the drawing; only her eyes brightened with a lively gleam of enthusiasm as she embarked on a new test of her strength and talent. Now her attention was immersed, not in the artist's idea or in the wistful feeling and poetics of the picture, but in the technique, which, grounded in knowledge and rich in means of execution, reached to the very foundation of the art, yet with the lightness of a bird's feather glided on its surface, creating beautiful things in small ways, implanting an idea even in the most subtle line, and using every part of the flat surface, which freely cast up areas of light and shadow. Marta had never drawn from nature, but in the past she had copied small landscapes, trees, flowers, and human faces. So the perfection of the drawing lying before her delighted but did not discourage her.

"I am certainly not such a great artist as the one who drew this lovely picture," she thought, "but probably I can copy someone's work. I must manage to do it."

With that thought, she opened a long box that held drawing tools. Maria Rudzińska, prompted by her kind heart and delicacy of feeling, had guessed what the poor woman needed next, and had given her the box together with the drawing that she was supposed to copy.

Marta's pencil moved over the smooth paper; she felt that her hand was light, that her thought melded precisely with the artist's thought, that her eye found no difficulty in perceiving the most complex curving of a line, the most subtle distinctions and convergences of light and dark. Her heart beat more strongly and joyfully; she breathed more freely; a rosy color appeared on her pale cheeks, and her eyes shone with cheer and enthusiasm. Work, the comforter of the afflicted, the companion of the lonely, the guardian of those battered by the storms of life—work entered the poor attic, bringing peace. In vain the sunbeam that had caressed the blank walls of the room since morning vanished behind the high roofs of the buildings; in vain the great city gave off its dull, mysterious, unremitting noises. Marta did not see or hear anything.

Every now and then she raised her eyes to look at her child as she played quietly in the corner. She spoke a few words to her and immersed herself in her work again. Once in a while she knit her eyebrows and a look of deep reflection settled on her forehead. The difficulties and enigmas of executing the drawing became apparent to her, presenting her with a hard, defiant front of resistance. But she struggled with them, and it seemed to her that she resolved them successfully.

When she lifted her head and looked at her work, she was smiling, but the smile vanished from her lips when she began to compare her drawing with that of the master. Evidently she had doubts and fears, but she pushed them away as if they were too bothersome, too painful and troubling. She worked with deep concentration and great exertion of will, with the spirit and ardor of an imagination in love with the object of its work. She worked with all her mind, soul, and strength, and she only stopped working when the first shadows of evening entered the room. Then she called Jasia, put her on her lap, looked into her face, and smiled at her. But this smile, unlike the smile of the morning, was not forced from a heart in pain, not belied by the gloomy expression in her eyes. It blossomed by itself, without any effort, from the heart of the young mother, who was calmed by work and warmed by hope.

Marta was telling her little daughter one of those fairy tales that weave together miraculous happenings, rainbow colors, birds' songs and angels' wings, absorbing the minds and delighting the imaginations of children. But as she was spinning out these long threads of fantasy for the poor little ear that for some time had yearned for such a treat, her head was filled with one thought that repeated itself like the theme of a musical accompaniment to her life: "If I had been able . . . if I am able . . . if I can do . . ."

"What could I do? What skill do I have?" Marta thought several days later as she climbed the stairs to the Rudzińskis' home.

She did not receive a firm answer to these internal questions this time. However, she would receive it before long because the next day there would be an editorial meeting at which competent people would expresss their opinions of the level of her artistic ability and the value of her drawing.

"Come the day after tomorrow, in the morning," Maria Rudzińska said. "My husband will bring definite news for you from tomorrow's meeting."

Marta came at the appointed time. The owner of the pretty drawing room met her with her usual courtesy and motioned to an armchair by the table on which lay the work Marta had finished two days ago. A middle-aged man with a refined, intelligent, gentle face was sitting at the table: it was Adam Rudziński. He rose to greet Marta, extending his hand to her with great respect. When she sat down, he also resumed his seat, glanced downward, and was quiet for a moment. Maria moved farther into the drawing room and, resting her visibly sorrowful face on her hand, sat silently with her eyes lowered like her husband's.

It was quiet for several seconds in the drawing room. The atmosphere was heavy. Each of the three found it difficult to speak the word that would start a conversation. Adam Rudziński broke the silence.

"I am very sad," he said, "that I am an envoy bringing news that will certainly be unwelcome. However, it was not in my power to make it different than it is . . .."

He stopped speaking and looked at Marta with an expression of large-hearted frankness and sincere compassion. He interrupted what he was saying, perhaps to give the young woman some time to gather strength and prepare to receive a blow. Marta turned a little pale and suddenly looked down as intently as she had looked into the man's face until that moment. No cry came from her lips; she did not even sigh. Adam Rudziński observed her posture and facial expression and felt intuitively that she knew how to be courageous and restrained.

After a while he continued:

"In the matter that presently concerns you, madame, I am myself not a competent judge. I am only repeating what I was directed to say to you. I will do it openly to save you new disappointments and disillusionments, and because nothing is more harmful morally and financially than for a person not to know his own resources as he enters life in society, and to have a mistaken vision of himself.

"Your work shows that you have studied drawing and you have some talent, but . . . you studied too little, and your studies were cursory and superficial. That is why your talent is insufficiently trained, why you are not initiated into the demands of art, why you did not attain an appropriate level of development and power.

"All art has two sides: one that proceeds from the nature of the man who is devoted to it—from his inborn talent—and a second that proceeds from something with which no one is born, but which can be attained only through work and knowledge. Inspiration arises from talent, but inspiration, once it exists, is guided by skill. Technical skill not enlivened by talent cannot create a genuine work of art, and is useful at best for works of craftsmanship. By the same token, talent, even at the highest level, without technical skill is a primitive force, blind, undeveloped, and undisciplined, capable at most of creating things that are incompetent, chaotic, incomplete. Madame, you have talent, even a high level of talent, since one can discover it in your work despite its flawed execution. But—"

"Adam!" exclaimed the lady of the house. Maria Rudzińska rose and approached the table, looking at her husband with a plea in her eyes for the woman who was listening to him sadly and apprehensively. Marta understood the kind woman's concern. She raised her head and said in a confident voice:

"Madame! I want to hear the truth, the entire truth. From my short experience, I am convinced that your husband spoke quite rightly a moment ago when he said that nothing is more harmful morally and financially than for a person not to know his own resources as he enters life in society, and to have a mistaken vision of himself."

Maria sat down at the table. Marta turned her eyes toward Adam Rudziński, who continued:

"Art has various levels; people practice it for different reasons. A rather low level of artistic education is enough to allow a person who possesses it a degree of pleasure that beautifies and diversifies moments of life for himself and those around him. This superficial acquaintance with art, the acquisition of a partial knowledge of it and the means used to create it, is called artistic dilettantism. It has some additional significance in drawing rooms and small salons because it fits agreeably with the style of life of the wealthy or at least well-to-do, seasoning it with charm, poetry, and a continual festival of impressions and activities.

"This dilettantism, however, though it is not completely devoid of noble and useful features and occupies a wide space in the spiritual economy of humanity, cannot be anything more than an addition, an adornment to life, a charming pattern thrown on the warp of existence to color and diversify it. To build a physical existence on it, to wrap it in a fiber of the spirit that is as long as human life—that is impossible and unreasonable.

"It is impossible because from an incomplete cause there could be no complete result. It is unreasonable because what offers the world a trifling and very limited service does not have the right to claim from the world a mutual favor of such magnitude as physical welfare and moral peace. Only above artistic dilettantism, in heights which often the dilettante cannot imagine, exists—art, a powerful force composed of inborn talent developed to the ultimate limit and solid, wide knowledge.

"Dilettantism is one of the toys of life; only art may be an anchor of it. It may be the bedrock that supports the physical existence as well as the moral one. But in art, as in science or craft, the one who receives the most puts the most time, toil, training, and skill into the work he offers society. Here, as everywhere else, competition exists; demand and sacrifice face each other, staring at and evaluating each other. Here, as everywhere else, the degree of a worker's well-being is in direct relation to the excellence of what he produces. In art, just as in any other field of work, a man may make a sufficient and often a very fine living. He may only attain that if he has talent that is not just innate, but cultured—if he is not only a dilettante, but an artist."

Having said all that, Adam Rudziński stood up and bowed respectfully to Marta, adding:

"Forgive me, madame, for speaking so long. I could not put all that I had to say into a few words. I feared you would suspect that those who rejected your work and notified you through me were influenced by caprice or prejudice, which in this case would be a crime. Your drawing does not suit the needs of the magazine. It is not accurate enough, not precise enough; it does not reproduce the concept and character of the model.

"For example, you drew the face of the young mother with warmth and feeling that are plain to see. Nonetheless her features seem blurred in comparison to the clarity given them by the skillful, trained artist. Because of this vagueness, much was lost in the expression of her eyes as they followed the movements of her beloved children, and in the appearance of her head, which is thrust slightly forward, ready to emit a warning or a tender cry.

"The tree, which has such a rich, dense growth of branches in the picture, looks poor and sickly here. The path leading from behind the house, which the artist intentionally veiled in a mysterious mist, in your drawing is almost completely covered with pencil strokes that are too thick, and becomes to the viewer's eye an almost enigmatic, incomprehensible black trail.

"Madame, you understood the artist's idea. You penetrated it, you appreciated it, that is clear; but it is no less clear that you struggled with every detail, every movement of your pencil. You struggled with the technical aspect of the art and you did not solve the problems it posed for you. They were beyond your comprehension because you do not possess the requisite skill and training. That is the whole truth, and I am doubly sorry to express it. As your acquaintance, I regret that you did not receive the employment you require; as a human being, I am sorry that you did not adequately develop your talent. You have talent, without doubt; it is a shame that you did not study more, more deeply, more widely, and that apparently you have no opportunity to study now."

Marta rose, slowly lowered her clasped hands, and said quietly:

"You are right. There is no way for me to study now. I do not have time for it," she added after a moment. She stopped speaking and stood silently, looking down. Adam Rudziński gazed at her with great interest, even with a touch of admiration. He had expected, perhaps feared, tears, moans, recriminations, fainting, and spasms. Instead he heard a very few words of regret at the impossibility of studying, the lack of time for studies.

A slender, delicate woman with a proud bearing and a beautiful face had a great deal of strength if she could listen without tears or sighs to a stern verdict that sentenced her cherished hope to death, and take on her shoulders the unspeakable burden of uncertainty that had fallen on her again after a short period of relief. Her heart and mind must have been very heavy, yet she did not burst into tears. She did not gasp or murmur.

The time of loud groans and tears unashamed of being seen had not yet come for her; her pride was not broken and her strength was not shattered. She stood at the beginning of her road to Calvary, having passed only two stations of the cross, having only twice burned with shame and trembled to her core with the sense of her lack of ability. She still had enough strength, enough pride and willpower, to control outbursts of feeling. She did not know herself well enough to stop expecting the best from herself.

Adam Rudziński respected the impoverished woman's wordless sorrow. He was a complete stranger to her, someone she had hardly seen more than once or twice, and at that moment he felt that he should leave. He bowed deferentially to Marta and left the drawing room. Only then did his wife grasp Marta's hands and press them in hers.

"Dear lady, do not lose hope!" she said quickly. "I cannot allow you to leave my house this time with no consolation, and with your quite reasonable requirements unsatisfied. I do not know your past, but I believe I surmise correctly that poverty took you by surprise, that you were not prepared to be a worker in society, earning a living for yourself and another—"

Marta looked up at her suddenly.

"Yes," she interrupted fervently. "Yes, yes . . ."

She looked down again and went silent. It was obvious that she had been struck by a clear formulation of something that had been nebulous before.

"Yes," she repeated firmly after a moment. "Poverty and the need for work took me by surprise. Nothing armed me for the one and nothing trained me for the other. My past was full of peace, love, and enjoyment. It gave me nothing to help me face trouble and loneliness."

"A terrible fate!" Maria Rudzińska said after a pause. "If every father and mother could foresee and comprehend all the dreadfulness of it!"

She moved her hand over her eyes and, hastily overcoming her emotions, turned to Marta.

"Let us speak of you," she said. "Though two roads have been closed to you for lack of appropriate skills, do not lose hope or courage. The professions of teacher and artist have turned out to be unsuitable for you, but intellectual and artistic work do not constitute the entire range of human activity, or even women's activity. There still remain industry, business, and craft.

"While you were talking to my husband, a happy thought came to me. I know the owner of one of the most prosperous fabric stores very well. I was even at school with her for a few years, and since then we have kept up relations—if not friendship, at least a pleasant acquaintance. The store is large, fashionable, and affluent, and needs an army of salespeople, agents, and other workers. What is more, no more than a week ago, Ewelina D. met me at the theater and told me that she lost one of her best sales assistants and is in difficulty without him.

"Would you agree to stand behind a counter in a store, receive customers, measure fabrics, create window displays, and do other such tasks? Such positions are very well paid. One only needs to fulfill all the requirements with honesty, politeness, and good taste. Will you go with me to Ewelina D.? I will introduce you to her, and if necessary I will ask her and induce her . . ."

A quarter of an hour later, a cab with the two women stopped before one of the most ostentatious stores on Senatorska Street. In front of the wide glass doors stood two chaises with very fine horses, and coachmen wearing livery in the drivers' boxes.

The two women alighted from the cab and entered the store. At the sound of the doorbell, a young man appeared from behind a long table that almost divided the store in half and, gracefully bowing, asked them what they wanted.

"I would like to see Madame Ewelina D.," Maria Rudzińska said. "Is she here?"

"I do not know for certain," the young man answered, bowing again, "but I will find out at once."

He hurried to the wall across the room, placed his lips to the end of a tube running to the upper floors of the building, and spoke into it.

"She has left, but she will be back soon," someone replied from upstairs.

The young man hurried back to the two women standing near the door. "Please sit down, ladies," he said, pointing to a velvet sofa in the corner of the store. "Or," he added, pointing to the carpeted stairway, "perhaps upstairs . . ."

"We will wait here," Maria Rudzińska replied, and sat down on the sofa with Marta.

"We could have gone upstairs and waited for Ewelina's return in her apartment," Maria said to her companion in an undertone. "However, it seems to me that it would be well for you if, before the interview with the owner of the store, you would observe the normal functions of salespeople selling the merchandise and see what they involve."

The scene that unfolded before the eyes of the two women was enormously lively. There were eight people speaking loudly and with exaggerated enthusiasm. There were piles of fabric rolled and unrolled, rustling, iridescent and flashing with the gleam of silk, in all the colors of the world. On one side of the long table, which was covered with lengths of expensive material—some piled on top of each other, others unrolled and lying in ripples—stood four women dressed in satin and sables, probably the owners of the two chaises waiting in front of the store. On the other side were four young men. One can only say "were" because it is impossible to describe all their positions: standing, walking, jumping, bending in all directions, climbing the walls to reach the higher shelves, bowing yes, bowing no, bowing slightly, bowing deeply, gesturing with their hands, chests, heads, lips, eyebrows, and even hair. The latter, though usually it plays a minor role in a man's physical state and appearance, in this case deserves particular attention.

Pomaded, perfumed, gleaming, fragrant, curled into intricate locks or falling onto the forehead in eloquent untidiness, it constituted a masterpiece of the hairdresser's art and lent the appearance of the young shop assistants a high degree of elegance. Perhaps these salesmen were not innately very elegant, but nature had given them great physical strength and large, firm muscles which would very adequately have enabled them to do heavier work, less meticulous and pleasant than unrolling silk fabrics, passing webs of lace between two fingers, and brandishing light, dainty, polished yardsticks. Their shoulders were wide, their hands were big, their fingers were plump, and their faces were not the faces of men in the first blush of youth; their mature features and full beards indicated that they were over thirty.

Black frock coats, made in the most fastidious style, enclosed their wide shoulders; colorful bow ties unfolded like butterflies' wings below their luxuriant beards; their big, muscular hands moved gracefully, and their stout fingers were decorated with rings that, without exceeding the bounds of taste, dazzled the eye! Nothing in the world except snow could excel the whiteness of their shirts, with their fluffy ruffles and the thick embossing on their bulging fronts. Nothing in the world could compete with their lithe movements, agile hops, darting eyes, and exquisitely practiced tongues—neither a string, nor a spring, nor a rubber ball, nor a woman's waist shaped by a corset.

"The color Mexique in white designs!" one of them said, unfolding a length of fabric before the eyes of two women customers.

"Perhaps you prefer Mexique as a solid color!" called another.

"Or grosgrain, sea green! It's the latest fashion . . ."

A sonorous male voice sounded from the other end of the table: "Here are Cluny laces to sew peplums and flounces."

"Laces made in Valencienne, Alençon, Bruges, machine-made, raw silk, tulle . . ."

"Thin grosgrain, color Bismarck. Perhaps too magnificent, too showy? Here is a different one with a black design."

"Bordeaux, a pattern in one color! Do you want something lighter, madame?"

"Mosambique! Sultan! Flesh color! Exquisite for brunettes!"

"The ladies want something in stripes! Horizontal or perpendicular?"

"Here is a fabric with stripes! White and pink, a delightful effect! Eye catching!"

"Gray stripes. Absolutely distinguished!"

"A stroke of blue on a white background! For young persons!"

"Lace for a pouf or a butterfly bustle? Here are the ones with points on the edges—dentelles—and the smooth ones. Which do you prefer?"

"You are buying Bismarck with a design? Very good! How many yards? Seven? No! Ten?"

"Do you prefer laces with dentelles on the edge? You have excellent taste! For a butterfly bustle?"

"For you, madame, gray stripes and for you, madame, a blue stroke on a white background? How many yards?"

The fragments of these conversations between the four young men and the four female customers created a kind of chirping, so to speak, which, coming from the mouths of men, had an uncommon effect. If it had not been for the sounds of voices with an unusual modulation that softly imitated the rustle of fabric falling in waves and the lighter rustle of unfolding lace—voices that nonetheless came from the chests of men with large lungs and flawless voice organs—one could not have guessed that this talk of designs, stripes, strokes, backgrounds, dentelles, flounces, peplums, and butterfly bustles; all that chatter so incomprehensible to the inexperienced ear; this unheard-of erudition about textiles, could really come from the mouths of men—men, who were supposed to be the embodiments of serious strength, serious thought, and serious work.

"Madame Ewelina D. has returned!" A deep voice from the opening of the tube resounded through the store.

Maria Rudzińska rose quickly.

"Wait here for a while," she said to Marta. "First I will speak to the owner of the store by myself, so you will not be unnecessarily upset in case of a refusal on her part. If everything goes well, as I hope it will, I will come for you."

Marta paid close attention to the strategies of buying and selling that were playing out on both sides of the long table. A smile appeared on her pale lips from time to time when the salesmen's hopping became most energetic, their hair bobbed hardest, and their eyes were most expressive.

Meanwhile Maria Rudzińska hurried up the stairs covered with the fluffy rug and through two large halls with breakfront cabinets all around them. She entered a beautifully furnished boudoir in which, after a few seconds, the rustle of a silk dress moving over the floor could be heard.

"Ah! *C'est vous, Marie!*" A woman's chiming, pampered, very pleasant voice sounded, and two graceful white hands grasped Maria's.

"Sit down, my dear, please sit down! This is a great surprise! I am always so happy to see you! How lovely you look! Is your good husband well, and does he always work so much? I read his last article about . . . about . . . I really do not remember now about what . . . but it was beautiful! And sweet Jadwisia—is she a good student? Good heavens! Where are the times when we studied together at Madame Devrient's? You cannot imagine how dear the memories of the moments we spent together at school are to me!"

Ewelina was a graceful, elegant woman of more than thirty, with her hair done behind her head in an artistic bun, features that were regular, though her face was slightly faded, and lively, dark eyes shaded by wide, black eyebrows. She emitted a rapid, almost breathless stream of words without releasing Maria, who sat down by her on a rosewood love seat covered with expensive damask. She would certainly have talked longer, but Maria interrupted her.

"Dear Ewelina!" she said. "Forgive me for shortening our greetings this time and, with no further introduction, opening the discussion of a business matter that is very close to my heart!"

"Maria, you have a business matter to discuss with me? Heavens! I am so happy! Tell me, tell me quickly how I can help you. I am ready to go barefoot to the end of the world for you."

"Oh, no, I will not demand so great a sacrifice from you, my dear Ewelina!" Maria laughed, then added seriously: "Recently I met a poor woman who is of great interest to me—"

"A poor woman!" the proprietor of the affluent store interrupted her animatedly. "Surely you want me to help her? Oh, I will not disappoint you, Maria! My hand is always open to those who suffer!"

She reached into her pocket and took out a large ivory purse. She was about to open it, but Maria stopped her.

"This is not a matter of charity," she said. "The person I want to talk to you about is not asking for charity and would never accept it. She wants work, and she is looking for it."

"For work!" the beautiful Ewelina repeated, raising her black eyebrows slightly. "What hinders her from working?"

"Many things. It would take too long to talk about them," Maria answered gravely. Taking the hand of her friend from school days, she added in a pleading tone, "I came to you, Ewelina, to ask you to offer her an opportunity to work."

"I . . . offer her an opportunity to work? How, my dear?"

"Hire her as a shop assistant."

The shop owner's eyebrows rose higher. An expression of surprise and uneasiness came over her face.

"Dear Maria," she began after a while, stuttering with visible embarrassment, "that is not my function. In general, my husband takes care of business matters relating to the store."

"Ewelina!" Maria exclaimed. "Why do you tell me what is not true? According to the law your husband is the owner of the store, but you are involved in the management of the store with him, and even more than he is; everyone knows that. So I know that you are very well versed in the business, and that you show a great deal of energy in carrying out your plans. Why, then—"

Ewelina did not allow her to finish.

"Well, yes, yes," she said quickly. "It would have pained me to refuse you, Maria, and I wanted to find a quick excuse, to throw the responsibility on my husband. It was wrong of me. I was not open, I admit it. But, my dear Maria, your wish is utterly impossible to fulfill. Utterly."

"Why? Why?" Maria asked in a no less heated tone. Both women had vivid, sensitive personalities.

"Because," Ewelina cried, "women do not sell merchandise in our store, only men."

"But why? Why do women not sell, only men? Does one have to know Greek or be able to bend steel bars with his hands to—"

"Of course not!" her hostess interrupted again. "Good heavens, dear Maria, you are putting me in a difficult position. How can I answer your question, 'Why?'"

"Are you one of those people who do not consider the reasons for their actions?"

"Obviously I am not one of those people. If I had been one of them, I could not have been, as I am, an active partner with my husband in a business venture. Only men sell because, you see—because that is the custom."

"Ewelina, you are trying to put me off again, but you are not succeeding. Old friendship gives me the right to speak to you without being guarded. You tell me that it is the custom, but every custom must have reasons that proceed from the interests or circumstances of those who adhere to it."

Her hostess rose hastily from the sofa and walked rapidly across the room several times. Her long train murmured as it moved along the floor. A light blush of embarrassment appeared on her face, which showed traces of rice powder not completely rubbed off.

"You are pinning me to the wall!" she exclaimed, stopping in front of Maria. "I am very sorry for what I have to say, but I cannot leave you without an answer. I will tell you: our clients do not like female shop assistants. They prefer men."

Maria blushed a little and shrugged her shoulders.

"You are mistaken, Ewelina!" she said hotly. "Or you are speaking insincerely again. This cannot be . . ."

"I am telling you how things are. Young, well-mannered, handsome salesmen are good for the store. They attract customers, especially women customers."

This time Maria blushed with chagrin and indignation. The latter overcame her.

"But that is horrible!" she cried. "If what you say is true, I really do not know why . . ."

"And I do not know why it is that way. To tell you the truth, I have never thought about the reasons. It is none of my concern—"

"What do you mean, Ewelina, it is none of your concern?" Maria interrupted again. "Do you not understand that if you adopt this custom, as you call it, you are pandering to a bad—I do not know exactly what to call it, but most certainly something bad."

The owner of the store stood in the middle of the room and stared at Maria with wide eyes. In those dark, shining eyes there was much cleverness and even wisdom, but at that instant, restrained simpers twinkled in them.

"What do you mean?" she said slowly. "Do you think that for some theory out there I should expose our venture, our own and our children's only asset, to losses and risks? It is all well and good for you literary people to reason in such a way, sitting over a book and a pen, but we entrepreneurs, we have to be practical."

"Should entrepreneurs believe that just because they are businesspeople they are exempt from the feelings and obligations of citizens?" Maria asked.

"Not at all!" the owner of the store exclaimed with new fervor. "That is why neither I nor my husband avoid fulfilling these obligations. We always give as much as we can . . ."

"I know that you are benevolent, that you are active in all the philanthropic societies and projects, but are donations the only thing? You are wealthy people and in many ways influential; you should take the initiative in everything that has as its aim the reform of bad customs and correction of social errors!"

Ewelina gave a forced laugh.

"My dear," she said, "reform and correction belong to such people as . . . your husband, for instance: scholars, writers, journalists. We are people of precise calculations. We must maintain the most exact calculations in our dealings with the public, with its tastes and demands. It is our master; our existence depends on it—the success and the future of our enterprise."

"Yes," Maria said firmly, "and for that you should cater to its senseless caprices and its dubious decency and tasteless proclivities? And just to annoy you at least a little in return for what you have said, I will tell you, my dear Ewelina, that your shop assistants, putting on airs and graces and chatting like parrots about designs and butterfly bustles, look enormously amusing!"

Ewelina exploded with chuckles.

"I know!" she cried, carried away with laughter.

"If I were in your place," Maria continued, "I would advise these gentlemen to busy themselves with a plow, an ax, a hammer, a trowel, or something in that line rather than silk and lace. It would be much more becoming to them."

"I know, I know!" Ewelina laughed.

"I would replace them," Maria concluded, "with women who are not strong enough to plow, forge, and lift rocks."

All at once Ewelina stopped laughing and looked seriously at Maria.

"Dear Maria!" she said. "These people also need to make a living, and their need is more pressing, more urgent, than that of women. They are fathers of families."

This time Maria smiled.

"My dear," she said, "I must remind you of our friendship again and tell you that you have just repeated automatically what you constantly hear but have probably never reflected on. Perhaps these people are fathers of families, but the woman for whom I am interceding with you also has a child to raise and feed. If I, for example, had the misfortune to lose my good, worthy husband, who offers me not only happiness but a secure existence because of his work, would I not be a mother and the person responsible for the care of my family? If within a few years both you and your husband passed away and, as often happens, left no estate, would your oldest daughter not be responsible for supporting, raising, and guiding the younger brothers and sisters?"

Ewelina listened to these words with her eyes cast down. Evidently it was difficult for her to formulate an answer. But it was not easy for her to refuse, without giving any reason, a request from a woman whose friendship was close to her heart and perhaps flattering to her self-regard. After a moment her exceptional shrewdness, which expressed itself in her face and eyes, furnished her with a new answer:

"Anyway," she said, raising her eyes, "my dear Maria, do you find it respectable for a young woman (your protégée is undoubtedly a young woman) to spend entire days behind the same counter with several young men? Would that not lead to developments that would be disastrous for her, unpleasant for me, and publicly compromising for my store?"

"Ewelina, you have repeated again one of the commonplace observations that circulates everywhere. You fear that working with men would impose a strain on a woman's virtue and honor, but do you not fear that poverty would do the same thing? My protégée, as you called her, lost her husband three months ago. She has a child whom she loves. She is sad, sober, completely occupied by the search for a means of earning money, and, I am convinced, very honest. Do you suppose that a woman in such a situation, with such emotions and recollections, with such a fear of tomorrow, could pay the least attention to your foppish assistants? I assure you that not a single frivolous thought would enter her head."

"Dear Maria!" Ewelina exclaimed. "You cannot prove what you have just said. Women are so frivolous . . . so frivolous . . ."

"True," Maria replied, looking gravely at her old friend. "But is pushing them away from every kind of work a cure for their frivolity? Ewelina, I repeat again that the woman of whom I am speaking is neither frivolous nor dishonest now. But if she walks away from many doors as she is about to walk away from yours, after begging for work as others beg for alms, I do not vouch for the sort of person she will become in the future."

"You are pinning me to the wall again!" cried the owner of the shop. "Very well; I believe you when you say that the person you want to help is the model and personification of virtue, sobriety, and honesty. But can you also assure me that she will be punctual in arriving for work, and that she has a sense of order, a knowledge of mathematics, and an ability to carry out tasks without the slightest delay or neglect?"

Now it was Maria's turn to hesitate. She recalled Marta's failures because she lacked competence at teaching and drawing. She recalled Marta's own words of a few hours ago: "Nothing armed me against poverty. Nothing taught me to work."

She said nothing. Ewelina, keen and lively as a spark, seized on her companion's moment of embarrassment and hesitation.

"Dear Maria, you said a moment ago that salespeople need to know nothing more than how to unfold, arrange, and measure material. It only seems that way. They have many other attributes; for instance, they are extremely well organized. Even one object put in the wrong place, one crease in a fabric folded poorly, one roll of lace carelessly thrown, creates chaos in the store or causes serious loss. The salespeople must also be able to calculate, and calculate accurately, because every hour, almost every minute, large sums of money flow in, altering the figures. An error of one penny can cause disorder in the accounts, which we must guard against diligently.

"Finally, and most important, the salespeople should know the world and people, and know how to deal with each person, how to please them, whom to believe, whom to refuse credit, and other such things. Women most often lack these capabilities. They are not in the habit of being organized. They are inaccurate. They must carry multiplication tables in their pockets to calculate the smallest sums. They are meek and innocent; they have barely left off clinging to their mothers' skirts. They hardly dare to raise their eyes and look the customers in the face; either they do not know how to talk to them and what to think of each customer, or else they are uncontrolled, loud, and scatterbrained. They invite improper attentions; they flirt, talk, and behave tactlessly, risking disgrace and compromising the institution in which they work.

"Men, however amusing they seem because their activities and deportment are not altogether manly, are convenient and useful for store owners. That is why every store employs men on a larger scale. Anyone who tried to replace them with women came out badly. My dear, women today are not brought up to resign themselves to rigorous duties, the despotism of numbers, and the demands of such a diverse population as the buying public."

The owner of the store stopped speaking and stared at her companion with a degree of triumph. Indeed, she had reason for triumph. Maria Rudzińska stood silently with her eyes down and a sad look on her face. Ewelina took her hand.

"Well, tell me, dear Maria," she said, "tell me honestly: can you guarantee that your protégée is orderly, accurate, clever at mathematics, tactful, and discriminating about people, just as you have vouched that she is honest?"

"No, Ewelina," Maria said with difficulty. "I cannot guarantee that."

"And now," the owner of the store pressed her more vehemently, "tell me, can you, people of theory and reasoning, justly demand of us, people of calculation—pragmatists—that we hire as a sort of philanthropic initiative, or, as you said, civic obligation, people with no aptitude for business, who will cause us trouble, expose us to losses, and perhaps bring on the complete collapse of our enterprises? Tell me, can anyone justly demand this of us?"

"Of course not," Maria stammered.

"Well, you see," Ewelina said, "you ought to excuse me for not fulfilling your wish. The fact that poor women are excluded from business is certainly regrettable, but it is necessary and inevitable because of the caprices and not altogether transparent instincts of wealthy women who require diversion, and because of God only knows what impressions on the part of society concerning women's incompetence, their timidity, and the shallow-mindedness of poor women who need work but are not skilled enough to do it. When the first group becomes wiser and nobler, and the second is better prepared to work with precision and responsibility, then I will dismiss my salesmen, and I will ask you to choose salesladies for me from among your protégées."

With those words Ewelina D. kissed both Maria's cheeks with her characteristic vigor.

Marta, sitting in the store, heard the rustle of a dress and the steps of her temporary protectress while she was still at the head of the stairs. The young widow's hearing was strained and her patience nearly exhausted. She rose and looked intently at the face of the woman who was coming down to meet her. After a few seconds her hand trembled slightly and she leaned against a chair. Maria's lowered eyes and the vivid blushes on her cheeks told her everything.

"Madame!" she said quietly as she approached Maria. "Spare yourself the grief of recounting the details. I was not hired, was I?"

Maria shook her head and pressed Marta's hand in silence. They left the store and stood on the wide sidewalk. Marta was very pale. One could say that she was cold because she trembled a little under her fur coat, and that she was deeply ashamed of something because she could not tear her eyes from the stones in the pavement.

"Madame!" Maria spoke first. "God sees how painful it is for me to be unable to help you on this difficult road. You are hindered on the one hand by your lack of preparation and on the other by custom, by a lack of initiative on the parts of employers, and by the bad reputation that has attached itself to working women."

"I understand," Marta said slowly and quietly. "I was not hired here because it is contrary to custom, and because I do not inspire confidence."

"Give me your address, madame," Maria said, declining to answer. "Perhaps I will hear of something useful for you. Perhaps I will still be able to help you."

Marta gave her the name of the street and the number of the house where she lived. Then, raising her eyes with an expression of warm gratitude, she reached out to press the kind woman's hands.

But the two women had hardly clasped each other's hands when Marta pulled hers away and took a few steps back. Maria Rudzińska had slipped into her hand the same envelope with lilac edges that Marta had not wanted to accept two weeks before.

Marta stood motionless for a moment. Her pallor vanished and a scarlet blush covered her face.

"Charity!" she whispered. "Charity!" A quiet sigh and a stifled sob shook her chest. Suddenly she began to run after Maria, but the endless wave of pedestrians filled the sidewalk between them, and she lost sight of her. Only at the corner did she see Maria sitting in a cab that was turning in the opposite direction.

"Madame!" she called.

Her voice was weakened, dulled, and stifled by the loud din of other voices and the rattle of vehicles on the street.

Having been endowed with money by a compassionate hand, she made her way toward Świętojerska Street, intending to return the gift that branded her forehead with a warm flush of humiliation. Her step, at first quick and feverish, after a few minutes became slower and less certain. Had the moral shocks of which she had experienced so many on this day undermined her physical strength? Was she overcome by some deep thought, by an inner hesitation that caused her intention of a few minutes ago to waver?

In her hand she pressed a delicate envelope in which several valuable banknotes rustled. She stopped at the corner of Świętojerska Street. She stood motionless for a while, rested her hand on a wall, and leaned over. Her face had lost its color. Suddenly she turned in another direction and walked toward her apartment.

In her soul, pride and fear had fought a great, rending battle in which the first gave way to the second. Young, healthy, not yet worn out and exhausted, with all her powers and desires channeled into a longing for work,

Marta had nevertheless accepted money she had not earned. She would perhaps not have accepted it, and her feeling of personal dignity would not have given way before the fear of poverty, if she had been alone in the world. But at the top of a tall building, between four bare walls, her child was shivering with cold and looking with longing eyes into the sooty depths of the empty fireplace as her pale face, sunken cheeks, and thin, sickly body demanded more substantial food.

It was a very important day in the life of the young woman, although perhaps she did not realize its significance. It was a day when for the first time she accepted charity, tasting the bread that is bitter enough to the elderly and handicapped, but is venomous, putrefying poison to the young and healthy.

That evening in the attic room, a cheerful fire burned on the hearth, and Jasia sat at the table over a bowl of broth. For the first time in many days the child experienced a pleasant feeling of warmth, and she ate her carefully prepared, nourishing food with a lively appetite. Her large, dark eyes moved by turns from the golden beams of light in the fireplace to the slices of bread covered with a thin layer of butter that lay next to her plate, and her mouth did not close even for a moment.

Marta sat very still in front of the fire, with her profile outlined against the red background of the flame. She appeared somber and preoccupied. There was a dry gleam in her eyes; her brows were knit, and her white forehead was deeply furrowed. In front of her, suspended in empty space, stood the figure of a woman wringing her hands with a look of deadly fear and a blush of shame on her face. It was a reflection of herself in the mirror of her imagination.

"Are you," Marta thought, arguing silently with the apparition, "are you the same woman who so convincingly promised herself and her child that she would work and make her own way and gain a place under the sun with her energy and endurance? What have you achieved since you made those heroic decisions? How have you fulfilled the promise made deep in your soul to the spirit of your child's beloved father?"

The figure of a woman moved in the space like slender boughs disturbed by the wind. Her only answer was to wring her hands more frantically and whisper with trembling lips: "I could not do it! I do not know how!"

"Oh, you incompetent thing!" Marta cried inwardly. "Are you worthy to call yourself a human being if your mind is so empty that you do not know what to think of yourself, and your hands so weak that they cannot shelter one child's poor little head? Why did people respect you once? Can you respect yourself now?"

The figure unfolded her hands and put them over her face, which was leaning down. Tears fell from Marta's eyes in a warm stream. Large drops seeped through her fingers as they covered her face.

"Mama, you are crying!" little Jasia exclaimed, jumping up from her chair.

She stood in front of her mother and looked at her for a moment, half amazed, half indignant. Then suddenly she crept over, put her thin arms around her mother's knees, and began to cover her legs and hands with kisses. Marta took her hands away from her face and sat as if turned to stone for a few seconds. Her child's sweet kisses burned her like slippery snakes of grief. The fierce love of this slender creature kneeling at her feet tore at her heart and tormented her conscience.

She leaned over, took the child in her arms and pressed her lips to the small forehead and cheeks again and again. Then she rushed from her seat to the window, fell to her knees, and raised her eyes and hands toward the patch of deep, dark sky that glittered with stars.

"God!" she cried almost aloud. "Give me a place on the earth! Even a tiny, poor place where I would have room for myself and my child! Do not let me be so faint and weak that I must accept charity again. Do not let me fail to fulfill my duty as a mother, and lose my clear conscience and my self-respect."

Indeed, the woman's pleas to the heavens were absurd and unjustifiably demanding, were they not, readers? She did not ask to sit in a chair at a ministry, or to make her name famous throughout the world, or with licentious freedom to indulge in forbidden pleasures. She wanted to live and be able to nourish the one being she loved with a piece of bread. She wanted to avoid the fate of a beggar and not burn with shame in her own eyes. How ambitious she was, how envious and unbridled in her self-indulgence, was she not?

Again she conquered herself; she stilled the voices of the shame, sorrow, and fear that tore at her, and beat them back. She rose from her knees with a serene face, took the crying child on her lap, and in a quiet, gentle voice began to tell her her favorite fairy tale. It was clear that she had great strength of spirit and will. Was her strength to remain useless to her—to help her only in her emotional struggles, and then meekly bend and collapse help-lessly before the adversarial force of her own incompetence and the oppres-sive external elements that surrounded her?

Throughout the long winter night Marta stared into the darkness that filled her room without closing her eyes even for a minute, listening invol-untarily to the calm breathing of her sleeping child and thinking of what she ought to do the next day.

|||

Around noon on the following day, a woman in mourning entered a small but very elegant store with windows full of bouffant dresses, and a display of graceful hats and caps gleaming like a cluster of colorful butterflies. In this store at an earlier stage of her life, Marta had often bought items needed to complete her costume.

At the sound of the bell that trembled on the door, a still-young woman with a beautiful figure and a very pleasant face came out of a room nearby. She looked at Marta, smiled, and bowed very politely. Obviously she recog-nized her former client and welcomed her again with pleasure.

"You have not been here for such a long time, madame!" the owner of the store said with the same polite smile. Then, glancing quickly at Marta's mourning dress, she added: "For heaven's sake! I heard about your misfor-tune. I knew Mr. Świcki well!"

An expression of pain passed over the young widow's face. The name of her beloved and now lost husband pierced the fresh wound in her heart like a stiletto. But she could not allow herself to stop for long and listen idly to her inner voices, the voices of grief and memory.

"Madame," she said, lifting her eyes to the woman standing before her, "I used to come here to buy things. Now I come to you with a request that you buy something from me: my time and my work."

As she spoke, she kept her voice from quivering and forced a smile.

"Honestly, I would be happy to be of use to you, madame, but . . . I did not exactly understand what you meant."

"Would you not hire me, madame, to work at your store as a seamstress?"

On hearing these words the owner of the store did not seem at all sur-prised or confused. Nor did she alter her expression, which was courteous and compassionate. For a while she stood thinking in silence. Then she pointed to the door of the adjoining room and said very politely:

"Please come to the workshop. We will be able to talk more comfortably about business."

The workshop next to the store was situated in a large room with a table beside its windows. On the table were piles of ribbons, lace, feathers, flowers, and pieces of fabric. Three young women sat beside it making hats, headdresses, and decorations for gowns, all of which demanded a delicate, skilled hand. Marta could hear the clacking of two sewing machines with two women leaning over them. In the middle of the room stood another table completely covered with patterns, large pieces of woolen fabrics, linen, batiste, and muslins, among which glinted steel scissors and lead crayons and pencils. All the women were very busy with their work; only one raised her head from her machine when Marta entered and nodded politely when their eyes met.

The owner of the store motioned Marta to a chair next to one of the tables, then turned to a young woman who was fastening a luxuriant ostrich feather to a velvet hat.

"Miss Bronisława!" she said. "This lady would like to work here. I believe that the circumstances are propitious for her. Yesterday we were saying that one more pair of hands would be very useful."

The woman so addressed, who was obviously the most important employee in the store, rose and approached the table.

"Yes, madame," she said. "Since Miss Leontyna's departure, one sewing machine has remained idle. Miss Klara and Miss Krystyna cannot keep up with the sewing. I also cannot do enough cutting because I must oversee the production of hats. The work is delayed and orders are not filled on time."

"You are right," answered the owner of the store after a moment's thought. "I have thought of that myself. And because Madame Świcka came with a desire to work here, it seems to me that nothing stands in the way of fulfilling the wish of a person who was kind to us in other times."

Miss Bronisława bowed politely.

"Indeed," she said, "if only madame is skilled at cutting . . ." The words were spoken as a question.

Just then one of the machines went quiet. The young woman who was sitting at it raised her head and began to listen attentively to the conversation.

Three women standing by the large table in the middle of the room were silent for a moment. The owner of the store and her assistant looked inquisitively at Marta. Marta looked over the patterns spread out on the table, which were covered from top to bottom with black lines, dots, and wavy marks that ran across and along the paper, running together, running apart, crossing each other, and making geometric figures of all kinds. They presented a chaos impossible to unravel for the unpracticed eye.

Marta looked up slowly and reluctantly.

"I cannot claim to be able to do something that I cannot do," she said. "It would be dishonest on my part, and it would not do any good. I only know how to cut a little, a very little—just how to cut a collar, perhaps a shirt. I do not know how to cut dresses, coats, or even the more elegant underclothing."

The owner of the store was silent, but a disagreeable smile appeared on Miss Bronisława's lips.

"It is strange!" she said, turning to the owner of the store. "Many people want to work at sewing, but it is so difficult to find someone who would be good at cutting. After all, it is the basis of the entire operation."

Then the excellent and no doubt highly paid seamstress turned to Marta.

"And how is your sewing?" she asked in an inquiring tone.

"I know how to sew well enough," Marta replied.

"On a machine, undoubtedly."

"No, madame, I have never sewn on a machine."

Miss Bronisława stiffened, folded her hands on her chest, and stood in silence. The owner of the store also looked a little stiffer and colder than before.

"I am really . . ." she began after a while, stammering and a little confused, "I am really very sorry. What I needed most of all was a person skilled at cutting and sewing, but on a machine. We only sew on machines here."

Again there was a moment of silence among the women standing by the table. Marta's lips trembled a little and her face went red and white by turns.

"Madame," she said, raising her eyes to the owner of the store, "could I not learn—I would work for free in the meantime . . . just to be able to learn—"

"Impossible!" Miss Bronisława cried in a sharp voice.

"It would be difficult," the owner of the store interrupted. Speaking more politely than her employee, she continued, "We make various types of garments, most of them to order, from expensive fabrics that could not be used for teaching and practice. We must complete our work quickly, and because of a lack of well-trained workers, we have too few hands and we are behind. That causes us losses and unpleasantness. That is why we can only hire workers who are adequately trained. I deeply regret—please believe me, madame, I deeply regret—that I cannot fulfill your wish."

Only when the owner of the store finished speaking did the machine that had gone silent at the beginning of the conversation resume its rattling. The woman leaning over it had a tear in her eye.

After leaving the store, Marta did not go toward her apartment, but in the opposite direction. From the look on her face one could guess that she was walking aimlessly. Her hands were pushed into the sleeves of her coat and clasped tightly together. She felt an involuntary but overwhelming desire to raise them and press her head, which was unspeakably hot and heavy. In that head one thought repeated itself obdurately, unrelentingly, and with unnatural rapidity: "I do not know how!" This thought burst into thousands of lightning flashes, thousands of stilettos that pierced her brain, pricked her temples and stabbed her chest. After several minutes she thought: "Always and everywhere the same thing . . ."

She did not think about anything else for a while, but rather repeated to herself mechanically but incessantly: "I do not know how!"

Suddenly she added a question: "What is it that always and everywhere follows me, and wherever I enter, pushes me out?"

She rubbed her forehead and answered herself: "I always go everywhere alone, and everywhere it is I who push myself out."

She made a great effort to think. In her mind she reached back to the moment in the information agency when she sat at the grand piano to play the unfortunate "Maiden's Prayer," then forward to the time a few minutes ago when, standing in the workshop of the affluent store, she had had to answer: "I do not know how!"

"It is always the same!" she thought to herself again. "I know how to do a little of everything, but nothing well enough . . . Everything for decoration or the small comforts of life and nothing for real use . . ."

These words forced themselves into her thoughts, became entwined like a net around one phrase—"I do not know how!"—and exhausted her. When she had left home that morning, she had been so worried, so busy—almost feverishly busy—with her new plan that she had not thought of eating. Watching Jasia drinking her usual morning glass of milk, she had even felt a certain disgust at the sight of food. Her psyche, torn and wounded, was expressing itself physically. Her legs were unsteady and her heart beat harder and faster than usual, although she was walking slowly.

Now her mind struggled with a new question embodied in one short word: "Why?" After a while, other words began to attach themselves to that one, first chaotically, then as a logical train of thought. "Why is this?" the young woman asked herself. "Why do people demand something from me—skill, knowledge—that I have never been given? Why has no one ever given me what people demand from me?"

At that moment Marta trembled. She felt someone's light touch on her arm and heard the gentle, even timid voice of a woman behind her.

"Would you allow me to introduce myself again?" said the voice.

Marta turned around and saw the same woman who had raised her head from her sewing machine and nodded politely when she entered the workshop, then stopped sewing and listened to the conversation that decided her fate. She was plain, not tall, but graceful, like most women of Warsaw, and very well dressed. Good sense and kindness radiated from her face, which was pitted from smallpox.

"Perhaps you do not recognize me, madame," she said, walking beside Marta. "I am Klara; I have worked at Madame N.'s store for nearly five years now. I used to make dresses for you. I brought them to you on Graniczna Street."

Marta looked at her with misty eyes.

"Indeed, I remember you," she said with difficulty after a moment.

"Please excuse me for being so bold as to approach you in the street," Klara continued, "but you were kind and polite to me then. You had such a lovely little daughter. Is your daughter . . ."

She hesitated, but Marta guessed her thought.

"My child," she said, "is alive."

The last word was torn from her lips against her will, probably because of a sudden, inarticulate bitterness that sounded in her voice as never before. Klara was silent for a while as if she were thinking. Then she said:

"I heard of Mr. Świcki's death and I wondered right away how you would manage, especially with a child. I was so happy to see you in our store, and I thought that you would be working there with us. That would have been very good because Madame N. is kind and she does not pay badly. Miss Bronisława is just a little capricious and makes a fuss once in a while, but when one is poor, one must put up with anything at times, as long as there is work. That is why I was sorry, very sorry, when I heard Madame N. refuse to hire you. I remembered my poor Emilia."

The seamstress spoke the last words more quietly, as if to herself, but Marta was struck by them more than by what had come before.

"Who is this poor Emilia, Miss Klara?" the young widow asked.

"She is my cousin, a few years younger than I. My mother and her mother were sisters, but as often happens, their lots in life were not the same. Her mother married a clerk, my mother a craftsman. When we were growing up together, Emilia was a young lady, and I a simple girl. She was also pretty, and I was blemished by smallpox when I was twelve years old. So my aunt always used to say: 'I will give Emilia an education and then I will marry her well.' At first she had a governess; then she was sent to a small private school.

"When the smallpox marred my face, my mother worried terribly, but not my father. 'So what?' he said. 'She will be homely, she will not marry. It's no great matter! A man does not marry and he lives well enough!' My mother retorted: 'For a man it is different! God forbid that Klara should die of hunger because she does not get married!'

"But my father did not worry like my mother; he laughed. Sometimes he was angry. 'Oh, you women, you women!' he would say. 'You think you will starve to death if you do not marry! Does the girl not have hands to work?' For you must know that he was a carpenter, and he liked to show off his strength. He used to say: 'Hands are the thing! God gives a head to one and not to another, but everyone has hands!'

"I was thirteen years old when my parents began sending me to a garment factory for training in sewing. Naturally, they paid for me, and they paid a great deal, but, thank God, I learned everything that was needed."

"And did you study for a long time?" Marta asked, listening with growing interest to the seamstress's simple story.

"Oh! I studied for a good three years," Miss Klara answered. "And even then I could not earn anything at first. For an entire year I worked for free at a store to practice cutting and sewing on a machine, and learn more about fashion. Now I know so much that I could open a small factory or shop of my own if I had money, because for that one needs some capital. But three years ago my father passed away, and besides me, two younger brothers stayed with my mother. One has an apprenticeship with a carpenter and the other goes to school. Their studies must be paid for, and my mother, who is no longer young, provided with some comforts."

"And you alone work for all this?"

"Almost alone. We inherited no money from our father, but he left us a small house on Solna Street. We live there and do not have to pay rent. Anyway, Madame N. pays us well and with what I have from her, somehow we make ends meet well enough to live and give my brothers some direction in the world."

"My God!" Maria exclaimed. "How happy you are!"

"Yes," Klara answered. "Actually, there is nothing joyful about sitting at work for whole days and only having time to go out on Sunday or a holiday. But when I think that my work gives me a way to support my mother and ensures a future for my brothers, I am very happy, and I feel great pity for all those who, as my father used to say, have neither a head nor hands. How I worried about Emilia! How I cried because of her!"

"She did not marry?"

"It did not happen somehow, although she was pretty and educated. Her father lost his position and that distressed him so that he became disabled; he still lies in bed, poor thing, neither alive nor dead. The mother is also sickly, and to tell you the truth, she is a very moody, snappish woman. Besides Emilia she has a younger daughter and a son, and she does not know what to do with them, because one has to pay for studies everywhere, and in their house there is poverty and hunger.

"At first, when they became poor, my aunt tried to force Emilia to work. She had been spoiled with balls and clothes, and did not want to. And it turned out that the fine education my aunt had given her had not taught her how to work with her hands or head. She wanted to be a teacher, but it was no good! She strums and strums on the piano and it is said that she speaks French pretty well, but when it came to teaching, no one wanted her. She only got two tutoring assignments at forty pennies an hour, but soon she lost them. Anyway, she does not know how to do anything well. Wherever she went looking for work, she was turned away.

"At home her mother scolds her for being lazy, her sick father groans in bed, and her brother fritters away his time on the streets and looks as though he will soon turn into a thief. The sister argues with the entire family out of spite and boredom. There is nothing to eat or to light a fire with. Emilia has a good heart, so she worries terribly. She has grown thinner. We thought she would get consumption, but only two months ago she found work—"

"She found it!" Marta cried and breathed deeply, as if a heavy load had been lifted from her chest. When she listened to the story of poor Emilia, though she did not know her, it seemed to her that someone was telling the story of her own last few months. The similarity between Emilia's sad lot and hers awakened in her a passionate sympathy and curiosity. But Klara was silent for a while. After reflecting and then hesitating, she said a little shyly:

"When you left our shop, I tried to catch up with you on the street. Fortunately, this is the time when I go home for two hours every day to have dinner and help my mother in the kitchen. Then I return to the shop for five hours. So I ran after you, madame, to ask you if . . . if by chance you were in the same situation that my poor Emilia was in two months ago, perhaps you would agree to work where she works now . . ."

She spoke so diffidently that it was clear that this suggestion was not the most desirable one. But Marta, as if awakened from a long sleep, quickly grasped her hand.

"Miss Klara," she exclaimed, "tell me more, and tell me quickly! I will agree to anything, anything in the world! I am driven to desperation."

Her voice was choked and trembling. She pressed the hand of the seamstress almost convulsively.

"Oh, my God!" Klara exclaimed in turn. "How fortunate that I thought of this, since you are in such an unpleasant situation, and with a child . . . with this lovely little angel that you allowed me to play with sometimes when I brought your dresses to Graniczna Street. Although, really, the fate of the women working at Madame Szwejc's shop is not to be envied—"

"Who is this Madame Szwejc? Where does she live? What does she do?" Marta asked, on edge with curiosity and anxiety.

"Madame Szwejc has a factory on Freta Street, madame, where they make all kinds of underclothes. It is a strange shop. It is large, it is even supported with a great deal of capital, and about twenty women work there, but not one has a sewing machine. For nearly six years now, sewing has been done on machines in all the shops, but Madame Szwejc did not buy even one. She and her daughter do the cutting, but she hires workers to sew, workers who do not know how to use a sewing machine but need work urgently. She pays them . . . it is sad and shameful to talk about what she pays them—"

"All this does not change my decision, Klara," Marta interrupted briskly. "I, like your cousin, do not know how to do anything well, and I must go where the requirements are lowest."

"And they pay the least," Klara concluded sadly. "But it is better to have something than nothing. So, if you wish, I can take you to Madame Szwejc's."

"Only give me the address and I will go myself. You do not have much time."

"No, I will go with you. I will only be late for dinner, and it does not matter. My mother will not worry, because sometimes they keep me at the shop longer than usual if there is urgent work. Anyway, I have not seen Emilia for a long time. We will go together."

Again Marta gratefully pressed the hand of the goodhearted seamstress and both women made their way toward Freta Street.

"Madame Szwejc is not a young woman anymore," Klara told Marta as they walked, "and people say all sorts of things about her past. She set up her shop twenty years ago, but she was not doing well as long as there were no sewing machines. After sewing machines were introduced, she became wealthier. Perhaps it seems strange, but that is how it was.

"I heard Madame N. tell Miss Bronisława that Madame Szwejc exploits poor workers who are not skilled and because of their poverty have to work for any wage at all. I do not understand the meaning of the word 'exploit' very well, but it seems to me that if Madame Szwejc mistreats poor women, then it is not only her fault, but someone else's."

Here the seamstress grew silent and reflected for a moment. Evidently something was dawning on her that she did not fully understand.

"I do not know whose fault it is, but, madame, why are there women in the world who can be mistreated—what am I saying?—who go and offer to be mistreated just to get a piece of black bread?"

Marta walked faster. She walked so fast that Klara could hardly keep up with her. Soon they found themselves on Freta Street.

"Here," said Klara, entering the low, damp gate of one of the tenements.

From the gate they entered a long, dark, narrow courtyard surrounded by high walls—old, damp walls under an elongated patch of cloudy sky. It must always have been cloudy and stifling there, because above the walls a number of chimneys could be seen venting smoke which, pressed down by the moist air, surged in the tight, enclosed space, spreading thick layers of gray fog through the courtyard.

At the far end of the courtyard, opposite the gate, a long, narrow sign hung above a few small stairs and a decaying door. Against a background of dirty sapphire blue, large yellow letters formed the following inscription:

SEWING FACTORY

MEN'S AND WOMEN'S UNDERCLOTHING

B. SZWEJC

With Marta behind her, Klara entered a large hall where, in deep gloom, one could see stairs leading to the upper floors. There were doors on both sides of the hall; she opened one and a thick wave of musty, damp air hit them both in the face. Nonetheless they entered and found themselves in a large room longer than it was wide. It was lit from three windows that faced the courtyard and were half covered with a white muslin curtain, so that the interior was plunged almost into utter darkness. The ceiling was low, timbered, and dusty; the floor was made of simple unpainted planks. The walls were plastered and ashy gray from dust, and, in the corners, covered above the floor with large black and blue spots of dampness.

Against the gray background of this dreary room, the figures of women appeared in blurred colors but with clear shapes. Some were grouped around the windows and tables; some sat alone near enormous cabinets with piles of material sewn or prepared for sewing behind their glass panes. In the middle of the room stood a large black-painted table. Two women bent over it, each with scissors in one hand and papers of pins in the other.

Klara took a few steps into the room, nodded to several workers who looked up at her, then turned to the black table.

"Good day, Madame Szwejc," she said.

One of the women standing by the table turned toward her and smiled very cordially.

"Ah, it is you, Miss Klara! You have come to visit your cousin. Miss Emilia! Miss Emilia!"

At the sound of the twice-repeated name, one of the women sitting alone in the shadows raised her head. She was obviously so busy with her work or preoccupied with her thoughts that she did not see what was going on around her. Now she looked out with bleary eyes and saw Klara. But she did not jump out of her seat and run toward her cousin. She got up slowly, placed her work on the chair, and took a few halting steps.

"Ah, it is you, Klara!" she said, extending a white, very thin hand with fingers pricked by needles.

Now the entire figure moved into the light that flowed through the window, and Marta recognized the young girl she had met on the stairs of the information agency on her first visit there. Emilia even wore the same dress, but it was grayer now than three months ago, and had been patched and mended. Her face had grown paler and thinner; it was enough to look at her to see that an ominous process of deterioration had begun prematurely and was swiftly progressing.

The two cousins shook hands. Their greeting was short and quiet. Emilia returned to the seat she had abandoned a moment before, and Klara turned to the owner of the shop.

"Madame Szwejc!" she said. "This is Madame Marta Świcka, who would like to work in your shop."

Madame Szwejc stared at Marta for a while, but it was impossible to see the expression in her eyes because it was obscured by the glasses she wore. Nonetheless her voice sounded very courteous, sweet, and almost tender when she answered Klara:

"I am very grateful that Madame . . . who? Madame Świcka thought of my modest shop, but really, I have so many employees, I do not know if I will be able to . . ."

Marta wanted to say something, but Klara pulled lightly at her coat sleeve and quickly began to speak.

"My dear Madame Szwejc," she said resolutely, like a person who is utterly independent and to some extent feels her own superiority, "why waste words? You said the same thing to Emilia when she came here for the first time, and then you hired her. The main thing is for everyone to agree to the lowest salary, is it not?"

Madame Szwejc smiled.

"Miss Klara always has such a spirited way about her," she said with the same monotonous sweetness. "You compare the salary employees receive at Madame N.'s with the salary that our poor shop can give, and that is why it seems to you that we pay too little—"

"Seems to me? Dear Madame Szwejc, I know it well," Klara interrupted. "I would only like for you to tell me right away if Madame Świcka will find work here, because otherwise we will go somewhere else."

Madame Szwejc clasped her hands on her chest and bowed her head.

"The love of one's neighbor," she began quietly, drawing out her words, "the love of one's neighbor does not allow me to refuse a person work."

Klara shifted impatiently.

"My dear Madame Szwejc," she said, "the love of one's neighbor has nothing to do with it. Madame Świcka offers you her work, for which you will pay her, and that is the end of it. It is the same as if a person comes to a shop, takes merchandise, and puts the money for it on the table. Why the need for love of one's neighbor here?"

Madame Szwejc sighed quietly.

"My dear Miss Klara," she said, "you know how I care about the health of our employees, and most of all about their habits . . ."

With the last word her face, which was long and wrinkled, took on a hard, stern expression.

Klara smiled.

"All that is none of my concern. I would like to hear, finally, if you will hire Madame Świcka or not."

"Well, what can I do? What can I do? Although, really, I have so many employees that there is not even enough work . . ."

"What terms, then?" Klara pressed her energetically.

"What terms? The same terms under which all these ladies work. Forty pennies a day. Ten hours of work."

Klara shook her head.

"Madame Świcka will not work for such a salary," she said firmly, and added, laughing, "Forty pennies for ten hours of work: that is four pennies an hour. You must be joking."

She turned to Marta.

"Madame," she said, "let us go somewhere else."

Klara turned toward the door, but Marta did not follow her. She stood for a moment as if nailed to the spot. Suddenly she raised her head and said:

"I agree to your conditions, madame. I will sew for ten hours a day for forty pennies."

Klara wanted to speak, but Marta did not allow her to say a word.

"I have made my decision," she said, then added quietly: "You said yourself an hour ago, Miss Klara, that it is better to have something than nothing."

The agreement was made. The next day, at Madame Szwejc's shop, Marta was going to enter the profession of seamstress. Finally, after a long search, difficulties vainly confronted, humiliations vainly endured, fruitless flailing in many directions and knocking like a beggar at many doors, Marta had found work and the possibility of earning the money that would secure her welfare and that of her child.

Nonetheless when she returned to her room, tired from walking around the city, she did not smile as she had on the day of her happy return from the information agency. She did not open her arms to the child who came running to her. She did not say to her with a tear in her eye and a smile on her lips:

"Thank God!"

Pale, lost in thought, with her forehead deeply furrowed and her lips set, Marta sat down by the small window. She stared with glassy eyes at the rooftops of the surrounding houses and listened, without being able to distinguish any particular sound, to the noise of the great city.

The low figure of her salary did not frighten her. Too little time had passed since she had begun to patch together the means of life like a rotten rag that was continually falling apart in her hand. She was still unpracticed at counting pennies as the poor do, and too unaware of the swarm of everyday details, each one smaller than the tiniest fly hovering in the air, that falls like a load of stone on the shoulders of a penniless person, to be quick to measure her future earnings against future needs and see clearly the insufficiency of the one and the acuteness of the other.

She did not yet know exactly if she and her child could manage to survive on forty pennies a day. That small number was large in comparison with yesterday's income, represented by zero. But if Marta was a novice—though a novice with harsh experience, to be sure—in the school of practical living and in the gloomy fraternity trudging through the world under the banner of poverty, she had enough knowledge and common sense to understand how far down the ladder of human labor she had descended without any visible possibility of moving up some day.

She was on the rung just above starvation, on which all kinds of incompetence huddled.

She was on the rung to which no one descended except those who lacked the strength to maintain themselves on higher levels.

It was a rung sunk in the low-lying realm of perpetual twilight, of strenuous, boring work that makes it impossible to breathe, giving the body dark bread while keeping the soul perpetually shackled to physical needs that are never completely satisfied.

Finally, it was a rung on which spiders wove thick webs to entangle flies who came willingly—where abuse ruled, crushing heads humbly bowed in acknowledgement of their own incompetence.

Not once—at no time either during her days of prosperity and success or in her moments of loneliness and poverty, or even during the time when she had taken various paths from which she had had to back away—had Marta imagined that she was so weak, and her knowledge so limited, that she would sink to such a sphere.

She had accepted that fate with almost irrational haste and unreserved, resolute willingness; nonetheless it was a surprise for her. Whatever might have prepared her for it in the days just past, she had never really expected it.

A loud, contentious, gloomy crowd of new thoughts filled the young woman's mind as she sat over a piece of fabric in the large, dark, damp room on Freta Street. She sewed meticulously, raising and lowering her hand in uniform rhythm with twenty other hands that rose and fell around her. As a new employee, Marta looked more attentively than the day before at the persons with whom she shared her work and her lot. She was greatly surprised to notice that the majority were women whose delicate faces, supple figures, and white hands showed that they had belonged to different social classes than the one into which they had fallen. The morning of their lives had been different from the noon and the evening.

These women varied greatly as to age, appearance, and disposition. Some sat silent and motionless on the stools except for their hands, which moved continuously. Their heads, bent for hours over their work, rose with evident heaviness when they left it. Their legs dragged slowly as they walked out of the room; their fading eyes, under lids that were always red, did not brighten even with one sparkle or beam at the sight of the traffic and the noon sun gilding the city's lively streets, or the sound of easygoing human voices surrounding them with chatter that was full of life as they, mute and numb, left their dismal workshop.

Their dresses were torn and stained with mud from the street. Their hair, hardly combed and rolled into shapeless buns on the backs of their heads, fell disheveled onto their gaunt necks. Only from time to time did a linen collar of impeccable whiteness, or a wedding ring glittering on a finger where its gold glint seemed at odds with the impoverished figure of its owner, recall old habits, warm emotions and ties that had sailed out of reach on the too-swift wave of a past that would never return. These were creatures already exhausted by the short road they had taken, faint in their hearts and minds, ailing in body and dying in spirit. They dragged out their dark, heavy, hopeless existence in silence as if silence were the last shroud left for them by fate to cover, stubbornly, their inner wounds.

However, it was not they, those fragile bodies and spirits dying of sorrow, who were the saddest sight in Madame Szwejc's shop. Nearest the windows, like enslaved birds searching for daylight from behind the bars of their cages, sat workers younger than the others, if not in calendar years, then in years of suffering, with more vivid personalities, with more determined desires in their hearts, and with smiles that were stifled and restrained but did not want to die either in their hearts or on their lips. Their faces were pale and thin, their clothes very poor. But under their white foreheads gleamed eyes that looked up from their work almost every few seconds—eyes looking for the eyes of other workers, eyes sometimes playful, defiant, or mischievous, their lines of vision still impatiently leaping out somewhere beyond the dank, dark walls of the room. From time to time on their sunken cheeks, almost every day more deeply yellow, appeared smiles similar to the expressions in their eyes: impish, satirical, longing, dreaming. There were heads resplendent with a wealth of braids, among which from time to time flashed a ribbon, a bow, or a pink or blue band. Sometimes a string of colorful beads encircled their necks, mocking the holes and patches in their bodices.

And all their glances, smiles, and adornments presented a more painful and puzzling view than the silence, fragility, and numbness of other workers. They revealed a malignant contradiction between their feelings and desires and the crushing conditions of their lives, between their dreams of wealth and their deep poverty. A passive fall had taken place with the other group, while here, every minute, an active fall seemed to threaten. Those deprived women were near the end of their earthly wanderings; these were approaching the beginnings of their lives, perhaps lives of vice. In front of the others a grave opened; before these, a quagmire.

When Szwejc and her daughter stood by the large black table, it seemed that there was silence in the shop, and the only clear sound was the click of the huge, sharp scissors almost constantly kept in motion by practiced fingers.

But that silence was only on the surface. Besides the one sound that could be heard clearly above it, there were many other sounds, indistinct, intermittent, but creating a continuous rustle that fluttered quietly, sometimes erupted as if in an impatient wave, then subsided again and almost merged with the silence. The rustle consisted of the flicking of almost twenty moving hands; the breathing of more than twenty sets of lungs; the whispers of lips that hardly moved; quiet, quickly muffled giggles, and occasional coughing, some dry and brief, some heavy and difficult to control. The workers sitting in the depths of the room coughed; the workers gathered by the windows whispered and giggled. Szwejc sometimes lifted her head and looked attentively around the room from behind her glasses. Her eyes shone with a sharp glow behind the thick lenses: she was supervising the work. Now and then she put her scissors on the table and launched into a long speech in her drawling, honeyed voice.

She talked about workers in other shops who lost their health sitting over sewing machines, which, as was known, exhausted their operators' strength and brought on all manner of ailments, and how she renounced all the advantages she could have gained by introducing sewing machines in her shop just to avoid burdening her conscience with the sin of destroying her workers' health. Conscience is the most important thing; everything else is empty mammon. Szwejc only demanded one thing from her workers: that their habits be impeccable. She was unyielding in this because she did not want her shop to have a bad reputation and lose its respectable clients, after which she would immediately be plunged into poverty along with her children and grandchildren.

The workers listened to these speeches in deep silence. Almost certainly there was not even one who believed them. Almost certainly they all knew that they were being exploited, but they kept quiet and listened meekly. They knew that beyond the walls of this room there was nothing for them besides the grave or a quagmire.

Occasionally Szwejc or her daughter left the shop by the door that led to the interior of the building. Through the open doorway the workers could hear the sound of a splendid piano played masterfully by someone who had been well taught. A row of luxuriously furnished rooms was visible through the door. Waxed floors and wide mirrors glittered there; the crimson damask that covered the furniture dazzled the workers' tired eyes, causing some of them to smile sadly, others to stare gloomily, and still others to wink spitefully. Pain, envy, and bile permeated the hearts of the twenty women.

At three o'clock, large ceiling lamps were lit, and the employees worked by artificial light until the wall clock in Szwejc's apartment struck nine.

When Marta had spent an entire day in this place, she returned home hardly able to stand on her feet. She was not utterly exhausted, after all, and she had met with no new sorrow. But to the depths of her heart and mind, to the very marrow of her bones, she was afraid.

‖‖

Discriminating readers, especially tender and impressionable feminine readers, will you forgive me for presenting a tale completely devoid of mysterious intrigues and the affecting picture of two hearts pierced by fiery arrows?

Anything that serves as the subject for a story may be handled in various ways. The tale of poor Marta, rather than being spun before your eyes as a single thread of one color, could have been embellished with many intersecting feelings, striking contrasts, and events like thunderbolts. They could have been woven into a garland of episodes, each of which would cast its spell, exert its charm, or arouse fear. Or they could have been treated episodically as the complement to a more effective, riveting whole, as a counterpart to stories of happy or despairing people, idyllic or heroic stories of people favored by fate or oppressed by it: Numa and Pompilius.

Excuse me! Having met Marta in the world, I looked around, I searched, but I never found anyone at all like Pompilius. Since I did not find him, I wanted to shorten the history of this woman, compress and enclose it into one episode. I could not because I had to acknowledge that each incident was worthy to form a separate whole. Finally, I intended to weave the incidents into knots of intrigue, a garland of episodes. I did not do so because it seemed to me that they would be set off to better advantage if they went into the world alone.

Pardon me for the simple way in which I present to you one of the most desperately sad social phenomena of our time, and follow me further along the road on which the sorrowful figure of a poor woman walks, a woman who perhaps deserves a better fate than she was offered by . . . what? By something which, like a fatal curse, crushes the heads, binds the feet and shatters the hearts of multitudes of human beings. Marta's history will tell you what it is.

‖‖

Warsaw was bright, joyful, noisy with chatter. It was the holiday week. For days the multitudes of lights that shone among the green boughs of Christmas Eve firs had hardly been put out. The laughter of children up and down the musical scale, and the lively conversations of happy families gathered around festively decorated tables, still seemed to quiver and dance joyfully in the air. The next day a mysterious guest was supposed to be welcomed into the world: the New Year. The interiors of homes and the windows of stores were decorated. The streets were covered with a thick layer of snow crusty with frost and gleaming with millions of sparks under the sunbeams that shone in the cloudless sky.

Swarms of sleighs darted in many directions. Crowds of pedestrians overflowed the sidewalk. For every head in this colorful, lively crowd, there was a train of thought secretly spinning itself out into space, invisibly pursuing through a wide world, near and far, a sublime or a banal object. Love, greed, adoration, hate, fear, hope, the most divergent interests and passions, the most varied desires and aspirations, wound and crossed through the thousands of minds in the huge city where people were walking, running, driving, spurred on by all the great goals of life and the small aims of the day. Amid this mysterious noise, with its elements indistinguishable by the human ear, in which, as on a lower deck, the words and actions of thousands of people were diffused, a train of thought that no one else understood or paid attention to ran quietly through the mind of an unassuming woman who passed along unnoticed.

"Two tens a day . . . eight złotys a week . . . ten pennies a day to the concierge's wife for looking after Jasia while I am sitting at Szwejc's . . . fifteen pennies for bread and milk for the child . . . fifteen pennies for dinner . . . for Sundays there is nothing left . . ."

So Marta thought as she walked slowly, with her head down, along the sidewalk beside Krakowskie Przedmieście.

"Two months' rent is forty-five złotys . . . I owe twenty at the store . . . I took a hundred for the fur coat I sold . . . sixty from a hundred . . . forty . . . Jasia needs shoes badly and mine are worn out . . . I have to buy some wood . . . The child is always cold . . ."

As she finished that thought, Marta's chest contracted with a dry, short, but persistent cough. A month had passed since the first day she had taken her place as a worker in Madame Szwejc's shop. During that time she had changed a great deal. On the transparent whiteness of her face, yellow blotches appeared here and there; there were dark circles under her eyes, which were now sunken and wider, and a furrow lay in the middle of her remarkably beautiful forehead. Her black dress was clean and whole, but had become reddish from wear; it looked neat, but old. On her head there was no hat and on her arms, no fur wrap. A black wool scarf covered her hair, enclosing her pale forehead and sunken cheeks in thick folds.

"Ten pennies and five . . . fifteen and two . . . seventeen . . . seventeen from forty . . . twenty three . . ."

What a low, boring, dry thought! It crept along the ground while the winter sky shone with a clear azure. It congealed among cold numbers while the flow and hum of people on the wide sidewalk along the elegant street simmered with desires, emotions, and hopes for the approaching New Year. Among them ran the quiet, commonplace, monotonous internal calculation of a pale woman pushing her way through the crowd. It was a spiritual action occurring inside a human being, but prosaic, not elevated— the petty, penny-pinching calculation of poverty.

Marta's thoughts had not always crawled so low. There was a time when she had raised her eyes to the azure sky and greeted the coming New Year with a throbbing heart and a smile of hope. She recalled it now. She looked up and glanced around. Her eyes, which at first had been shadowed with worry from counting, adding, and subtracting pennies, brooded and then flashed with rising emotions. First there was longing, then regret, and finally the impatient rebellion of a spirit oppressed by a fatal necessity to which it could not reconcile itself.

Fires kindled in Marta's sunken eyes; something in her arose, shouted with pain, moaned in fear, revolted with the yet unexhausted energy of her will. She stopped for a moment, lifted her head, and whispered with trembling lips:

"No! This cannot go on any longer! It should not always be this way!"

She took a few steps and thought that it was impossible, utterly impossible, that her unalterable, inescapable, lifelong destiny should be to sit on the stool in Szwejc's shop and sew for entire days in the dark, amid dampness and musty air, surrounded by emaciated, dying faces, unable to earn enough to sleep peacefully at night or to be free, during her moments off work, from the tyranny of numbers—numbers that represented only pennies.

By birth and through all her past she had belonged to the enlightened class; she had been considered an educated woman, and that was how she thought of herself. Why, then, when the hard hand of destiny touched her, was she standing on the lowest rung of the social hierarchy—the domain of work, profits, and honors—on which, it seemed, only those who were the least fortunate, the most cruelly disenfranchised of the wealth and tools that bring people education, were supposed to stand?

Was that education her chief handicap? Was it only a sculpted trinket made beautiful for the enjoyment of a calm spirit living in a well-nourished, satisfied body, then disintegrating into useless dust every time the spirit wished to use it to protect itself from exhaustion or collapse, and to save the body from losing the strength it needed to serve the spirit? Was her education only an illusion? The degree and kind of education Marta had had awakened desires without offering anything to enable her to satisfy them. It aroused longing for elevated things while shackling the spirit to the ground with bonds to the hungry body. It increased the heart's capacity for feeling, only to fill it with bitterness and make it tremble with deadly fear.

Marta thought about this and felt all its implications, but she did not generalize her thoughts or feelings. She did not precisely comprehend the enormously complicated issue that had determined her lot. She clung to one recollection, one conviction: that she belonged to the layer of educated people to whom many, many roads are open.

Was she to stay forever on the road she was taking now? Was there no other place for her than the one she had entered with shame and thought of from a distance with fear? She begged God for a small, modest place in the sun, for a place where two beings who shared the closest and most holy bonds and feelings could live. The place they had secured after much effort was not a place in the sun but a dark pit in which two human beings were not living but dying by degrees, shackled to the lowest, most primitive, perpetually unsatisfied, never-ending needs.

Indeed, they were dying slowly. That was not a metaphor but a terrifying reality. It was still not long since Marta, reflecting on the situation she had fallen into and the duties that weighed on her heart and conscience, had encouraged and consoled herself by repeating, "I am young and healthy." Today only half that statement was true. She was young, but no longer healthy. Physical and psychic elements together had created something like an invisible saw that was wearing out and weakening her body.

She coughed. For several weeks she had been experiencing weakness unknown to her before. She had feverish dreams; she woke from them with headaches and chest pains.

It was in this way that these workers had to start their careers: today half dead, with consumptive flushes on their faces. Not long ago one had left Szwejc's shop a few hours earlier than the rules of the establishment allowed, and never returned. When Marta asked the other workers about her the next day, a muffled but piercing whisper from more than a dozen lips ran around the room:

"She died!"

She died? Marta knew that the woman had been barely twenty-six years old, and that two small children had lived somewhere in an attic or basement, waiting every day for her return.

"What happened to her children?" the young mother of beautiful dark-eyed little Jasia asked her companions with feverish curiosity.

The reply she received sounded sharp and rough to her ear:

"The girl was accepted at an orphanage, and the boy was lost somewhere."

At an orphanage? So onto the shoulders of the philanthropic public, into the hands of strangers, for no one knew how long. And the boy—lost? Where could he have gotten lost? Perhaps in his childish naïveté he was looking for his mother, who had been taken from a high attic; perhaps he had died quietly somewhere on the snowy streets in the frosty winter night and been covered by a shroud of white drifts or, horrors! joined other social outcasts like himself.

Marta could no longer think about this gloomy story, which perhaps mirrored her own future. Her own? Never mind! The people she loved were already beyond this world; she felt exhausted and so sad that she would have been happy to close her eyes in the eternal sleep that her faith promised would reunite her with those her wounded heart longed for! But the future of her child . . . what would it be, what could it be if she no longer existed on the earth, if hot, blood-red flushes appeared on her face, if her forehead became deathly white and the breath went out of her lungs, like that poor worker who walked unsteadily out of Szwejc's shop a few days before and never returned?

As she became lost in thought, Marta had been leaning forward, but now she sat up straight.

"No!" the young woman said quietly but firmly. "This cannot happen! It should not!"

As she spoke those words, she felt the inborn desire that every person has to rise from misery and the right of every person to better himself, to improve the conditions of his life.

Marta looked around. Energy and curiosity beamed from her eyes, replacing worry and exhaustion. From the multitude of things that surrounded her, her glance singled out one: a wide, tall window with a rich display, the window of the most affluent bookshop in the city. At the sight of several dozen volumes whose colorful covers could be seen behind the bright windows, the young woman experienced three emotions: nostalgia, longing, and hope. She recalled the happy days when, leaning on the arm of her young, cultivated husband, she had come to this place more than once.

Longing for the higher joys of the mind that she had tasted occasionally in the past, that she had been deprived of for a long time, and that shone with spellbinding radiance against the dark background of her present life, she saw women's names printed below the titles of a few of the books. One of the names belonged to a person she had known once—a person who was never suspected of having talent until she showed it by degrees, with slowly increasing success. Yet now her name figured with honor among the many great, famous names of the nation's writers. Now this woman, who, Marta knew, had been alone and poor as she herself was, had a place in the sun. She had the respect of others, and she had self-respect.

"Who knows?" Marta whispered with trembling lips, and her pale face flamed red between the black woolen folds that enclosed it in a somber frame.

She advanced a few steps and stood in front of the door of the bookshop. She looked through the window and saw its owner inside a large room. Once his thoughtful, honest, kind face had been very familiar; she had seen him often in the days of her prosperity.

A bell rang at the glass door and Marta entered the bookshop. She stopped near the threshold for a moment and glanced sharply and anxiously around. She was afraid of finding customers in the shop; she could not say what she had come to say in front of them.

The bookseller stood alone behind the counter, writing accounts in a large book that lay open on a small lectern. When the door opened he looked up, saw her entering, and assumed a welcoming, expectant posture. Marta walked over slowly and stood before him; he was obviously waiting for her to speak first.

For a few seconds her eyelids remained lowered and her pale lips trembled slightly. However, she quickly raised her eyes to the bookseller's face with a look in which all her powers of mind and will were concentrated.

"You do not recognize me, sir?" she said in a low but confident voice.

From the moment she entered, the bookseller had been looking at her closely.

"Indeed!" he cried. "Why, I have the pleasure of seeing Madame Świcka! It seemed to me at once that I recognized you, but I was not certain."

He glanced quickly at the young woman's shabby clothes.

"What can I do for you, madame?" he asked politely, with a trace of sadness in his voice.

Marta was quiet for a while. Her face was very pale and her eyes were deep and still when she began to speak:

"I have come to you with a request which will seem unusual . . . strange . . ."

Suddenly she broke off. She raised both her hands and moved them over her blanched forehead. The bookseller stepped quickly from behind the counter and moved a velvet-covered stool in her direction, then returned to his former place. He seemed sad and even more confused.

"Please sit down, madame," he said. "You have my attention."

Marta did not sit down. She rested her clasped hands on the counter and looked into his face again with deep but brightening eyes.

"My request is special and unusual," she said, "but . . . I remembered that you were on friendly terms with my husband once—"

The bookseller bowed.

"Yes," he interrupted. "Everyone who knew Mr. Świcki well remembers him as a fine man and a friend."

"I recall," Marta continued, "that I received you several times at my home, sir, as a welcome guest."

The bookseller bowed respectfully again.

"I know, sir, that you are not only a bookseller but also a publisher . . . that . . ."

Her voice weakened and gradually grew quiet. She was silent for a moment. Suddenly she lifted her head again, extended her clasped hands a little way, and breathed deeply a few times.

"Give me work, sir . . . Show me a path . . . Teach me what I am supposed to do!"

The bookseller seemed astonished. He looked closely at the woman who stood in front of him, almost scrutinizing her. But Marta's beautiful young face did not present a riddle that was difficult to understand. Poverty, anxiety, futile desires, and desperate pleading had left very intelligible marks on it. The bookseller's wise gray eyes looked sternly and searchingly from under his elegant forehead; then they slowly grew softer until they seemed almost to close in pensive brooding. There was a moment's silence. He interrupted it first.

"So—" he said with a slight hesitation in his voice—"Mr. Świcki did not leave any estate after his death?"

"None," Marta replied quietly.

"The two of you had a child."

"I have a little daughter."

"And until now you have not been able to find work for yourself?"

"I have. I sew, for which I receive forty pennies a day."

"Forty pennies a day!" the bookseller exclaimed. "For two people! But that is poverty!"

"Poverty!" Marta repeated. "If it were only poverty, and poverty only for me, with no possible help on earth! Oh, believe me, sir, I would be able to suffer with courage, live without begging, and die without complaining! But I am not alone, I am a mother! If I did not have a maternal heart that loved, I would still hear the voice of my conscience, which reminds me of my responsibilities. If I did not have a conscience, I would still hear the voice of my heart.

"I have both, sir! I despair when I see the thin face of my child and when I think of her future, but when I remember that until now I have not been able to do anything for her, I am so ashamed that I would like to fall on the ground and roll my head in the dust! After all, there are poor people who lift themselves and their children from poverty; why can I not do that? Oh, sir! Indeed, poverty is hard to bear. But to feel powerless against it, to attempt everything and turn away from every place with the sense of one's own incompetence—to suffer and to see a beloved person suffer today, and to think that that suffering will last through tomorrow, the day after tomorrow, and always—to tell oneself: 'I cannot do anything to stop this suffering,' is a torture for which there is only one name: the life of a poor woman!"

Marta spoke rapidly and hotly, but with those last words her voice became subdued. She could not restrain the two streams of tears that poured down her cheeks. She covered her face with her scarf and stood still for a moment, struggling with the tears that would not stop, trying to control the sobs that shook her more and more violently. She was crying before a witness for the first time, giving voice for the first time to the complaint she had carried inside her for so long. She was no longer as strong or as proud as when, at the Rudzińskis' home, with dry eyes and a calm face she had voluntarily given up the work she was unable to do.

The bookseller stood motionless behind the counter with his hands crossed on his chest. He was somewhat taken aback by the outburst of emotion he had witnessed, but after a moment it became clear that he was moved.

"My God!" he said in an undertone. "The fates of people in this world are so changeable! Having known you before, could I ever have expected to see you in this state of sorrow and poverty? You lived so well! You were such a loving, happy couple."

Marta pulled the scarf away from her face.

"Yes," she said in a muffled voice, "I was happy. When the man I loved died, I thought I would die, too. But I lived. I still grieve; I still miss my husband; but I tried to find relief by being a mother to my child. Yet to this very day I have not been able to do what I should do for her. I went into the world alone and sad to fight for some peace for myself, and for my child's life and future. It was futile."

The bookseller's sober, thoughtful eyes stared into space. He had a large family. He was a brother, a husband, a father. Perhaps Marta's words brought before his eyes moving images of women he loved: his young sister, his little daughter, his beloved wife. Might any of them not someday undergo the same fate as the woman standing before him—this lonely woman without a home, with an aching heart and lips parched with the fever of hunger and despair? Why, just a moment ago he had mentioned the cruel changefulness of fate!

His eyes slowly fell on Marta's face and he stretched out a hand to her.

"Be calm, madame," he said mildly and gravely. "Please sit down and rest for a while. You will not think me indelicate if, in order to be useful to you, I inquire about some essential details. Have you tried other work than this, which offers you such a miserable wage? What work best suits your inclinations and abilities? If I know that, perhaps I will think of something ... perhaps I will find something."

Marta sat down. Her tears dried and her eyes took on the look of good sense and lucidity that they always had when she brought all her mind and will to bear on a matter. She felt hope reviving; she understood that its fulfillment would depend on this conversation. She felt her courage return, and she appeared composed.

The conversation did not last long. Marta spoke candidly and concisely; she only dwelled a little on the facts of her past. Her pride reasserted itself and she said little or nothing about her feelings. The bookseller understood her very well. His shrewd eyes lingered on her face, but it was evident that he saw more in her story than one young woman and her fate.

Great social questions, perhaps a great injustice pervading the social organism, were in the thoughts of this good, educated man as he listened attentively and with feeling to the story of the poor woman who could not find a place of her own in the world despite her energy, her effort, and the hardships she had endured.

Marta rose from the stool on which she had been sitting for several minutes. Giving her hand to the bookseller, she said:

"I have told you everything, sir. I was not ashamed to tell you of all the disappointments I have encountered so far, for if my strength has failed me, my inclinations have been honest. I did everything I could, everything I knew how to do. My misfortune is that I was not able to do much; I did not know how to do anything well enough. But within the realm of human activity, there are still many forms of work that I have not attempted, and among them something may be found for me. May I hope that it will? Tell me, sir, honestly and without hesitation. I ask you in the name of your former friend who no longer lives, and in the name of those who are dear to you."

The bookseller pressed her hand. His own was warm and kind. After a moment's thought he said:

"Because you asked me to be honest, I must tell you the unhappy truth. The hope that you can better your situation with work is slim and very uncertain. You mentioned the realm of human activity; the realm of human activity in general differs altogether from the realm of women's activity. You have almost exhausted the latter in your fruitless attempts."

Marta listened with downcast eyes, not moving from where she stood. The bookseller looked at her with eyes full of compassion.

"I have told you all that so you would not delude yourself with high hopes and experience a new, perhaps more painful disappointment than before. However, I would not wish you to leave here thinking that I did not want to offer you help. For five years you were the daily companion of an educated man; that means a great deal. I know that during autumn and winter evenings you had a habit of reading together, and you must have amassed a store of knowledge. Besides that, allow me to say, madame, that your view of life and your way of expressing yourself indicate that your mind is not uncultivated. That is why I believe that you could and should attempt work in a new field."

As he spoke the last words, the bookseller took a medium-sized book from a shelf. Marta's eyes brightened.

"It is a new work by one of the French thinkers. A translation of it would be useful for our public and my business. I intended to entrust it to someone else, but now I am happy that I can use it to help the wife of my dear and still lamented Jan."

He wrapped the volume in blue paper.

"This is a work treating one of the current social questions. It is written clearly and accessibly: it should not be difficult to translate. And so you know what you will be working for, I can offer you an honorarium (pardon this official terminology) of six hundred złotys. If this work turns out to be suitable for you, perhaps there will be something else for you to translate.

"Finally, I am not the only publisher in the city, and if you win a name as an able translator, you will be asked to translate here and there. You said that you know only a little German. That is a pity; translations from that language are more in demand and better paid. But if one or two jobs go well, you will be able to take dozens of lessons. You will translate French works during the day and improve your German at night. Such is woman's work: step by step with little help but one's own."

Marta took the book with trembling fingers.

"Ah, sir!" she said, pressing the bookseller's hand in both of hers. "May God repay you by ensuring the happiness of those you love."

She could say no more. A few seconds later she was on the street, walking very fast. She was deeply moved as she thought about the bookseller's generous act, and his courtesy and helpfulness. These thoughts led to another thought.

"For Heaven's sake," she said to herself, "I meet so many good people along the way. Why is it so difficult for me to live?"

The book she carried seemed to burn her hands. She wanted to fly like an arrow to her room and look through the pages that might be her salvation. On the way she went into a little shoe shop, however, and bought a small pair of boots.

When finally she hurried in through the gate of the tall building on Piwna Street, she did not go straight to the stairs. Instead she walked to the courtyard and through the small door of the concierge's apartment. Every day Jasia spent long hours there under the care of the concierge's wife, whom Marta paid to watch her while she sewed at Szwejc's shop.

Lately the child's appearance had changed more, and more profoundly, than the mother's. Jasia's cheeks were sunken and covered with a sickly yellow color. Her mourning dress, now faded to rusty red, was torn in several places and hung loose on her thin body. Her dark eyes had grown larger but lost their former luster and animation. From them came the mute, painful complaint often seen in the eyes of children who are suffering physically and psychologically.

On seeing her mother, Jasia did not throw her arms around her neck, did not start to chatter as she used to, and did not clap her little hands. With her head down and her thin, cold hands pressed around the woolen scarf that enfolded her, she entered the room in the attic with her mother, and was soon sitting on the floor in front of the empty fireplace, looking shriveled and harassed. Marta placed her book on the table and took two logs from behind the stove. Jasia followed her with dull, widened eyes.

"You will not go anywhere today, Mama?" she asked after a while in a sober, muffled voice that contrasted jarringly with her tiny, childish figure.

"No, my child," Marta replied. "I will not go anywhere today. Tomorrow is a great holiday and we were told not to come this afternoon."

She put wood in the fireplace, then knelt and tried to embrace her little daughter. Hardly had she touched her arm when Jasia gasped with pain.

"What is it?" Marta asked.

"It hurts me here, Mama!" the child said quietly, with no tone of complaint in her voice.

"It hurts you! Why? How long has it hurt?" the mother asked solicitously.

Jasia said nothing. She sat motionless with her eyes down. Her pale lips only trembled a little, as is common when children try to restrain a violent fit of tears. Marta worried more about the child's stubborn silence than her visible pain. She quickly unfastened the little girl's loosely hanging blouse and removed it from her arm. On that thin white arm a black and blue mark was growing darker. Marta wrung her hands as if an awful thought had come to her.

"Did you fall or bump into something?" she asked, quietly staring at the dark spot.

Still Jasia said nothing. Then suddenly she looked up with eyes full of tears. But she tried to keep from crying; her little chest heaved and her thin lips trembled like leaves.

"Mama," she whispered after a moment, leaning toward her mother, "today I was sitting by the stove. I was cold. Antoniowa was carrying water to the fire. She tripped over my dress and spilled the water. She was so angry, she hit me hard . . . so hard . . ." She spoke the last words very quietly, then pressed her head and chest to her mother and trembled all over.

Marta neither moaned nor screamed. Her face looked as if it had turned to stone, but her pale lips were pursed more and more tightly and her eyes, staring fixedly into space, flashed and darkened by turns.

"Oh!" she finally groaned, and took her burning forehead in her hands. Dull anger and pain beyond measure could be heard in that short groan. For a while the mother and child formed a tableau of two bosoms tightly embracing, and two faces: the face of a woman with dry, gloomy, glittering eyes leaning over the second face, a child's, pale and covered with tears.

After a while Marta brushed the child's tangled hair away from her forehead, wiped the tears from her gaunt cheeks, buttoned her blouse, and warmed her tiny, cold hands in hers. She did it without a word; she opened her lips a few times as if she wanted to say something, but could not. At last she rose from the floor, lifted Jasia, laid her on the bed, and took the shoes wrapped in paper from her pocket.

She had a smile on her lips, a strange smile! There was something artificial about it, but something quite sublime. Besides an effort of will, one could see the love and courage—the *manly* courage—of a mother who transforms her own pain into a smile to dry her child's tears.

The day ended, the city clock struck midnight, and in the attic room a lamp still burned. The room looked even sadder than when the young widow had crossed its threshold for the first time. Now there was neither a cabinet nor a chest of drawers, nor two leather bags. The tenant, unable to pay for them any longer, had returned the furniture together with two new chairs to the building's supervisor. The bags she had sold during the days of heavy frosts to buy more wood. Nothing remained in the room except the bed on which Jasia slept wrapped in her mother's black scarf, the two chairs with uneven legs, and the small table painted black.

Bathed in the white light of the lamp and encircled by a thick wreath of black braids, the face of the woman sitting at the table loomed out of the dusk in beautiful, austere outline. Marta was not working yet, though all the materials for her upcoming labors lay before her: the book, paper, and a pen. She was in the grip of an irresistible, overpowering dream. Grand perspectives were opening unexpectedly before her and she could not tear her eyes, which were so tired of gloom, away from them. She was no longer as full of confidence as when she sat at the same table with a drawing pencil in her hand, but she did not have enough strength to listen to the soft whisper of doubt. It was in her, that whisper, but she turned her ear away from it and listened only to the words of the bookseller, which filled her thoughts. From these words a long golden skein of dreams spun itself out: dreams for the woman, dreams for the mother.

To do challenging, rewarding work that would elevate the soul and fulfill its deepest needs: what a pleasure! To earn six hundred złotys in a few weeks: what wealth! When she became a wealthy woman, a great lady, the first thing she would do would be to hire an honest servant, no longer young, who would have children of her own, or would like children, at least, and would take good care of Jasia. Then (here Marta asked herself if she were not too bold in her dreaming) . . . then perhaps she would leave this bare, cold, gloomy room in which she was so sad, and which was so unhealthy for her child, and rent two warm, dry, sunny little rooms on a small but clean, quiet street.

Then, if she became known as a capable translator and got calls from here and there; if that huge sum of six hundred złotys came to her hands several times; she would look for teachers of language and drawing and she would study. Oh! She would study day and night without rest. She would study eagerly and patiently because that is how it must be with a woman's work: step by step on her own.

Then Jasia would begin to grow. With what an attentive eye her mother would follow her and discover her inborn talents so as not to leave any of them undeveloped, but to forge from each of them, for the woman Jasia would become, a treasure for the spirit and armor for the struggles of life! Jasia's studies, her education, her strength and happiness and the security of her future, would be the fruit of her mother's work.

How peacefully then Marta would close her eyes for refreshing sleep, and with what delight she would open them every morning, welcoming the new day that would bring difficulties and responsibilities, but at the same time peace and satisfaction! With what pride she would take her place among people, feeling that she was equal to them in strength and dignity! With what relief, with what a full heart she would kneel at the grave of the man she loved, whose image was always before her, and say: "I was worthy of you! I did not surrender to evil fate! I avoided starvation and a life of begging! I was able to care for and bring up our child!" Then . . .

Then Marta's eyes rested on a picture hanging near her on the wall. It was the drawing rejected by Adam Rudziński's employers and returned to her. She had decorated her poor, bare room with it; now, as she looked at it silently with burning eyes, she became absorbed in it. A country cottage, a spreading tree, a bird singing in a lilac bush, the clear air of the countryside, the deep silence of the fragrant fields . . . Oh, God! If she could work enough to have a modest, fresh, green corner like that for herself! She would be a woman approaching old age then. The wind rustling in the branches would cool her forehead when it was furrowed from the difficulties of life. Her tired eyes would drink in the fresh green. When she lay asleep forever, the bird that had sung when she was in her cradle would chime above her head, singing the last song that would be sung for her on earth.

These were the poor woman's dreams. That night in her attic room, the lamp was lit until dawn. Marta read the book she had been asked to translate. At first she read slowly and attentively, then eagerly, almost feverishly. She understood the author's thought; the subject of the work penetrated her mind and articulated itself clearly for her. Her comprehension of it formed an expanding circle that more and more widely and completely embraced the whole of it. Intuition, that rare and great gift that makes a man a half-god, rose from the depths of the young woman's soul and illuminated issues that had previously been beyond her awareness.

The dawn was white when Marta turned off the lamp and seized a pen. She wrote, from time to time turning her eyes from the paper to look toward the bed where her child was sleeping. By the wan light of the winter morning Jasia looked pale and unwell. When the first sunbeam entered the room, she opened her eyes. Then the mother got up, knelt by the bed, embraced the half-sleeping child, and let her own hot, tired head sink onto the pillow.

At that moment the city was awakening. Carriages rattled, church bells rang, and loud conversations began. People laughed and called to each other. Warsaw was greeting the New Year.

|||

After New Year's Day, six weeks passed. At one in the afternoon Marta, as always, left the shop to return home and prepare the midday dinner for her child and herself. She kissed Jasia, who was sad and distressed in the concierge's small room but livened a little at the sight of her mother. The young woman placed the pot with the food on the small fire, then pulled out the drawer in the table and took out more than a dozen large sheets of paper: the completed translation of the French book. She had worked five weeks translating it and one week making a clean copy. Now she looked with a smile through the pages filled with well-formed, clear writing.

Changes had taken place in her appearance during the past weeks, but those changes were very different from the previous ones. She had had two occupations, one during the day and the other at night. She had sewn for ten hours each day and written for nine hours each night. She had spent one hour each evening talking to her child, and slept for four hours. It was a style of life certainly not in keeping with the rules of hygiene; nonetheless the sickly yellow marks had vanished from Marta's face, her forehead had smoothed out, and her eyes had recovered their luster. She coughed less often; she looked healthy and almost free of care. Her spirit, bathed in peace and refreshed by hope, had revitalized her exhausted body; a sense of her own worth once more held her slender figure erect and restored her good humor.

After a dinner consisting of one very simple dish and a piece of black bread, Marta wrapped the manuscript she had just inspected in thin white paper. She did this with great care, and with feelings of solicitude and deep inner joy that were reflected in her face. When a clock on one of the city's towers struck two, she took Jasia back to the concierge's room and went to town. At three she had to be in her usual place at Szwejc's shop, and before that she wanted to call in at the bookshop.

The bookseller and publisher stood behind his counter as usual, writing numbers and notations in the large book. He looked up when Marta entered and bowed politely.

"You have finished your work," he said, taking the manuscript from Marta. "Good. I have been waiting for it eagerly. This book should be published now or never. It concerns a timely issue, a burning question, and cannot wait. Today everyone is interested in it; tomorrow everyone may be indifferent. I will look over your manuscript right away. Please come at the same time tomorrow and I will be able to give you decisive news."

That day at Szwejc's shop, Marta did not do much work. She tried as best she could to fulfill what, in spite of everything, she considered her responsibility, but she could not. Her hands trembled, now and then a dark mist covered her eyes, and her heart pounded so that she could not breathe. Perhaps at this moment the bookseller-publisher was unwrapping her manuscript and reading it . . . perhaps he was running his eyes over the fifth page. Oh! If only he would scan through it quickly, because on that page was a passage which was the most difficult to understand and came out the least well in the entire translation. But the final pages were translated superbly. As she wrote them, Marta felt that she had been seized by inspiration, that the thought of the master was reflected in her words like the brilliant countenance of a sage in a crystal mirror.

The clock struck nine in Szwejc's apartment and the workers dispersed. Marta returned to her room. At midnight she imagined that the bookseller-publisher was just closing the book that she had translated and he had read.

What would she have given to see his face at that moment! Was it pleased or frowning, stern or covered with the smile she hoped for? Daylight was entering the room when Marta, leaning on her pillow, stared with eyes that had not closed all night at the fragment of sky that showed from behind the small window panes. From her eyes, wide open and unmoving under her pale forehead, streamed a look of deep pleading, a mute but feverish prayer. At eight o'clock she was supposed to go to the shop as usual, but her legs trembled, her head burned, and her chest hurt so much that she sat on a chair, took her forehead in her hands, and said:

"I cannot . . ."

As she got up, brushed her long, silky hair, put on her old black dress, made a morning drink for her child and talked with her, her thoughts still revolved around one question: "Will he accept my work or not? Am I capable of translating or not?" *"He loves me, he loves me not,"* the lovely Gretchen whispered, plucking off the snowy petals of a wild aster. "I can, I cannot," the impoverished woman mused while lighting two poor logs in her fireplace, cooking miserable food, sweeping her gloomy room, and embracing her dear, pale child.

Who is able to say whether a more profound, dreadful drama lies in Gretchen's story or Marta's? Which of the two women would be more cruelly shattered by fate's reply? Which was the unhappier, the less demanding and therefore the more endangered in this world?

Around one in the afternoon Marta was again on the sidewalk along Krakowskie Przedmieście. The closer she came to her destination, the more slowly she walked. She found herself at the door of the bookshop, but she did not enter at once. She walked in the opposite direction; she placed her hand on the balustrade encircling one of the magnificent palaces and stood there with her head down for a while. Only after several minutes did she cross the threshold beyond which joy or despair awaited her.

This time, besides the owner, there was an older man in the bookshop. He was bald; he had a large face with wide, plump cheeks, and he wore glasses. He sat far back in the spacious room at a big table that had several dozen volumes scattered over it, holding a book in his hand. Marta did not pay the least attention to this man, who was unknown to her; she hardly saw him. All her powers of mind were concentrated in her eyes, which fell on the bookseller's face while she was still on the threshold and remained fixed on it. This time he was sitting behind his counter reading a newspaper. In front of him lay a roll of papers.

Marta recognized her manuscript and felt a shiver running over her from head to foot. Why was the manuscript here, and wrapped as if it were supposed to be returned to someone? Perhaps the bookseller was getting ready to go the printer right away and that was why he had put the translation there; perhaps he had not read it yet, had not had time. In any case it could not be lying here to be given back to the one who had spent many nights over it, fallen in love with it, cherished it, and invested her greatest hopes in it . . . her only hope! No, that could not be! Merciful God, that could not be! Like a volley of lightning bolts these thoughts crossed Marta's mind in a few seconds.

She made her way toward the bookseller, who rose, glanced at the older man, and shook her hand. Marta noticed that he was laboring under a difficulty, but she attributed it to the presence of a witness. That man, however, seemed to be immersed in reading, and he was more than a dozen steps away from where Marta was standing opposite the bookseller. Marta breathed deeply and asked quietly:

"Have you read my manuscript, sir?"

"Yes, madame, I have read it," the bookseller replied.

For God's sake! What could the sound of his voice as he pronounced those words mean? In his lowered tones she could hear a certain displeasure mollified by honest regret.

"What news do you have for me, sir?" she asked more quietly than before, staring into his face with wide eyes and bated breath. Oh, if only her eyes were deceiving her! His face showed abashment mingled with the same compassion she had heard in his voice.

"News, madame!" the bookseller began slowly, in an undertone. "The news is not good. What I must tell you pains me, pains me greatly. But I am a publisher with a responsibility to the public, and an entrepreneur who must protect my business. Your translation has many merits, but it is not suitable for publication."

Marta's lips moved weakly without making a sound. The bookseller began to speak again after a moment of silence during which he searched for the proper words:

"In saying that your translation is not without merit, I told you the truth. What is more, based on my knowledge of the subject, I can say with confidence that you have an obvious talent for writing. Your style, madame, is energetic: it is firm, lively, full of verve and zest in places. But . . . from the work of yours that I have seen, madame, your unquestioned talent remains in—forgive me for so expressing it—an elementary, unpolished state. It needs the assistance that only study and familiarity with the technical art of writing could offer. You know too little of both the languages you had to deal with; you have not mastered them to the degree demanded by the subject and its scholarly terminology.

"Moreover, a significant part of the advanced literary vocabulary is made up of a multitude of expressions that do not exist in colloquial language, and you do not know them very well. That is why you often changed the meaning of words, employed inaccurate expressions, and created an unclear, tangled style. In a word, you have talent, but you have not studied enough. The art of writing, even when limited to translation, nonetheless demands a certain range of study. Breadth of knowledge—general knowledge and more specialized technical knowledge—is indispensable."

He grew quiet, then added after a moment:

"That is the whole truth, and I am sorry to tell it. As your acquaintance, I regret that you did not get the opportunities for work that you wanted. As a fellow human being, I am sad that your talents have not been developed to a higher degree. You have talent; that cannot be denied. It is a pity, a great pity, that you have not studied more, more widely, more deeply."

The bookseller took the manuscript from the table and gave it to Marta. But she did not put out her hand, did not make the least movement. She stood straight, rigid and unmoving except for her pale lips, which trembled as a strange smile played over them. It was one of those smiles that are a million times sadder than tears, because they show that the spirit is beginning to express contempt for itself and the world. The bookseller had repeated almost word for word what the writer Rudziński had said of her drawing months before. The similarity brought a spasmodic smile to her trembling lips.

"Always the same thing!" she whispered after a moment. Then she lowered her head and said more loudly: "My God! God! God!"

A quick, stifled, but piercing moan came from her lips. Not only did she cry in front of witnesses; she also moaned. What had happened to her former pride and her courageous restraint? These qualities, so characteristic of Marta, had dissolved by degrees, in part because she had become accustomed to constant humiliation. She retained them enough that after several seconds she was able to lift her head, hold back her tears, and even look at the bookseller with clear eyes. But her look was pleading! Again, pleading and humiliation!

"Sir!" she said. "You were so good to me, but I could not take advantage of your goodness. It is my fault . . ."

She stopped suddenly. Her eyes became glassy and she seemed to withdraw into herself.

"Or is it?" she whispered very softly.

The question she was posing to herself, the social problem of which she was a representative and a victim, enclosed her more and more tightly in its hard arms and forced her to look into its terrible face. But she quickly shook herself free of her involuntary brooding and raised her eyes, which were brightening again, to the face of the man who stood before her.

"Could I not still study now? Is there no place in all the world where I could study something? Tell me, sir, tell me! Tell me!"

The bookseller was moved, but he was at a loss.

"Madame," he replied with a gesture of regret, "I do not know of such a place. You are a woman."

At that moment one of the shop assistants came out of a neighboring room and approached the bookseller with something in his hand: a long list or invoice.

Marta took her manuscript and gave her hand to the bookseller. Her fingers were stiff and cold as ice; her face was motionless as marble. Only her lips trembled with a glittering, unnerving smile that seemed to repeat *ad infinitum* the words: "Always the same!"

Hardly had the door closed behind Marta when the older man with the bald head and chubby face threw down the book he had appeared to be reading so intently and burst out laughing.

"What are you laughing at, sir?" the bookseller asked in astonishment, raising his eyes from the document that had been handed him a moment before.

"It is impossible not to laugh!" the man exclaimed, and his eyes gleamed from behind his thick, cloudy glasses with pure glee. "It is impossible not to laugh! Her nibs wanted to become a woman of letters, an author! There you go! Ha, ha, ha! But you gave her her walking papers! I wanted to jump out of my chair and hug you for it!"

The bookseller looked a little sternly at him.

"Believe me," he retorted with a hint of disapproval in his voice, "it was painful for me. I am deeply sorry that I had to give that woman an answer that grieved her."

"What? Are you are speaking seriously?"

"Very seriously. She is a widow whose husband I knew. I was fond of him. I respected him."

"Bah! Bah! I give you my word that she is an adventuress! Decent women do not ramble around the city looking for things that are not lost. They stay home, they attend to their households, they raise their children and praise God."

"Have a little compassion, Antoni. This woman does not have a household. She lives in poverty—"

"Oh, be quiet, Laurenty! I am surprised that you are so gullible. This is not poverty but ambition! Ambition! She would like to shine, to be famous, to occupy the highest place in society, to be able to do as she pleases and cover her caprices with her imaginary superiority and fraudulent work!"

The bookseller shrugged.

"Antoni, you are a writer. You should know more than that about women's education and work—"

"The 'woman question'!" the man shouted, sitting bolt upright in his chair. His face had suddenly gone red and his eyes were burning. "Do you know what that 'woman question' is?"

He was silent for a moment because a transport of emotion had left him breathless, and he had to inhale deeply. Then he added more calmly:

"Anyway, why should I speak to you about this? Read my articles."

"I have. I have read them, and I did not find them convincing—"

The writer in thick glasses interrupted him. "Well, if you do not believe me," he said, "you will not disregard all that is said by authorities on the subject. Eminent authorities. Not long ago, Doctor Bischoff . . . Do you know who Bischoff is?"

"Bischoff is indeed a great scholar, but apart from your distortion of his words and exaggeration of their meaning, I do not think that he could be an oracle sentencing thousands of unfortunate women—"

"Adventuresses!" the writer broke in again. "Believe me: only adventuresses, proud, ambitious creatures without any morals. Tell me: why do we need educated, or, as some say, independent women? Beauty, gentleness, modesty, submission, piety—these are the virtues appropriate for a woman. The household: that is her field of endeavor. Love of her husband: that is the only suitable and useful virtue for her! Our great-grandmothers . . ."

At that moment several people entered the bookshop, and the tale of our great-grandmothers hung unfinished on the writer's full, open lips. But what strong arguments he could have drawn on just then to give voice to his theory, how much that was new he could have said and written about the ambition and envy that leads women to cross the barriers set for them by nature and eminent authorities, if only he could have guessed Marta's thoughts as she walked along the street!

At first, after she left the bookshop, she seemed deaf and devoid of emotion. She did not think or feel anything. The first conscious thought that came to her formulated itself in these words: "How happy they are!" The first feeling to awaken in her was—envy.

She was walking along the sidewalk across the street from the wide, resplendent buildings of the Kaźmirowski Palace. Over the spacious palace courtyard swarmed youthful figures: young men with animated faces wearing the dignified garb of university students. Under their arms some held large books with plain covers or none, worn and half torn apart from use. Others were wrapping things in paper—elastic items or objects glinting with steel, probably scientific equipment that they would carry home and use to engage in experiments and make observations.

For several minutes they filled the courtyard with chatter, some quiet, some loud. They debated, they spoke with vigorous gestures; now and then, from this group or that, came notes of youthful laughter or a louder shout that revealed the exultation and enthusiasm of the young heart and the zeal of an inspired mind for its favorite subject. After a while the groups dispersed. The young men could be seen shaking each other's hands, smiling cheerfully or lost in thought, while others still carried on spirited conversations. Singly or in pairs, they left the university courtyard and mingled with the crowd that filled the wide sidewalk.

Marta walked very slowly with her head turned toward the large building that now acted on her imagination as a temple with mysterious powers of attraction. The young men with the books under their arms, with bright or soberly thoughtful faces, appeared to her privileged, distinguished, fortunate—almost half-gods. The poor woman sighed deeply.

"They are happy! Ah! Happy!" she whispered, once again sweeping her eyes over the magnificent buildings that by now she had left behind her. "Why was I not there? Why can I not be there? I cannot; why not? I do not have the right! Why not? What boundless differences exist between me and those young men? Why do they receive education, without which it is so hard to live, while I did not and cannot receive it?"

For the first time in her life, Marta was overwhelmed by a wave of burning indignation, numbing anger, and bitter envy. At the same time she felt an inexpressible, crushing humiliation. It seemed to her that the best thing she could do was fall on the stone sidewalk with her face to the ground and lie under the feet of the passersby. "Let them trample over me!" she thought. "What more am I worth? I am incompetent, useless, good for nothing!"

As the last word echoed in her mind, the manuscript she was carrying slipped out of her hand, fell under her feet, and opened. She leaned over to pick it up. On a page covered by her handwriting she saw two three-ruble notes.

It was a gift from the compassionate bookseller, who had rejected her inadequate translation but wanted to offer her a proof of his kindness. Marta stood up straight with her portfolio in one hand and the rustling papers in the other. At that moment her eyes had a sharp, piercing gleam and her chest trembled with hollow, muffled laughter.

"Yes!" she said almost aloud. "For them, education and work. For me—alms."

The words came hissing through her lips, which were almost as white as the paper she held in her hand.

"Very well!" she whispered after a moment. "Let it be! Why they did not give me the knowledge that today they demand from me? Why do they demand from me what they did not give me? Let them give me money now. Yes, money . . . for nothing. I will take it. Let them give it."

Quickly and nervously she put the banknotes into the pocket of her worn dress, and noticed that she was unsteady on her feet. Only now, when her spirit was thrown into another terrible storm, did her body remind her that she was hungry, that she had spent many nights in labor that had brought her nothing. She could not walk any farther.

Through the mist that covered her eyes she saw stairs in front of her. They were the stairs of Holy Cross Church. She crept onto them, rested her head on her hand and closed her eyes. After a while her tense face relaxed, the ice that had congealed in her heart melted, and tears began to flow from under her drooping eyelids onto her marble-white cheek. Drop after drop, copious, heavy, they fell onto her thin hands and hid among the folds of her mourning dress.

As this was happening to Marta, a man and a woman were strolling briskly along Krakowskie Przedmieście, carrying on a high-spirited conversation. The woman was young, beautiful, and elegantly dressed. The man was also young, handsome, and smartly turned out.

"Say what you like, give me your word if you like; still I will not believe that you have ever truly been in love!"

Having said that, the young woman laughed with her lips and her eyes. From behind those coral lips appeared two rows of small white teeth. Her amber eyes shone as she cast quick glances around her. The man sighed. It was a parody of a sigh, more playful and jocular than the woman's laughter.

"You do not believe me, beautiful Julia, but God is my witness that I was in love for an entire day, not only truly but madly, obsessively! Only imagine such a divine creature! Tall as a poplar, large, dark eyes, alabaster skin, hair like a raven's wing, a huge cloud of it and not artificial. Not artificial, I tell you, but her own! I know that difference very well. Sad, pale, unhappy . . . oh, a goddess! But all that is nothing. She pleased me at first sight, that is true, and I told my heart: 'Be silent!' because I knew my cousin liked her very much and had decided to protect her from me as if I were a fire. Then when she came to my cousin and said in her wonderful, endearing, nightingale's voice: 'I cannot teach your daughter . . .'

"But, my lovely lady . . . Julia . . . I told you that story. At that moment I fell truly in love. Then I walked around the streets like a drunkard for a whole day, looking for my goddess."

"And you did not find her?"

"I did not."

"You did not know where she lived?"

"I did not. My cousin knew, but—bah! Every time I asked her for the beautiful widow's address, she always answered, 'Olek, why do you not go to your office?'"

The woman burst out laughing.

"What a terribly serious person your cousin must be!" she exclaimed.

The man did not laugh or sigh this time.

"Let us not speak of my cousin, Miss Julia," he said firmly. "Better to listen to the ongoing drama of my life. Ah! That was a drama. Imagine that on that same day I met Miss Malwina X. on the street. I bowed to her from afar. I passed near Stępkoś's door with my head down and I looked with a sigh at a poster of Offenbach's *Beautiful Helen.* But I did not go to the theater; in a word, I was plunged into such gloomy despair that if good old Bolek had not taken me the next day to a certain apartment on Królewska Street, where I saw one of the most beautiful of earthly goddesses . . ."

"Oh! Oh!" Half laughing, half with coquettish indignation, the woman interrupted him. "No compliments. No compliments."

"I would by now," the man continued, "I would by now have found the one who disappeared before my eyes . . ."

"For whom you no longer looked."

"I did not look."

"And you forgot about her."

"I did not forget. Oh, I did not forget. But the wound to my heart scarred over somehow. What can one do? *Vivre c'est souffrir . . .*"

With the last words, the young man raised eyes full of melancholy and quietly whistled Kalchas's aria from *Beautiful Helen.*

Suddenly he stopped whistling, stood still and exclaimed:

"Ah!"

The woman walking next to him looked at him in astonishment. Cheerful Olek's eyes were fixed on one point, and, wonder of wonders! the perpetual smile vanished from his face. The shapely, delicate line of his lips, like all the lines of his face, quivered a little and their color changed slightly, as is common with people of exceptional sensitivity when they are suddenly moved.

"What is it?" the beautiful woman asked reluctantly. "I really should be offended," she added flirtatiously. "I should be offended, sir! You are walking with me and you are staring at someone else—"

"It is she!" Olek whispered. "Ah, how beautiful she is!"

It was a moment before the young, stylish woman named Julia could see the woman her companion was staring at. Suddenly she leaned forward a little, extended her hands, which were covered by a sable muff, and exclaimed:

"Why, that is Marta Świcka!"

They were only a few steps from the stairs of Holy Cross Church, where a woman sat wearing a mourning dress, with a black woolen scarf thrown over her head and crossed on her chest.

Marta was no longer crying. With the tears she had shed frantically but quietly a while ago, she had sobbed out a part of the anguish that had thrown her, weak and half fainting, onto the stairs. Her face was pale as ashes; her dry, hot, glittering eyes stared, fixed and unwavering, at the blue sky. Her entire figure was motionless. Neither her raised eyes, her set lips, nor her cold hands, which were clasped between the thick folds of her dress, made the slightest movement. From a distance she appeared to be a monument decorating the entrance to the magnificent church, or a statue representing the soul of a woman praying or asking a question, or praying and asking a question at the same time.

Marta stared at the sky. There was a fervent prayer in her eyes, but at the same time a deep, passionate, insistent question.

"How beautiful she is!" cheerful Olek repeated quietly. Leaning toward his companion, he added still more quietly: "If one could move her with those stairs to the theater, to the stage . . . what an effect!"

"That is true. She is beautiful," his companion whispered back, "but I know her very well. What has happened to her? Why is she sitting here? And dressed that way! Is she begging, or what?"

The young couple drew nearer to Marta, who did not realize that she was the object of anyone's attention. Since she had sat down there, powerless and battered by a tempest of feeling, to take a moment's rest, many people passing by on the street had glanced at her, but she did not see anyone. Her entire soul was wandering in the blue sky in which her eyes were immersed, searching for a good and powerful force that could overcome the circumstances that oppressed her. Just then, above her brooding head, two voices sounded.

"Madame!" a man's voice said quietly, in a tone of compassion or perhaps respect.

Marta did not hear that voice.

"Marta! Marta!" called the other voice, a woman's voice.

Marta heard that voice. It had a familiar ring from long ago. It seemed to Marta that at this moment her past called her by name. Slowly and with great difficulty her eyes tore themselves away from the blue expanse high above her and wandered over the face of the woman who stood before her, throwing her sable muff on the snow under her feet and reaching out with two small hands in gleaming lilac gloves.

"Karolina!" Marta whispered in astonishment at first. Then a brighter beam crossed her face and her tense features relaxed.

"Karolina!" she said more loudly. She rose and grasped both the woman's hands.

"Karolina!" she repeated. "Good heavens! Is it really you?"

"Is that you, Marta?" asked the woman in satin and sable, whose eyes glistened with sadness as she looked at the pale, thin face that was quivering with joy at the sight of her.

But sorrow could not remain in those eyes for long. The woman in satin laughed and turned to her companion, saying:

"Do you see, sir, how people meet in this world? Why, Marta and I have known each other since childhood!"

"Yes, since childhood!" Marta repeated. Only then did she see Olek, and she greeted him with a bow.

"For whom are you in mourning?" the woman in sable asked, glancing quickly at Marta's shabby clothes.

"For my husband."

"Your husband! You are a widow! That is a pity. He was a good-looking man, your Jan. So you are a widow! Where do you live? In the country or here?"

"Here, in Warsaw."

"Here? Why did you not return to the country?"

"My father's estate was sold at auction a few months after my wedding."

"At auction! Well! That is a shame. So you have no fortune, because your Jan loved you to distraction, and he must have spent everything he had on you. What do you do now? How do you live?"

"I am a seamstress."

"Very hard work!" the woman in satin laughed. "I tried it for a little, but I did not succeed."

"You, Karolina! You were a seamstress?" Marta exclaimed. Now it was her turn to be surprised.

The other woman laughed again.

"I tried to be a seamstress, but somehow it did not work for me! What could I do about it? That is what my fate decreed, and I do not complain at all."

Again she laughed. Her continual half-giddy, half-flirtatious laughter seemed to flow rather from habit than from real joy. Now Marta glanced at her expensive costume.

"Did you marry?" she asked.

The woman laughed again. "No!" she cried. "No, no! I did not marry, my dear! That is—how can I tell you this? But, no, no! I did not marry."

She was still laughing, but this time her laughter sounded unpleasant and rather forced. Olek, who had not taken his eyes off Marta, glanced at Karolina after that last question, smoothed his mustache, and smiled.

"But what am I doing?" exclaimed the woman in satin. "I am keeping you in the cold with my chatting. We could take a cab and drive to my apartment. Marta, you will go with me, will you not? We will talk for a long time and tell each other our life stories."

She laughed again and, looking around with sparkling eyes, added:

"Oh, the stories of our lives! How amusing they are! We will tell them, will we not, Marta?"

Marta seemed to hesitate.

"I cannot," she said. "My child is waiting for me."

"Ah! You have a child! So what? She can wait a little longer."

"I cannot . . ."

"Then come in an hour. Well? I live on Królewska Street."

She gave Marta the house number and pressed her hand.

"Come! Come!" she repeated. "I will wait for you. We will recall old times."

Old times: they always have great charm for those to whom new times have brought nothing but tears and sorrow.

Marta felt refreshed and emotionally revived by the unexpected encounter with a companion of her youth.

"In an hour," she said. "I will come, Karolina."

An observer who was closely watching these three people standing on the sidewalk would notice that when Marta said, "I will come," Olek felt an almost irresistible desire to leap up and cry, "Victory!" However, he did not do either; he took a step backward and snapped his fingers. His black eyes glowed like burning coals and he looked deeply into Marta's pale face, which was brightening just then. When at last she walked away, the man of the perpetual smile turned to his companion.

"As I live," he cried fervently, "as I live, I have not seen such a sweet, attractive creature! Even that ugly scarf that she wears on her head is becoming to her. Oh! I would dress her in satin, velvet, and gold."

Karolina suddenly raised her head and looked at the young man's impassioned face.

"Really?" she asked, drawing out the word.

"Really," Olek answered, and gave her a long look that they both understood.

The woman in satin burst into a brief, dry laugh.

|||

The winter day was coming to an end. In a drawing room with windows facing Królewska Street, in a graceful fireplace with an artistic wrought iron grating, enough coal burned to bathe the room in an even warmth without overheating it.

In front of the fireplace stood a love seat upholstered in wine-red damask, a low-backed rocking chair covered with a flowery carpet, and a footstool with yarn embroidery depicting a pretty, long-eared pointer. A tall woman in a black dress with a wide white band at the bottom lounged on the love seat.

On the chair another woman rocked lightly with her dainty, elegantly shod feet on the stool. She wore a fashionable ensemble of lilac satin richly finished with velvet and fringe of the same color, and a linen collar white as snow and fastened with a gold-framed cameo. Her light hair was combed high above her forehead and sprinkled with hardly visible powder; it fell in long, curly strands to her back, bosom, neck, and hands, which were small and white as they peeped from her linen cuffs. Entwined on her satin tunic, they were set off by the gleam of the large diamond that adorned her only, but very expensive, ring.

The drawing room in which both women were sitting was not large; for that reason the elegance of its decor was all the more striking. Silk curtains hung over two large windows and adorned the tall doorway. A wide mirror reflected clusters of low-backed, soft furniture. A large bronze clock stood on the mantel. Tables and side tables held crystal vases filled with flowers, silver bells, carved bonbonnières, and candelabra. Through the half-open door one could see, plunged into half-dusk, the adjoining room, with a fluffy rug on the floor, a round, varnished table in the middle, and, hanging over the table, a glass ball with a rose-colored flame in it. The delicate fragrance of greenhouse plants blooming under the windows filled the small apartment. Near the fireplace, shaded by a green screen, stood a table with a porcelain dinner service and left-over tidbits of food.

The women sitting in front of the fireplace were silent. Their faces, lit by the pink glow of the fire, were quite distinct in character.

Marta rested her head on a soft cushion on the love seat. Her eyes were half closed and her hands hung limp on her black dress. For the first time in many months her lips had touched tasty, plentiful food. She found herself in a warm room among beautiful, harmoniously assorted objects. The warmth of the room and the delicate fragrance of the flowers intoxicated her like a drink. Only now did she feel how exhausted she was and how much of her strength had been drained by cold, hunger, sorrow, fear, and struggle.

Half-lying on the soft furniture, embraced by the wave of heat that warmed her body, which had been cold for so long, she breathed slowly and deeply. Looking at her, one might say that she had suspended all thought and pushed away all the disquieting phantoms of pain and anxiety. Marveling at the peace, fragrance, warmth, and beauty of the unfamiliar paradise she had entered, she was resting before stepping again into the dark pit into which fate had cast her.

Karolina looked at her companion with her wide, keen, searching eyes. Her white cheeks were tinted with a wholesome blush, her lips were coral, and her dark eyes had a lively, youthful gleam. But the blooming freshness of this woman was not altogether natural. Everything about her was young and apparently serene except her forehead. On this forehead, an eye experienced in reading human faces could see traces of a long, as yet unfinished history of a life, a heart, and perhaps a conscience.

In contrast to her young, fresh, beautiful face, her forehead was shriveled and beginning to show signs of age. Over it ran hardly visible but dense networks of wrinkles; between her dark eyebrows lay a motionless, perpetually carved furrow. Despite the freshness of her cheeks, the bright red of her lips, the luster of her eyes, and the richness of her costume, the expression on her forehead might awaken, in a diligent and astute observer, three feelings: distrust, curiosity, and pity.

For a few minutes there was silence between the two women. Marta interrupted it first. She raised her head from the pillow on which it had rested for a while, looked at her companion, and said:

"Karolina, your story comes as a great surprise to me. Who would have supposed that Madame Herminia would treat you so cruelly? She brought you up, after all; by all accounts she was your close relative."

Karolina leaned against the backward-curving frame of her exquisite chair and, pressing the dog embroidered on the stool harder with her dainty foot, rocked faster. She began to speak, smiling slightly and staring at the ceiling:

"Madame Herminia was not my close relative, but a rather distant one. But I had the same last name—my father's—that she had. That was enough for this proud, wealthy woman to raise an orphan and make her a housemate or companion. She did me a great service; until the end of my life, whatever happens, I can boast that I grew up with dogs, favorites of Madame Herminia, who was well known in the world. Our education and style of life, mine and her dogs', were very similar. I and the dogs slept on soft pillows, ran around on waxed floors, consumed delicacies. The only differences between us were that they wore silk caps and golden collars while I wore silk dresses and golden bracelets, and that in the end they remained in that paradise while I was drummed out by the avenging angel of maternal pride."

With those last words the woman in lilac laughed—a dry, brief laugh that belied her youthful appearance, but was in keeping with her furrowed forehead and, like it, could arouse distrust or pity. Marta experienced the latter emotion.

"Poor Karolina!" she said. "How you must have suffered, going out into the world alone without the means of life . . ."

"Add to that, my dear," Karolina exclaimed, staring continuously at the ceiling, "add to that that I went out into the world with my heart broken by an unhappy love.

"Yes," she added, sitting up straight and turning her eyes on her companion, "you should know that I was really in love, terribly in love, with Edward, Madame Herminia's son, who (you surely remember him) sang so tenderly: 'Oh, angel who from this earth!' He had sapphire eyes that seemed to look into the depths of one's soul. Yes, I loved him very much. I was so ridiculous . . . I was in love."

She spoke in a jocular tone and with the last words burst into a long, loud, ringing laugh. "Yes!" she cried. "I was so silly . . . I was in love! Oh, how silly I was!"

"And he," Marta asked sadly, "did he really love you as well? What did he do when his mother ordered you out of her house into misery, loneliness, and a life with no home?"

"He!" Karolina said with exaggerated pathos. "He looked at me for a whole year with his beautiful sapphire eyes as if he wanted to enter my soul and conquer it with them. He sang songs at the piano that made my heart melt. He pressed my hand when we danced, then he kissed both my hands and swore by heaven and earth that he would love me until he died. He wrote ardent notes on the spur of the moment from whichever room he was in to the room where I was.

"Then, when his mother read one of his notes by chance and ordered me to leave with no place to go, he went to Warsaw for the carnival. He met me in the street, and by then I was hungry, desperate, dressed almost in rags. He blushed like a peony, looked away, and passed me as if he did not recognize me. A few days later at the Church of the Visitation he took a vow of faithfulness and love until death to a beautiful, wealthy heiress. That is how he loved me and what he did for me."

Again she laughed, but this time briefly and dryly.

"Despicable!" Marta said quietly.

Karolina shrugged her shoulders.

"You exaggerate, my dear," she said in a tone of complete indifference. "Despicable? Why? Because he made the most of an advantage he knew he had and would always have in the world, as will all the men he knows? Despicable because he amused himself with a young, poor girl who was so foolish as to believe that she was the object of his love? By no means, my dear. Edward was certainly not a saint or a hero, but he was also not, as you said, despicable. He had great qualities, I assure you, and he only did what the world gives him full permission to do: he took advantage of a right that it offers him. He was like all young men, and often not so young men."

She spoke quite seriously, without the slightest joke or sneer, in the voice of one who is utterly convinced. Then she crossed her hands on her chest and, without taking her eyes from the ceiling, hummed a song from *Ten Daughters for Marriage.* Marta looked at her in astonishment.

After a while, the woman in satin stopped humming, shifted from her half-reclining posture, and sat up. She leaned a little way toward her companion, resting her elbow on her knee and her face on her hand.

"Because in the end," she continued in a thoughtful voice, "when one is judging people, one must consider their habits and their points of view on life and its issues. If, for example, the colors white and black could have the power to think and feel, then the first, accustomed to the superiority that is constantly attributed to it, could imagine that the black was only created for the pleasure, diversion, and amusement of the white. The most important thing in human relations, my dear, are the differences that occur, and between Edward and me there were immense differences—"

"Indeed"—Marta interrupted spiritedly—"he was a rich man and you a poor girl, but does wealth entitle its possessors to mistreat those who are not rich?"

"To a certain extent," Karolina replied. "I was not thinking of wealth and poverty when I spoke of differences, for after all, if I had not been a poor woman but a poor man, Edward, who, I repeat, had many fine qualities, would not even have thought of harming or offending me. A wealthy, honorable man does not harm or offend a poor man. If he ever did, it would cast a blemish on his character and he would feel the lash of public censure. But I was not a man; I was a woman. To offend, to harm a woman in such a way as happened between Edward and me is a different thing than offending or harming a man. *Ca ne tire pas à conséquence!* Indeed, a certain glamour is attached to it. It is spoken of as success. Masculine boldness makes a young fellow interesting; it casts an aura of fame around him. 'Edward is a brave fellow!' 'A lady-killer!' 'He has the devil's own luck with women!' 'He was born with the gift!' 'Seducing a girl is like cracking a nut to him!' and so on.

"Everyone, my dear, likes to be praised, and fears a reprimand as he fears fire. Many people refrain from doing evil because they fear condemnation, and do good because of their desire for praise. Edward liked me; no wonder. I was eighteen years old and I was beautiful. He indulged his liking for me in a way that was pleasant for him. No wonder! He has known since childhood that such indulgence is his inalienable right, that if he does not take advantage of that right, the world will call him a bungler and a milksop, and that if he takes advantage, he will be called a stout fellow and an interesting young man. He did what any man would do in his place. That is why I do not hold any grudge against him. Indeed, I am grateful to him. He pushed me into the world. He taught me about life and its great truths."

She reached out and took a pink candy from the crystal saucer sitting on the table, bit it in her white teeth, and again pressed the yarn pointer hard with her little foot. The runners moved briskly, rocking her as she lay on the long chair. Her eyes, wandering slowly over the objects around her, looked like the great diamond that gleamed on her finger in the firelight. Bright rainbow colors gleamed in them as in ice crystals polished by frost. But Marta's eyes, as she looked at the companion of her childhood and youth, were deeply thoughtful, yet smoldering with alarm.

"He pushed you into the world, you say," she said slowly in a quiet voice. "What kind of goodness is that? For a poor woman, the world is terrible, suffocating. He taught you the truths of life? Or those that show a woman, who is, after all, a human being, the infinite differences between some people and others? These are awful truths! They are not God's truths, but people's—"

"And why should we care?" Karolina cried with her dry, short laugh. "Whether they are from God or from people, it is enough that they exist. They say to a man: 'You will study, work, achieve, enjoy!' They say to a woman: 'You will be a bauble for a man to play with!' We should know these divine or human truths so as not to eat away our hearts with fruitless worries, not to waste our youth grasping in vain at sunbeams, but to give up what does not exist for us in the world, and not die of starvation pursuing virtue, love, respect, or other such beautiful things."

"Yes," Marta said in a barely audible voice, "not to die of starvation. That is the highest good that a poor woman is allowed to dream of and reach for!"

"Really?" Karolina asked in a drawling voice. With the finger on which the diamond gleamed, she pointed to the objects that surrounded her and added:

"Nonetheless . . . see. Look around."

Marta did not look around. She only opened her lips as if she wanted to ask a question, but she quickly restrained herself. Both women were silent for a long time. Karolina still rocked slowly, nibbling candy after candy without moving her eyes from Marta, who sat lost in thought with her head on her hand and her eyes down.

"Do you know, Marta," said the woman in satin, breaking the silence, "you are really very beautiful. What magnificent height! You must be at least half a head taller than I. So far, poverty has not been bad for your appearance at all. The pink firelight falls on your face like a delicate blush. It makes you more beautiful, and looks lovely next to your black hair, which is so rich and thick! What would happen if, instead of this ugly, rusty-looking wool dress, you wore vibrant colors and finely cut clothes? If instead of this plain linen collar, you could wrap your neck in transparent lace? If you raised your braids higher and decorated them with a red rose or gold pins? You would be lovely, my dear. You would only need to appear a few times in the second-floor box at the performance of a fashionable comedy for young men from all over Warsaw to ask with one voice: 'Who is she? Where does she live? Will she let us place our homage at her feet—'"

"Karolina! Karolina!" Marta broke in, sitting up very straight and looking at her companion in astonishment. "Why are you saying all this? What does it have to do with my situation, with the grief of a widow or the anxiety of a mother? Why do I need beauty? Why should there be fine clothes for me?"

"Why? Why? Oh! Oh! Oh!"

These cries flew into space together with sudden, intermittent windfalls of brief, dry laughter, and they all died away together. Both women were silent for longer than before.

"Marta, how old are you?"

"I turned twenty-four not long ago."

"And I am twenty-three. I am one year younger, but so much wiser than you! I have advanced farther in my life than you, you poor victim of dreams and illusions!"

Again they were silent. Marta raised her head with an expression of determination on her face.

"Yes, Karolina, I see that you must be wiser than I am, and you have advanced farther in life. You are well off; you are not worried about tomorrow. If you had a small child, as I do, you would not have to let her be poorly treated or see her grow weak and pale and waste away before your eyes.

"I have known you for as long as I can remember. We spent our childhood and early girlhood together; we liked each other. But until now I have not dared to ask you where this wealth that I see around you came from—how you managed to pull yourself out of the poverty and misery that you mentioned in your story. I did not dare ask you because I saw that you were avoiding my questions, but, forgive me, Karolina, that was not well done on your part. I was your companion in the enjoyments of child-hood, the confidante, not so long ago, of your youthful dreams. You should tell me how you battled the fate that trips poor women up and deals them crushing blows. Perhaps it will cast some light on my path—"

"Oh, without any doubt it will cast a very bright, illuminating light on your path!" said Karolina, who had now let down her blond hair. Again her eyes looked like two cold crystals in which rainbow colors were reflected and a glittering smile trembled on her small lips, but her voice sounded calm and confident.

Marta continued to speak.

"When I went into the world alone for the first time to fight for my life and my child's, I was told that a woman only achieves victory in that strug-gle if she has some exceptional skill, some genuine, highly developed talent. Karolina, did you have such a talent?"

"No, Marta, I do not have any talent. I only know how to dance, enter-tain guests, and dress well."

"I have never heard that you had a talent."

"I never had any talent at all."

"Perhaps you had wealthy relatives who passed on their fortune to you?"

"I had wealthy relatives, but they did not pass anything on to me."

"So . . ." Marta began.

"So—" the woman in satin interrupted. Suddenly she rose from her chair, which was still rocking. The yarn dog lurched violently; the rockers hit the floor with a thud. The woman stood erect in front of the love seat on which Marta was sitting.

"I was beautiful," she said, "and . . . and I understood what the only possible place in this world was for me."

"Ah!" Marta exclaimed quietly, and she moved as if she were going to rise hastily from her seat. But the woman who stood before her fixed her with a look that kept her chained in place. She stood absolutely still, with her pale hair and slender figure bathed in the rosy light of the fire. She raised her eyebrows slightly and stared deeply and obdurately into Marta's face. Her eyes burned with a fierce, dark brilliance.

"Well?" she began after a while. "You took fright, you ninny. You want to run? Very well. Go! You have every right to pick up a handful of mud and throw it in my face. Who will deny you this right? Today you still have it."

Marta covered her eyes with her hand.

"You are covering your eyes. You do not want to look at me. You ask yourself if I am really that innocent, naïve, ideal Karolina who ran around your father's flowery meadow with you and flitted over Madame Herminia's polished floors in a giddy waltz, who loved white roses and the fragrance of lilies of the valley, and saw Edward's sapphire eyes in a flood of moonlight. Oh, it is I, I myself. But if the sight of me sets you on edge, do not look at me. Only listen."

She took a few steps forward and sat down by Marta on the love seat.

"Listen!" she repeated. "Have you ever asked yourself, have you ever comprehended, exactly what a woman is in the world? Certainly not. Then I will tell you. I do not know how it is according to the laws of God that you spoke of a while ago, but according to human law and custom, a woman is not a human being, a woman is an object. Do not turn your head away. What I am saying is the truth, perhaps relative, but the truth.

"Do you want to see people? Look at men. Every one of them lives in the world in his own right; he does not need anyone to assign him a number so he will not be a zero. A woman is a zero if a man does not stand next to her as a completive number. A woman, like an artistically polished diamond in a jewelry store, is given a gleaming frame so she will attract the eyes of as many buyers as possible. If she does not find someone to buy her, or if she loses him, she is covered with the rust of perpetual suffering and the taint of misery without remedy. She becomes a zero again, but a zero gaunt from hunger, shivering with cold, tearing rags in pieces in a useless attempt to carry on and improve her lot.

"Think of all the old maids and the abandoned or widowed women you have known in your life. Look at your colleagues at Madame Szwejc's shop. Look at yourself. Of what significance are all of you in the world? What are your hopes? Where is the possibility of pulling yourselves from that mire and getting on to where people go? You are plants raised in greenhouses, whose stems have no strength to resist winds and storms. That is how it must have been ever since the seers and sages of this world called woman 'the fairest of nature's flowers.' A woman is a flower, a woman is a zero, a woman is an object incapable of independent movement. There is no happiness or bread for her without a man. A woman must somehow attach herself to a man if she wants to live, otherwise she goes into Madame Szwejc's sewing shop and dies slowly. And what does she do if she has a passionate desire to live? Guess! Did you guess? Good! Cover your eyes with your other hand so you cannot even see the hem of my dress, but hear me out.

"I was young and beautiful and accustomed to luxury and idleness. When I was thrown out of my relatives' wealthy home, I had only a few dresses, my mother's golden bracelet, and the blue enamel ring you gave me, Marta, on your wedding day. I sold the bracelet and the ring. I thought that would bring me enough money to last until I found work. I imagined that I was a human being, and because of that mistake I suffered the pains of hell for several months. I would have suffered even longer if I had not met Edward on Nowy Świat Street. I still loved him. When he passed me by without a greeting, I finally realized that I am an object that one can take and then throw away as one pleases. Would anyone ever have treated a man as I was treated by that one whom I dreamed of in my days of peace, and whose features I recalled in hours of hunger and suffering?

"The moment I lost faith in my humanity, my suffering ended. Perhaps you have heard of a young gentleman named Vitaly who has an aging wife, a large estate near the city, and a fine house here in town. He often visits a little store on Ptasia Street. I helped the owner of that store sell candles and soap in return for a straw mattress in the corner of her children's bedroom at night and a bowl of barley soup and a glass of milk during the day. To tell the truth, my work was worth much more, but the worthy woman took advantage of an assistant whom she brought in from the street exhausted, hungry, and in rags. Two days after that encounter with Edward, after two nights I could not now describe, I stopped selling candles and soap. I said 'Yes!' to Vitaly. I left the store and the room in which five filthy children screamed and quarreled, and I moved in here."

Marta sat as if turned to stone. Her face, which showed from under the hand that covered her eyes, was still and pale as marble. A hardly noticeable shiver ran from her head to her feet, while almost next to her ear sounded a dry, short laugh like the night watchman's rattle.

"I do not know how it happened, but I believe I drifted into a rant!" the woman with loose fair hair exclaimed, laughing. "Marta, your mourning dress darkens my drawing room. I do not like darkness. I love the light. I love to laugh at comedies and eat candy at home. Believe me, it is better that way."

She took the widow's hand, which was dangling among the folds of her black dress, and drew closer to her.

"Listen, Marta," she began, leaning over almost to her companion's ear, "I loved you once, and today I am deeply sorry for you. The ring you gave me provided me with food for several weeks, so now I will help you and advise you. Until now I have spoken to you in theory; now I will speak of practical things. Next to my apartment there are three rooms for rent, almost like these. Do you want them? Tomorrow we will be neighbors. You will bring your child here. She will be comfortable and warm. The day after tomorrow you will take off this unsightly mourning dress—"

Marta took her hand from her eyes and raised her head.

"Karolina!" she said, standing up. "Enough. Do not say another word."

"What?" cried the woman in satin. "No?"

The woman in mourning did not reply for a moment. A look of excruciating pain alternated with a crimson blush on her face. Her voice trembled and broke off from time to time as she began to speak.

"Not long ago, if anyone had dared to say what you did to me, Karolina, I would have felt mortally offended, perhaps violently angry. Now I feel nothing except great pain and even greater shame. I must truly be something less than a human being since, without having done anything wrong, not the slightest evil, without having searched for anything in the world but honest work, I have met with something that . . . I have met with . . . oh, how low, how low I have fallen. And for what? For what fault?"

She stood still for a moment, staring gloomily at the floor. After a while she added gently:

"I do not despise you, Karolina. I will not throw at you, as you said, a handful of mud. My God! I know the life of a poor woman. I have been tasting it for months. Today I swallowed the bitterest drop of it. So I do not despise you, but I cannot follow in your footsteps. Never. Never."

She grew silent again. This time she stared with clear eyes at one point in space, where in her imagination she saw one of the pictures from her past. It was not a picture of joy and happiness; indeed, it reflected a moment of infinite pain. Marta saw, lying on his deathbed, the only man she had ever loved.

His face had stiffened under the hand of death. His breath had stopped in his ailing chest. But his eyes, lit with the last glimmer of life, rested on her face. His hand, twitching as his fingers went rigid in the final spasm, squeezed hers. "My poor Marta, how will you live without me?"—with those words on his blue lips he left her forever.

"Oh! How I loved him! How I still love him!" the widow whispered, wringing her hands. Then they fell on her black dress and her chest heaved with an immense sigh.

"No, Karolina! For God's sake, no!" she cried. Her face seemed to glow from under its pallor as she raised her head very high. "I was happier than you. The man I loved did not turn me into an object. He married me, loved me, respected me. Even in dying, he thought about me and my future. I still love him although he is no longer in this world. I respect his name, which I carry. His memory and my love for him rise inside me like altars. A lamp burns before him, filled with the tears of my heart, and lights my dreary path—"

"Which will soon take you to the Elysian Fields, where white angels will unite you with that dead husband of yours!" Karolina said in a penetrating voice punctuated by harsh laughter.

Marta was already standing several steps away. She put her black woolen scarf on her head.

"Be well, poor Karolina, be well!" she called in a muffled voice and ran out to the adjoining room, where a rosy lamp above a round mahogany table was already lit. She was near the door when she felt a hand on her arm. Karolina was standing beside her. Her lips trembled with laughter; her shriveled forehead was covered with wavy wrinkles. There was a dark gleam in her eyes.

"Listen!" she said. "I really feel like laughing at you! You are overwrought; you are strangely naïve. You are, my dear, still a great child. Despite that, I feel sorry for you! I do not even know why, because in the end, why should I care what will happen to you? It is better for me that you will not be my neighbor; you are too beautiful. But . . . but your ring fed me through several weeks. It is not necessarily the duty of one in my calling to be ungrateful."

She held the young widow's arm tightly with one hand and extended the other toward the window.

"Just think," she said, "it is so cold there, so crowded, yet so empty. The crowds will trample you. The emptiness will swallow you. Come back."

"Let me go," Marta whispered fervently. "I say nothing against you, but I cannot talk to you. I came here for a moment of friendship and rest, and I found new pain and the greatest shame of my life. Let me go!"

"You must hear one more word. The young man who was walking with me in the street today is madly in love with you. He will give everything he has—"

"Let me go!" Marta screamed aloud, and moaned. With spasmodic movements she tore her arm from the woman who was leaning toward her. The hand that had held her fell, and she ran toward the door.

She had taken several steps down the brightly lit stairway when she heard the rustle of satin behind her.

"Come back!" called the voice from above. "You will be a beggar!"

The woman in mourning ran down the stairs without replying.

"You will steal!" the voice called again.

Without turning her head, Marta hurried farther down the stairs.

"You and your child will die of hunger."

At the sound of the last words, Marta stopped. Her face was deathly pale; her eyes, smoldering with gloomy fire, were riveted on the woman who stood at the top of the stairway.

She saw a figure bathed in radiant gaslight that painted the lilac of her dress with silver. A large cameo at her neck gleamed with a bluish tint, and her golden earrings quivered amid the dense mass of her long hair, which was blown lightly upward by the wind from the door that opened to the street. She was leaning forward; her lips were trembling with laughter, and her cold eyes cast rainbow gleams from under her wrinkled forehead.

Marta stared at her for a moment with dry, burning eyes full of fear and melancholy. Then suddenly she turned, stepped quickly forward and vanished instantly onto the dusky street.

A few minutes had hardly passed before cheerful Olek ran in by the same door through which Marta had disappeared. He took the stairs in a few quick bounds and entered Karolina's apartment.

"Well?" he asked, standing on the threshold of the drawing room with his hat in his hand. "Has she left? I thought I recognized her on the sidewalk across the street. When will she come again?"

He asked the question briefly and hastily. His black eyes flashed with the impatience of a man who is in the grip of a strong sensation, but has no will or capacity for reflection.

"She will not come again," replied the woman, who was sitting before the hearth in the same place where Marta had sat a few minutes before. Her hands were crossed on her chest; her eyes did not move from the burning coals. She did not turn them toward the young man. She replied to his impatient question briefly, not merely with indifference, but reluctantly.

"She will not return?" Olek exclaimed, throwing his hat onto the nearest piece of furniture and walking into the room. "How can it be that she will not return? Have you ladies not been friends since childhood?"

The woman was silent. The young man grew more impatient.

"What did she say?" he urged.

"She said," the woman answered slowly without changing her position or the direction of her eyes, "she said that she still loves her husband."

His eyes opened wide.

"Her husband?" he said as if he did not believe his ears. "Her dead husband?"

He burst out laughing, raised his face toward the ceiling, and went on laughing loudly for a long time.

"Her husband!" he repeated. "And what does she still want from that poor devil? Why, he is not even alive! Oh, faithful heart . . . an inconsolable widow. How affecting!"

He went on laughing, but in that laughter after a while there were false notes—notes of something like remorse and painful irritation.

"By God!" he began again, pacing through the drawing room with long strides. "This is an uncommon woman! Still to love her husband several months after his death! How noble! What if now she were to fall in love with a living man? Oh, if I could be that fortunate one!"

"It is certainly possible that you could be that fortunate one," said the woman sitting before the fireplace. But she did not turn her head or move at all. He rushed toward her, flushed with excitement.

"I could be!" he cried. "Then she did not deprive me of all hope! Oh, beautiful, lovely Karolina, precious jewel, have mercy on me! I really am madly in love! I could be that fortunate one, if I—tell me, I beg you, I beseech you, if I did what?"

She looked at him for the first time. Deep in her eyes, in her slightly raised eyebrows, and in the playful corners of her delicate mouth lurked the subtle hint of a sneer.

"If," she said slowly, "if you courted her and wanted to marry her."

Her words left Olek numb, even stupefied. He stood paralyzed for a moment with his mouth half open and his eyes fixed on the woman who gazed unflinchingly at him.

"Marry!" he repeated in a choked voice.

His lips trembled as if he were about to laugh, but he did not. He only waved a hand, shrugged his shoulders and said, half irritably and half indifferently: "You must be joking!"

He moved away from the fireplace. The woman glanced at him with cold, scornful eyes. In the space of a minute, a myriad of arch, derisive, and contemptuous smiles played over her face. Again cheerful Olek stood before her.

"Karolina, you are cruel!" he exclaimed. "You talked of marriage, and to me! Is that not ridiculous? To tie myself for life to a person I hardly know, a widow who still loves her dead husband? To become the father of some child, to have the weight of the world on my shoulders—all those responsibilities, all that trouble? At my age? With my fortunate position in the world? This is an idea worthy of an honest bourgeois who longs for tasty homemade food and a dozen chubby children. I do not think that you were speaking seriously. I know that you like to joke! It is one of your most charming qualities."

Karolina shrugged.

"Of course I was joking," she said curtly, and gazed again at the flaming coals.

Cheerful Olek was increasingly irritated.

"What sort of humor are you in today?" he grumbled. "Will I not find out anything more?"

"You are boring me to death."

"Where does she live?"

"I do not know. I forgot to ask her."

"Splendid! What will I do now? I will have to look for her, but the city is like a forest. Before I find her, I will forget about her again."

He spoke with extraordinary exasperation, regret and something like anger. He was afraid that his inconsistent memory and the multitude of sensations that diverted him every day would pull him away from what now engaged him passionately. Suddenly he snapped his fingers, shouted for joy, and approached the fireplace again.

"Eureka!" he cried. "She is a seamstress? Where? In which shop? Beautiful, lovely, precious Karolina, tell me . . ."

The woman stood up and gave a wide yawn.

"There, on Freta Street, in Madame Szwejc's shop," she said with a look of profound weariness. "Go now. I have to dress for the theater."

Olek looked happy again.

"At Szwejc's shop! I know! I know! I used to go there. One of her daughters, the one who does the cutting, is a scarecrow, but the other, the young one, is married to a brewer, and Szwejc's son's daughter, Miss Eleonora, is not bad at all. So my goddess is there! Oh, tomorrow . . . tomorrow . . . I run, I fly, I'm off!"

He seized his hat and stood on the threshold. "Goodbye!" he called.

He crossed the threshold but turned back.

"You are going to the theater this evening. What is playing?"

The woman stood in the doorway to her bedroom with a lighted candle in her hand.

"*Flik and Flok,*" she said.

"*Flik and Flok!*" exclaimed the man of the perpetual smile. "I must go and see Laura performing her Egyptian dance! But is it not late? I must drop in at Bolek's! Goodbye! Goodbye! I run, I fly, I'm off!"

||I

All great cities, especially Warsaw, have among their permanent residents a certain number of men of various ages who enjoy wide, firmly established reputations as lady-killers and destroyers of feminine virtue. From the time Mother Nature sprinkles their upper lips with the first down of a mustache until, and sometimes even after, she adorns their heads with a frost of whitish gray, they take as their profession and their daily practice in life to admire feminine graces, platonically if they are unable to admire them otherwise, and not platonically everywhere they can. They are very pleasant, lively, witty, cheerful, and ready to be of service. They are sought after in society and highly regarded within their own circles. Often they have not only tender feelings but good hearts, and insofar as they consider and reflect on their actions, they would not deliberately harm anyone for the world.

And if they do often harm others, a forbearing mind that understood them very well might justly apply other expressions to their behavior, such as this from the gospel: "Lord, forgive them, for they know not what they do!" Considering what a common phenomenon they represent, the usual level of their achievements, and what they amount to in life and society, in general they are very insignificant figures: small pawns on the great chess board of humanity, microscopic insects sliding easily with their outstretched wings over the bark of life that is so rough for others.

Considering how insignificant they are, one might completely omit these cheerful rascals from one's consideration of social phenomena. At the sight of them one might even smile and parody the poet's famous cry, "Woman! O paltry feather in the wind!" But these paltry feathers—these tiny pawns perpetually in motion, these innocent insects, always full of the joy of life—are dangerous to a certain class of people: poor women. Leave aside the danger to the heart, for that, whether under a silk or woolen or percale bodice, is a susceptible, weakly defended place for the so-called fair sex; anything can conquer it, anything can wound it. That is why there are pains and regrets, tears and moans, pulling of hair and gnashing of teeth in drawing rooms as well as in garrets.

But what is very rarely harmed by these pleasant buffoons in drawing rooms, while in attics, basements, garment workshops, and other factories it remains completely under their power and is fatally damaged by them, is a woman's reputation. In this regard there are some so adept at conquest that often without prolonged attempts, and even unintentionally, by taking a few steps near a woman or glancing at her a few times, they kill a good reputation, creating evil suspicions. That is the sweet fruit of their wide and well-established fame—truly sweet for them because it demonstrates to the world their virility, the immense power of their influence, the rich inventory of sensations they have experienced and inspired, and the impressiveness of their exploits. But perhaps it is not so sweet for those on whom, by chance, the eyes of these lords of creation rest.

The lord of creation walks down the city street wielding his cane, with its curving handle, like a scepter. The hat on his head glitters, the gloves on his hands glitter with double seams, the golden chain on his chest glitters and sways gracefully against the background of the dark frock coat made by the august hands of the master tailor Chabou. What grandeur! He hums in an undertone a song from *Beautiful Helen*, casting glances around with his shrewd eyes. He often touches the brim of his hat; he bows to everyone and everyone bows to him, because he knows everyone and everyone knows him. What a distinguished position in society!

He breaks off his humming; he extends his neck and holds his foot in the air like a pointer who has tracked down an animal. He squints; he smiles. There at the street corner a pretty face is passing by, a white cheek gleams, black eyes glow. Forward! To the chase! Attention! The quarry is close! One must bring her to bay quickly, for she is about to run away! He approaches from the side, doffs his hat, bows with great respect (oh, irony!), and in a voice that is a faithful imitation of the Parisian voice he heard yesterday on the stage, asks:

"Will madame permit me to accompany her?"

She permits him; he walks with her. She does not permit him; he still walks with her. Is he not the lord of creation? On the way he encounters acquaintances (he has as many as there are drops in the sea); he winks playfully and looks at his companion so as to call their attention to her. Now and then his heart throbs harder. These are the first tremors of butterfly love, or perhaps the intoxication of triumph? Most often, both. The lord of creation, whenever he sees a beautiful or even a pretty specimen of a female face, swears before everyone, most of all himself, that he is madly and incurably in love. He does it in the utmost good faith. His heart is a volcano that erupts several times a day. And he enjoys drawing people's eyes to a new episode in the epic poem of his life. Those eyes are so accustomed to see him unvanquished that from the start they predict his victory!

He approaches, and so he charms. He sees, and so he conquers. Neither he nor anyone who knows him supposes that it could be otherwise. The fame of a bold man increases; the reputation of a poor woman drowns. A new laurel leaf sprouts in the crown he wears on his jolly head; a stain appears on her forehead. So it was with cheerful Olek, who was one of many such men. His very approach compromised a woman, and a conversation with him certified her as disgraced.

Madame Szwejc had three daughters and a few young granddaughters, so she knew Olek. He had often visited her home, and she herself even let it be known that one of her girls, the one who did the cutting with her, had not married because of him. Although she was homely, she had a pretty figure and a lively tongue, and she had turned the head of that lord of creation.

No wonder, then, that Madame Szwejc pushed her glasses close to her eyes and glued her face to the window pane one morning when she saw one of her workers crossing the courtyard in the company of the invincible Olek. The girls in ragged dresses, with sallow faces and fading bows in their hair, also peeked through the windows and made signs to each other with their eyes and fingers, smiling.

Madame Szwejc's daughter noticed all that as she stood by the round table. She rose to her tiptoes and glanced through the window. From her vantage point, she could see Olek's mustache and beard, and because it was his mustache and beard, she was overwhelmed by emotions and recollections. She stretched her neck even farther and saw a black woolen scarf covering a woman's head.

"Mama! Which one of our workers is walking with Olek?"

Madame Szwejc turned her head from the window.

"Madame Świcka," she said, approaching the table. Clouds gathered on the sober matron's forehead and she pronounced the S in Marta's name with a long hiss.

The younger workers exchanged stealthy glances. The look on their employer's face and the ring of her voice did not bode well for someone. One of them said quietly: "There will be a storm!"

"Perhaps she will dismiss her?" another asked more quietly.

"Oh!" a third whispered still more quietly. "Perhaps she does not care by now."

At that moment Marta walked into the shop. Her very expression on this day would have drawn the attention of everyone present if they had not already been looking curiously at her. Her eyes were dull and had dark circles around them. There were round blotches of blood red on her hollow cheeks and a deep furrow between her eyebrows. As she entered, she raised her heavy, swollen eyelids and saw more than a dozen eyes fixed on her. She did not show surprise or any other emotion. She took her scarf from her head, picked up the work that lay ready for her on her stool, and sat down silently. Her hands trembled as if she had a fever when she unrolled the linen and slipped the thread through the needle. She lowered her head with its braids, which were somewhat disheveled that day, and immersed herself in her work. Her hand was still trembling and red from cold; it rose and fell quickly, as if it were keeping time to an agitating, overpowering thought. She breathed quickly and heavily; several times she opened her lips to catch her breath.

Two pairs of scissors clicked long and harshly at the round table. Madame Szwejc glanced sidewise from under her glasses at the newly arrived worker. The corners of her thrust-out lips hung down, indicating that she was in a bad humor. She stopped cutting, but her wrinkled fingers did not let go of the scissors as she said in a quiet, drawling voice:

"Madame Świcka was not with us yesterday afternoon."

Marta heard her name and raised her head.

"Did you say something to me, madame?"

"Madame Świcka was not with us yesterday afternoon."

"No, madame. I had some business in town and I could not come."

"Absences from work bring great losses to our shop."

Marta lowered her head. She resumed her sewing without a word.

Only one pair of scissors made ringing and scraping noises at the round table, but the sounds were harsher and harsher. It was clear that the young woman who had not married because of invincible Olek felt increasingly perturbed.

Her mother stood with her face to the seated workers. The scissors in her swarthy hand were still.

"Yesterday I saw Madame Świcka in town. Madame Świcka was standing with two persons by the stairs of Holy Cross Church."

Marta did not say anything. What could she say? She could not deny the fact to which Madame Szwejc had alluded.

"I also know the persons with whom Madame Świcka was talking in the street yesterday. One of them even worked for a time at our shop a few years ago. Not for long, however, because I noticed very soon that she might set a harmful example for our workers. Do you know that woman well, Madame Świcka? Her company can have a very unsound influence."

"Not on me, madame." Marta spoke up for the first time. She did not lift her head from her work, but her trembling voice rang with the muffled rebellion of a proud woman who feels that someone is trampling on her.

"Ah!" Madame Szwejc gave a long sigh. "One cannot be too sure of oneself. Pride is the mother of all sins. Better to avoid, far better to avoid dangerous company . . . And is Mister Olek Łącki also your close acquaintance, madame?"

The ringing and scraping scissors stopped ringing and scraping. The young woman with the homely face who had once drawn the glance of the lord of creation raised her head.

"He must be her close friend, Mama, if Madame Świcka goes for walks with him every day."

The words were like snakes that wrapped themselves around Marta from head to foot and sent venom into every part of her body. Suddenly she straightened up, lifted her gaze from the linen on her knees, opened her eyes wide and looked the young woman in the face.

"What is the meaning of this?" she said in a heavy, choked whisper, looking around the room. All the workers, even those who usually looked numb and inert, sat with their heads up, staring at her. Their faces expressed a range of attitudes: regret, curiosity, and mockery. For a moment it seemed that Marta had turned to stone. The crimson marks on her face slowly widened until her forehead and neck were covered with purple.

"There is nothing to be angry about, madame, nothing to be angry about," Madame Szwejc began. "For twenty-some years I have been the manager of this shop in which twenty or more young persons have always worked; hence I have a great deal of experience. I know what my responsibilities are to the souls Providence entrusts to my care, and I cannot look on indifferently if one of them voluntarily exposes herself to danger. I have daughters and young granddaughters. What would people think of them if our shop presented, God forbid, examples of debauchery?

"The apartment windows of a certain wealthy and God-fearing lady face the courtyard. She is a true protectress and benefactress of our shop. A saintly lady! What would she think if she saw one of my employees strolling in front of her windows and mine with a young, worldly bachelor? Perhaps she already has! I am afraid, I am deeply disconcerted, when I think of what I will tell my protectress if she asks me about it. That I dismissed the worker? But perhaps that would not be in accord with Christian charity . . ."

"You will tell her, madame, that the employee who had the misfortune to meet that young, worldly bachelor in the courtyard left your shop alone and of her own accord."

These words, spoken in a ringing, penetrating voice, resounded throughout the large room. Marta rose from her seat and with her head high and her lips trembling looked straight into Madame Szwejc's face.

"I am a poor woman, very poor," she continued, "but I am honest and you had no right to speak to me in that way. Providence did not entrust me to your care and lead me here, but my own inability. I came here because I could not get work anywhere else. You knew that very well, and you knew how to take advantage of my situation. My work is worth several times more than you pay me for it, but I did not intend to talk about that. I made a voluntary agreement with you and I fulfilled all the requirements. I have to endure poverty, but to bear insults—despite everything, I cannot. I cannot. Goodbye, madame!"

With those words she threw her scarf over her head and turned toward the door. The workers followed her with their eyes, the younger ones with admiration and something like triumph, the older ones with pity but mostly with astonishment.

Everything that had happened to Marta since the previous day: the disappointment at the bookseller's; the bitter envy that had overwhelmed her for the first time when she saw the hopeful young men studying at the Kaźmirowski Palace; the visit to Królewska Street and the depressing proposal offered her there; the sleepless night when her face was streaming with tears and burning with shame; and most of all the meeting with this man who, she knew, had been waiting there with the thought of debasing her—all that put her spirit into a state of feverish tension which cannot last for long in silence, and explodes at the slightest touch into an irrepressible storm.

And the touch administered by Madame Szwejc and her daughter in their words to Marta was not just any touch. In her heart a tendon of feeling, stretched to the utmost, burst and emitted a mournful moan and a cry of rebellion. Had she done well, giving in to an exhausting outburst of womanly pride and human dignity, throwing her last bite of bread under the feet of the woman who had affronted her? She did not think of that. She did not take account of the consequences of her action as she ran through the long courtyard toward the gate leading to the street.

As soon as she entered the gate she took a step backward, as if she had seen some hideous apparition. A look, the look of one who has been offended past all possibility of conciliation, came over her face. Olek was still standing in the gate, talking in an undertone with a young man who was standing near the bottom of a stairway by which he had descended a moment before on his way to town.

Marta sprang aside. It was clear that she was trying to dart past them near the wall without being noticed. But when was the nimble deer able to evade the eye of the practiced hunter?

"Madame!" Olek called, turning around. "What a surprise! I did not think that you would leave that cave so early today, that cave"—here he lowered his voice—"which for some time has been the paradise for which I long!"

The man with whom Olek had been talking a moment before hurried down the last few stairs and into the street, darting a glance at the woman his companion had turned to and obscuring his knowing smile under a song from *Flik and Flok*. Marta stood by the wall, pale but perfectly erect, with eyes flashing like lightning. Cheerful as usual, Olek approached her with a smile on his face and a dreamy look in his eyes.

"What do you want from me, sir?" she exclaimed.

"Madame!" the lord of creation interrupted her. "A quarter of an hour ago you pushed me away with very stern words, but I have not lost hope that my persistence—"

"What do you want from me?" she repeated, recovering her voice, which she had lost for a moment. "Yes, I left that cave, which, nevertheless, provided me with my last earnings, the last piece of bread for me and my child. I did that because of you. What right do you gentlemen have to cross our paths when it is so difficult for us to make our way even without your interference? Do you have no heart or conscience, that you pursue persons who do not know where to find a place in the world? Oh! It is certain that nothing bad happens to you men because of this! People praise you in these situations, and insult us. We lose our good name and often our last bit of bread; you have your exquisite diversion."

She said all that rapidly, hardly taking a breath. There was a biting sneer in her voice and eyes.

"You will amuse yourselves," she repeated with a pained smile, "but, sir, permit me, a woman you condescended to choose as an object of your amusement, to repeat a few words from the old tale of the frogs: 'Boys, you do badly, amusing yourselves. For you it is play, for us it is life!'"

She passed the young man, leaving him speechless with astonishment, and disappeared beyond the gate.

The lord of creation was left alone. He lowered his head, touched his mustache, fixed his clouded eyes on the ground, and stood that way for a long time. His expression was one of embarrassment and regret—embarrassment because of his defeat, and regret because the attractive and resistant (the more attractive because resistant) creature had vanished before his eyes. And perhaps seeing the woman with smoldering eyes, a clouded forehead, and lips trembling with pride and grief stirred a more serious feeling in him. Perhaps he felt that he had done something wrong and harmed someone unintentionally. Oh, yes! Unintentionally! "For us it is life!" she had said.

What a thought! Had he intended to kill someone? Nothing in the world was more foreign to his tender heart or farther from his mind. He was not at all inclined to anything so dramatic as deliberate murder. Yet she had made her argument to him so powerfully! What dazzling sparks of grief had shot from her eyes! How pale she was, and how beautiful! At that moment Olek would have given, without hesitation, a few years of his sweet, privileged life to see her again, to plead for her forgiveness, to compensate her for her injuries if he had harmed her—and to take her to her apartment.

But where was that apartment of hers? He did not know. He frowned, snapped his fingers impatiently, lifted his head, and exclaimed almost angrily:

"Now I will have no chance of finding her!"

At the same moment a very young lady, wearing a snugly fitting fur-lined coat and strikingly graceful shoes, hurried in through the gate. Olek saw her and his expression changed at once. He quickly removed his hat, bowed to the pretty teenager, and said, smiling:

"It is such a long time since I have been so fortunate as to see you, Miss Eleonora."

The girl did not seem to be displeased at meeting him.

"Ah! You are so kind, Mister Łącki, truly! Very kind! But you have not visited us for a month. My grandmother and aunt have said several times that that is not polite of you."

Olek followed the movements of the chattering pink lips with his dreaming eyes.

"Miss Eleonora!" he said. "My heart pulls me toward your home, but my mind dissuades me."

"Your mind! I am curious as to why your mind dissuades you from visiting us."

"I am afraid of losing my peace!" the lord of creation whispered.

The girl blushed to her ears and hair.

"Well, do not be afraid of that. Come to us, because otherwise my grandma and aunt will surely be angry with you."

"And you?"

There is a moment of silence. The eyes of the teenager stare at the nail protruding from the floor under the gate; the eyes of the conqueror count the golden locks that have fallen from under her hat onto her white forehead.

"I will be angry with you as well."

"Oh, if that is the case, then I will come. I will certainly come!"

The teenager hurries into the courtyard, but the lord of creation dares not follow her. With a poor working woman it is different, but with the granddaughter of a woman in whose home he visits—with Miss Szwejc, who, they say, will have a dowry of a hundred thousand złotys—it is not permissible to stroll around the courtyard.

Olek walks out to the street and the figures of two women pass before his eyes: the poor working woman with the fire of indignation in her eyes and the pretty young girl with golden locks around her white forehead. He does not know which is more beautiful and more alluring. "That one," he muses "is a proud, flaming goddess; this one is a lovely little goddess! The sages speak truly: what inexhaustible riches are lavished throughout the kingdom of nature! How many shades, how many types! When a man is to make a choice, his head spins and his heart melts. But what does the choice amount to? *Tous les genres sont bons, hors le genre—vieux et laid!*"

Man! You paltry feather in the wind!

|||

And Marta?

Marta, after her storm of strong emotion, again fell to counting pennies. She had used the six rubles she had received from the bookseller to pay the manager of her building her arrears and the next two weeks' rent for the attic.

"You must still pay for the furnishings," the manager said as he took the rent money from her hand.

"Take them from my room, sir, because I cannot pay for their use."

A wealthy couple on the second floor needed a table, a few chairs and a bed for their kitchen or anteroom. By evening there was no furniture in Marta's apartment. She made her spartan bed on the bare floor, then sat on the floor in front of the empty hearth, while Jasia sat near one end of the hearth. The mother sat motionless, even stiff, and the child hunched forward, trembling from cold and perhaps sadness. The two pale faces immersed in the evening twilight and the deep silence of the lonely room presented a dreary sight. It was also a sight that would have presented an observer with a mystery. Two unhappy lives shared a place there, in front of the cold opening of the sullen chimney. What would become of them?

Jasia slept restlessly that night, waking from time to time.

Until then, if she often cried during the day, at least she slept peacefully at night. But that evening the last objects that had served to amuse and comfort her had been taken from the room: the two old crippled chairs. She grieved for them as for good friends with whom she had played in her more carefree moments and to whom she had quietly confided her resentments and woes—hunger, cold, and Antoniowa's slaps—when, led by the instinct of a good child, she did not want to complain to her mother. The child had cried as she saw her beloved broken furniture taken away. Later, lying on the floor, perhaps she recalled her old mahogany bed, surrounded with spindles and covered with the yarn quilt from whose varicolored pattern she had learned to distinguish colors and admire beauty.

Midnight came on. The little girl moved on her low pallet, groaning now and then and crying in her sleep. Marta still sat on the floor in front of the fireplace, plunged in darkness and bitter self-reproach.

Harshly and painfully she chided herself for the way she had behaved to Madame Szwejc. Why had she let herself be carried away by her injured pride? Why had she left a place in which there was some possibility of earning money? The insult that had been hurled at her there was undeserved and very great, even cruel, perhaps, but what of that? Could a woman in her situation retaliate against an insult by throwing a crust of bread in someone's eye—hard, black, bitter bread, but the last crust? Not to be able to raise herself from her humiliating situation, and at the same time not to be able to bear the blows and humiliations of that situation patiently: what inconsistency! Because of her own incompetence, she had been in the hands of a woman who exploited that incompetence but who nevertheless demanded respect and justice for herself! How mindless!

"No!" she thought. "Only one of two things is possible. One must be strong and proud in the world, or weak and humble. One must know how to maintain and protect one's personal dignity, or renounce all pretensions to it. I am weak; I ought to be humble. I cannot, by my actions, raise myself to a position that enables me to command respect.

"In any case, why should people respect me? Do I really respect myself? Can I look without shame or pangs of conscience at this child, whom I should support and care for, and I have no power to do it? How humiliated I am when I think of how I bowed my head before that unscrupulous woman like a silly, defenseless sheep, allowing, even begging her to use the labor of my days and the sweat of my brow to build a fortune for herself and her children!

"Anyway, what does the whole world take me for? One person rejects my work because I have no ability; another does not hire me because she is convinced beforehand that I will not succeed; still another wickedly exploits me precisely because I have no ability; and finally, another does not see me as his equal in virtue and respectability, but only as a reasonably good-looking woman whom he can . . . buy!

"Why did I demand from Madame Szwejc what the entire world refuses me—what I could not win from other people or from myself?"

As the night gave way to a gray winter dawn, Marta was still sitting in the same place, with her elbows on her knees and her head in her hands. Now she felt humble, very humble. She smiled to herself at the thought that as recently as yesterday she had still believed that she had some pretense to respectability. She was certain that humiliation would never again take her by surprise, and that she would not murmur against the hand that dealt it.

Together with the daylight, the thought of daily necessities entered the attic room. Marta took a złoty from her pocket. She had no more money and no work.

"I must go and ask," she thought.

She went out to town and made her way toward the bookshop. She was going to the man whose compassionate hand had once offered her work and, another time, alms.

Marta was astonished when she opened the door of the bookshop. Before leaving home she had imagined how difficult it would be to cross this threshold, and assumed that as before, when she put her requests into words, she would be embarrassed and lose her voice. But her heart did not beat harder and she did not blush when she met the eyes of the bookseller.

He stood, as usual, behind the counter, leaning over a large pile of notes and bills. When he heard the bell he looked up. His forehead was less smooth than before, and his eyes expressed a slight uneasiness or worry. He was visibly troubled or saddened. Perhaps one of his ventures was not going well although he had expected much from it; perhaps a friend or member of his family was ill. With difficulty he tore himself away from what was occupying him and looked at her, as she entered the shop, with eyes that were not so bright, kind, and courteous as before.

Marta noticed that, and several days ago she would have withdrawn and gone away, or at least concealed the aim of her visit. Now, however, she approached the counter, exchanged greetings with him, and said:

"You were so kind as to help me with advice and a gift, sir, so I have come again."

"How can I help you, madame?"

He spoke politely but more coolly than before. His distracted eyes turned now and then to the papers lying on the counter.

"I lost my employment in the sewing shop in which I earned forty pennies a day. Do you know of a suitable place for me, of any . . ."

The bookseller lowered his eyes and stood silently for a moment. His already troubled air was deepened now by a little embarrassment and even impatience.

"Ah!" he said after a moment with a gesture of regret. "That is hard, madame! One must be skilled at something, one must certainly be skilled at something . . ."

He did not finish his thought. He said no more. Marta squeezed the ends of her scarf in both hands.

"Then," she said after a pause, "what will I do?"

She said it in such a way that the bookseller raised his eyes and looked at her closely. Her voice was curt, even a bit sharp. Her sunken eyes burned, not with pain as they had before, not with silent, poignant pleading, but with dull, stifled anger. One who saw and heard her might say that she felt some resentment toward the man she was talking with, that in her mind he was partly responsible for what she was experiencing.

The bookseller thought for a while longer.

"I am sorry," he said, "very sorry to see the wife of a man I knew and respected in such a situation. It seems to me that I may be able to do something for you, although it would involve a new test of your abilities. Acquaintances of mine, the Rzętkowski family, need someone . . . someone . . . a housemaid . . . if you wish to accept such a position."

"Yes, please," Marta said without a moment's thought.

"Then I will write a few words to the Rzętkowskis. If you like, you will go to them with this note."

"I will certainly go."

The bookseller hastily wrote a dozen words on a sheet of paper and handed it to the waiting woman. He was rushed and ill at ease, and he still seemed worried. He bowed immediately after giving her the letter. His bow was clearly a polite form of dismissal; it meant, I have no more time and I cannot do any more.

Marta left the bookshop. The letter she held in her hand was not sealed. She opened the paper, which was folded in two, and turned it a few times. She seemed to be looking for something between the thin sheets. Indeed, the thought had crossed her mind that, as he had previously placed something in her manuscript, now the bookseller might have put a gift for her in the letter. But there was no gift. Marta thought:

"It is a pity that he did not give me anything!"

The bookseller was a kind man and he had a very compassionate hand. But compassionate hands are inconvenient for those who need them, because the souls to which they are attached are not always in the same mood. Even the best man may not be uniformly inclined to do good deeds at every moment of his life. Good deeds are a form of luxury for the soul whose daily bread is its primary responsibility. In the moment when responsibility is pressing, a compassionate hand may be not disposed to do compassionate things.

What a change! Several months ago Marta moaned with pain and shame when she received alms. Now she resented not having received them!

She glanced at the address on the paper she was holding and turned into Świętokrzyska Street. A few minutes later she was in the kitchen of a large, well-kept residence. There she found a cook, and gave her the note from the bookseller. The cook went to another room while Marta sat on a wooden bench, where she remained for a good ten minutes while the Rzętkowskis deliberated and conferred.

After ten minutes a pleasant-looking, expensively dressed middle-aged woman entered the kitchen, holding the note from the bookseller. She approached Marta, who rose on seeing her and looked at her attentively for a few seconds.

"I am very sorry, madame," she said in a slightly embarrassed voice. "A few days ago we needed a maid, but now we do not need one. I am very sorry. My apologies."

She bowed far more politely than one usually bows to a person seeking work as a maid, and then left the kitchen. She went to a room where a gray-haired man was sitting with a pipe in his mouth and two young ladies were embroidering by the window.

"Well?" the man asked. "You did not hire her?"

"Of course I did not hire her. An official's widow . . . she would surely demand special favors. And she is so thin and delicate! Sweeping rooms and standing over an iron for whole hours is not for her. She probably does not even know how to do the washing and ironing. We would have trouble with her and nothing more."

"You are right," said her husband, "but it is too bad that you turned her away with nothing. She must be very poor if, being as delicate as you say and an official's widow, she wants to work as a maid. Perhaps you should give her a chance."

"But, my Ignacy, Laurenty writes that she has a child! Even if there were no other objections, could we hire a maid with a child?"

"True! True! It would be impossible with a child. There would be great expense and trouble. And God only knows what kind of child! But Laurenty recommended her. I am afraid he might be offended because we turned her away with nothing. He might take us for heartless people."

"Well, we must give her something! I would rather give her a ruble than bring constant trouble on us . . . nuisances . . . and have a strange child in the house."

Marta was already on the stairway when she heard quick steps behind her and a voice calling twice:

"Madame! Madame!"

She looked around and saw a young, pretty girl running after her, wrapped snugly in a warm caftan.

"Madame," the girl began, stopping before the widow, "Mama told me to apologize to you for giving you the trouble of coming to us for nothing. It is so cold today, and you had the bother of coming to us. Mama told me to ask your pardon."

She spoke rapidly and was somewhat abashed, but she reached out shyly with a ruble note. Marta hesitated for a second, but only a second, before she took the rustling paper from the pretty girl's hand, said: "Thank you!" and left. On the way home she bought a bundle of wood, a little black bread, coarse flour, and milk. The bread was for herself, the milk and flour for her child.

That day she did not go to town again. She boiled the milk and flour, poured it into a clay bowl, and seated Jasia before it.

But the girl ate very little. She was silent and unusually subdued. It was clear that her head was painfully heavy because she rested it on her thin hand. She sat on the floor by her mother, lay down on her lap, and fell into a long, deep sleep.

The next day Marta looked at her child's face by the morning light and was frightened. Jasia was paler than the day before; from her sunken, ringed eyes came a silent but heartrending plaint. The young woman turned toward the window and wrung her hands convulsively.

"If I do not provide her with better food and a warm room," she thought, "she will become ill. Better food and a warm room: a wild idea! In two or three days I will have no way to heat the room and cook warm food for her!

"Ah!" she said to herself after a moment. "There is nothing else to do! I must go and apologize to Madame Szwejc!"

She went to Freta Street. When she opened the door of the gloomy shop, she was even more astonished at herself than when she had entered the bookshop. True, she felt a little embarrassed, but that feeling was nothing in the face of her overwhelming desire to be hired again in this place that she had left of her own accord two days ago.

Madame Szwejc did not show the least surprise on seeing her. Only a quick smile fluttered over the grave matron's sagging lips, and her eyes glittered sharply behind her glasses. The workers lifted their heads and looked at the woman who had just arrived, some with curiosity, others sarcastically, with malicious satisfaction. Under the scrutiny of twenty pairs of eyes, Marta felt a hot flame on her cheeks and forehead.

It was torture, but it lasted only a second. The manager of the shop and her daughter stopped cutting linen, obviously waiting for the first word from their former employee.

"Madame," Marta said, turning to Madame Szwejc, "two days ago I was rash, impulsive. I was offended by what you said and I replied to you discourteously. I apologize. If it is possible, I would like to work for you again."

As a moment ago Madame Szwejc's face had not betrayed surprise, neither did it express triumph now. Indeed, she smiled sweetly and nodded politely.

"O, my dear Madame Świcka!" she began in a honeyed voice. "I am not offended, not offended at all. Why, it is very salutary to hear some impoliteness, to bear with painful words. Our Savior ordered us to repeat morning and evening: 'Forgive us our trespasses as we forgive those who trespass against us!' I would not be obedient to our Lord if I were angry at you,

Madame Świcka. But I cannot hire you back. I am very sorry, but I really cannot, because since yesterday I have had a new employee in your place."

She pointed with her scissors to a young woman who was sitting in Marta's former seat.

"Our shop, God be praised, has the finest reputation. We do not use sewing machines, which so terribly undermine the strength and impair the health of working persons. That is why workers come thronging to our shop, thronging—a crowd of them, really. There is not a single day in which two or three persons do not come asking for work. We are not lacking, thank God, for employees. We have no shortage of them and we cannot take more because my daughter and I do not want to be burdened with excessive work. So now, when there is a full complement of workers, even more than a full complement, there is no place for Madame Świcka—"

"But, Mama, perhaps there would still be work for Madame Świcka as well!" the homely girl whispered, leaning toward her mother. She looked at Marta keenly and curiously for a few minutes, with something like pity in her small, slightly crossed eyes.

But Madame Szwejc shrugged her shoulders.

"No," she said, "there is no work, none! We cannot dismiss Zofia, who was engaged yesterday, to hire Madame Świcka again after she left us voluntarily."

At those words the woman sitting in Marta's old place lifted her head from her work and looked almost with terror at the owner of the shop.

"You will not hire me again, madame?" Marta asked. "There is no hope?"

"None, dear Madame Świcka, none! I truly regret it, but the place has been taken. I cannot."

Marta nodded almost imperceptibly and walked away. As she opened the door of the shop, she heard behind her the murmur of very soft whispers and even softer giggles. She understood that she was the object of the mockery or the idle pity of twenty people, and again her face and chest felt hot. Yet when she found herself on the street, a single thought gripped her:

"I cannot return with empty hands! I absolutely must warm the room, and tomorrow I must prepare a meat dish for my child or she will fall ill."

She walked for a while as if she did not know where she was going. She turned to the left and to the right; she stopped in the middle of the sidewalk with her head down, thinking. Then, more confidently, she began to walk straight forward along Długa Street, looking long and carefully at the displays in the shop windows. She stopped in front of one store; it was a jewelry store, not very large and not especially elegant. She was evidently looking for such a store because she walked up a few small stairs and opened its glass door.

The exterior of the store had misled her. It was not as modest as it looked. In a rather large room there were a number of pieces made from gold and precious stones. The opulence of the store did not reveal itself to passersby outside, either by intention or because it was not artfully exhibited. One might suspect that the simplicity of the exterior was an effect deliberately created by the owner, seeing how closely he worked with his assistants and apprentices. He was a sturdily built, florid man with gray hair and a good-natured smile, and great cleverness in his small gray eyes. On seeing the woman enter, he stood up and asked politely how he could help her.

"I apologize, sir, if I am in the wrong place," Marta said. "I thought perhaps you could buy an item of gold from me."

"Why not, my good lady, why not?" the jeweler replied with a shrewd glint in his eyes. "What sort of item?"

For a moment there was no reply. Marta stood in the middle of the store with her eyes fixed on the floor. Her face was as white as a statue's, and as rigid. It seemed that she had concluded a conversation with herself and was now marshalling her strength to speak aloud the final word of that conversation—the word that would express a decision she had reached after great struggle and difficulty.

"What sort of item?" the jeweler repeated, glancing a little impatiently at his worktable.

"A wedding ring," she replied.

"A wedding ring!" the jeweler repeated slowly.

"A wedding ring," the apprentices whispered, raising their heads.

"A wedding ring," Marta said again. She took her hand, which was still cold, from under her heavy scarf and pulled the gold ring from her thin finger. As she did so, she staggered like a person who is about to faint and reaches involuntarily for something to support herself.

"Sit down, madame, please sit down!" the jeweler exclaimed, and his good-humored smile vanished. One of the apprentices pushed a stool toward Marta, but she did not sit down. She was living through one of the most difficult moments—perhaps the most difficult—that she had known on her toilsome march through poverty. When she took the gold wedding ring from her finger, it seemed to her that once again, and for the last time, she was being separated from the only man on earth she loved, and from the happy, unforgotten past. Her heart tightened and there was a buzzing in her head.

But the moment passed. Through sheer willpower she kept her grip on her flickering consciousness, regained all her presence of mind, and offered her wedding ring to the jeweler.

"Is this necessary? My God! Is it necessary?" the jeweler asked sympathetically.

"It is necessary," she replied dryly and briefly.

"Ah! If you wish, madame, it is better for you to sell it to me than to someone else. At least you will receive what it is worth."

He stood behind a table covered with glass boxes of gold jewelry and dropped the wedding ring onto a small brass scale. There was a long, pure chime as the two metals touched each other.

"Fine gold," the jeweler whispered.

Marta averted her face from the swaying scale. Her eyes were arrested by something else, something to which she had not paid any attention. It was something very simple. Five young men aged fifteen to twenty-five were sitting on both sides of an oblong table with delicate tools in their hands. Some were grinding and polishing precious stones of various sizes; others were melting gold in small flames that licked the rims of iron tripods. One was drawing designs for chains, bracelets, brooches, earrings, watch covers, and other such artistic products.

Marta stared at each pair of hands that she saw moving over the long table. Her eyes, which had been losing their glow a moment before, began to shine brightly with burning curiosity and almost covetous desire. In these few minutes she saw and understood more details of the jeweler's art, and more about the nature of it, than someone in different circumstances would have understood in several hours.

"My dear lady," the jeweler said from behind his table, "your ring is worth three and a half silver rubles."

Marta turned from watching the workers and quickly approached the jeweler's table.

"Sir!" she said. "These gentlemen are your assistants?"

"Yes, madame," the jeweler replied, a little surprised at such an unexpected question.

"And your pupils, surely . . ."

"Yes, madame, in a manner of speaking, pupils."

Marta looked deep into his face with flashing eyes.

"Could you accept me as an assistant and pupil?"

The jeweler's small eyes opened wide.

"You, madame! You, madame!" he stammered. "How . . . why . . . but . . ."

"Yes. Me," the woman replied firmly. "I am without any means of living. I see that a jeweler's work is not beyond my strength. Indeed, it seems to me that I could do it well, because it requires good taste, and there was a time when I had the opportunity to form that. It is true that you would have to teach me in the beginning, but that would not take long. I swear that I would work hard, and that I would understand the work. I would accept the lowest salary . . . anything. Anything."

The jeweler recovered from his astonishment. He understood what the woman who had come to sell her wedding ring wanted. His low forehead wrinkled deeply and a fleeting glint of confusion appeared in his shrewd eyes.

"You see, my dear lady," he began, "I really do not have novices in my store. These gentlemen are already seasoned, trained . . ."

Marta glanced toward the table where the workers were sitting. The one who had been drawing had just gotten up and gone to the adjoining room.

"I know how to draw," Marta said. "That is," she corrected herself hastily, "I know how to draw well enough to create designs for jewelry."

Having spoken with almost frantic eagerness, she approached the long table and sat down at the place vacated by the designer. The young men at the table moved their chairs a little, stopped working, and stared with surprise mingled with irony at the woman who was sitting among them. Without irony, but with great astonishment, the jeweler also stared at her. She paid no attention to them; she did not see them. She seized a pencil and began to draw on a sheet of white paper that she found in front of her.

There was dead silence in the shop. On the woman's face, which was bent over her work, a flush appeared. Her breath came slow and deep. Her hand, without the least tremor and with sure, accurate motions, threw light, short or trailing lines onto the paper.

The draughtsman who had gone to the neighboring room a moment before returned. He saw that his place was taken and stopped on the threshold. He was a man of perhaps twenty-three, well dressed, with neatly cut hair and a sleek mustache. He put his hands in his pockets, leaned carelessly against the corner of the wall, smiled, and exchanged jocular, knowing signs with his companions.

"But, my dear lady . . ." said the jeweler, whose patience was wearing thin.

"Just a moment! Just a moment!" Marta rejoined without taking her eyes away from her work. After a while she got up and gave the paper with her drawing to the jeweler.

"Here is a design for a bracelet," she said.

The jeweler looked hard at the drawing. The design was beautifully executed. It consisted of a garland of wide, shapely leaves fastened by a smooth, round clasp with two entwined curving stems. A bracelet made according to this design would embody the two finest attributes of such products: simplicity and elegance.

"Pretty! What can one say? Very pretty!" the jeweler said, inclining his head in both directions and looking at the drawing with the satisfied expression of a connoisseur.

"Pretty, very pretty!" he repeated, but this time with some embarrassment. "Your drawings could be very useful, but . . . but . . ." He was silent, obviously groping for words to express his thoughts. He ran his hand through his thick gray hair.

The young man standing on the threshold was still smiling. "For goodness' sake!" he said, shrugging his shoulders. "If you are refusing to hire this lady as a draughtsman . . . well, how would you say it . . . draughtswoman . . ."

A fifteen-year-old boy sitting at the table burst out laughing. The young man with neatly cut hair continued:

"If you are refusing to fulfill this lady's wish because of me, do not, please do not let that be a hindrance. You know very well that I will not be working here more than a few weeks. I am certain that in that time I will be employed in the bureau of architecture in Warsaw."

He spoke carelessly, with a touch of irony. It was obvious that for him, the jewelry store was only a stop on the way to higher, more lucrative positions.

"Yes, yes," the jeweler said, "I know that you will leave me soon . . . but I cannot—"

"How much do you pay this gentleman?" Marta interrupted. The jeweler named the figure of the daily wage given the smartly barbered young man.

"I will take half that wage," the woman said.

This time the jeweler ran both his hands through his hair.

"Oy! Oy!" he cried, pacing from one table to another. "You are presenting me with a vexing dilemma, madame!"

In spite of himself he glanced once more at the design she had drawn for a bracelet.

"Pretty! What can one say? Very pretty! Oy! Oy!" he repeated, and his sharp eyes ran anxiously around the shop. He was struggling with himself, or rather his desire for good, cheap labor was struggling with his fear of introducing into his shop something previously unheard of.

He stopped in the middle of the store and, staring at his employees, asked:

"Eh? What?"

He was probably putting this laconic question to himself, but he met his answer in the faces of the four employees who were sitting at the table. They expressed a little surprise, but far more ridicule. As for the young man with the well-cut hair, he snickered almost aloud and, as if intending to laugh to his heart's content, withdrew hurriedly to the adjoining room.

Why did these people smile and laugh? It would be difficult to say, or rather it would take a long time. In those smiles the jeweler found reinforcement for his misgivings and reluctance. He made an expressive gesture with both hands and exclaimed, looking at Marta:

"But, my dear lady! You are a woman!"

The words, as he blurted them out, were perfectly good-natured. They carried the ring of an entrepreneur's regret that, for a reason that is of no concern to him, he has lost something that would have been good for business.

Marta smiled.

"I am a woman. Yes," she said. "That is true. What of that? I can draw designs."

"Well, yes, yes!" the jeweler exclaimed, rubbing his hair again and taking his seat among his employees. "But, you see, madame, it would be something new, altogether new. I have to admit that I do not like new things! As you can see, young people work here . . . The world is mean-spirited. Do you understand . . ."

"I understand," Marta interrupted. "And thank you, sir, for the explanation, which is nothing new to me. Will you buy my ring?"

"I will, dear lady, I will."

He rose from his chair and hurried to another table. He pulled out a drawer and stood over it, brooding.

"Here is the money," he said, giving her two banknotes.

Marta nodded and walked toward the door. At the threshold she turned toward the jeweler.

"You said that my ring is worth three and half rubles, and you gave me four. I received half a ruble too much."

"But, my dear lady," the jeweler stammered, "I thought . . . I believed . . . I wanted . . . You created a design for me—"

"I understand," Marta interrupted. "Thank you, sir!"

How many times had it been, since she had begun going from door to door in poverty and pressing need, that instead of the work she had asked for, she had received charity?

Marta left the jeweler's store without tears, and without quickening or slowing her steps. Without tears, without a smile, and without a sigh she walked straight toward her apartment at a steady, even monotonous pace.

An hour before she had thought that after receiving the money from the sale of her ring, she would buy wood to make her room warmer for the night and groceries to prepare nourishing food for her child. But she did not do as she had intended. She did not go to the store. One might say that she had forgotten about everything in the world, or that she did not have the strength or courage to go anywhere else, only to the high, bare, cold den that was her apartment.

Until today, whenever she returned home, she had always hurried up the stairs. Today she started up them slowly and stumbled a few times because in the deepening twilight she did not see a steep step in front of her, or anything in front of her. She was cold and silent as the grave as she entered her room; she glanced only fleetingly at the girl, who sat hunched over in front of the fireplace. She did not speak to her. She took the scarf off her head and walked over to the bedding on the floor. Her glassy eyes stared into space.

"An outcast from society!" she whispered. She sank to the floor and lay motionless with her face buried in the pillow and her hands clasped over her head.

Jasia crawled rather than walked to the place where her mother rested quietly. She sat at the foot of the pallet with her thin, cold arms around her raised knees, resting her drooping little head on them.

Deep silence filled the room. Only beyond the window, far down in a wide space, the great city hummed and chattered, sending its dull waves of sound to that place where—abandoned by God and other people, it seemed—a woman and a child were turning to stone in the arms of misery, gasping out their souls, dying slowly.

Marta lay on the hard pallet immobile as a stone, with no thought in her head, no other feeling than mortal exhaustion. Work, ably undertaken and fairly compensated, is the most powerful and probably the only powerful hygiene for illnesses of body and soul. Nothing exhausts the physical and moral strength so quickly and deeply as being thrown from one kind of work to another, or the feverish search for work and despair at not finding it.

By now Marta did not see any road before her. There was one that was always open to her, but that one would lead to the apartment on Królewska Street. Then she would have to say to that woman with the wrinkled forehead and loose hair: "I have come back! You told the truth! I am not a human being, I am a thing!"

Inside the young woman, however, there were instincts, feelings, memories that turned her from that path, made it impossible for her to take it. She did not think about it; at that moment, she did not think about anything. Suddenly she heard as if through her sleep a hoarse, wracking cough. The sound sent a shudder through her and instantly wrenched her from her stony immobility. She shifted on her pallet and sat up straight.

"Was that you coughing, Jasia?"

"It was I, Mama!"

The mother's voice was trembling and choked. The child's was faint and cracked.

Marta seized the girl and laid her on her lap. She touched her forehead: it was hot. She pressed her hand to her chest, where her little heart was pounding spasmodically.

"Oh, my God!" the woman moaned. "Not this! Anything but this!"

In the deep dusk she could not see her daughter's face clearly. She lit a small lamp and, lifting the four-year-old in her arms as if she were a tiny baby, held her head under its light. The girl had red blotches on her face—signs of fever—and her wide pupils stared out with an expression of deep, mute suffering. She coughed again and languidly rested her heavy head on her mother's arm.

At midnight a woman wearing a black scarf ran from the attic down the tall staircase. She was surrounded by darkness, but she did not stagger as she had a few hours ago. She did not stumble on the steep steps or stop in the street to catch her breath. It was as if she had wings, and that was no idle metaphor. She was almost lifted from the ground by fear and anguish.

In a little less than half an hour she returned, but not alone. A young man wearing a hat and an expensive fur coat walked in with her. They entered the room and approached the pallet on the floor. A child with a red, feverish face was writhing there in a deep malaise, coughing incessantly.

The doctor looked around for a chair. He did not see one, so he knelt on the floor. The woman stood at the foot of the pallet neither moving nor speaking, with grim fire in her eyes.

"How cold it is in here!" the man said, standing up.

The woman did not answer.

"What will I write on?"

There was a bottle of ink on the windowsill. Pens and a sheet of paper lay next to it. The doctor bent over and wrote a prescription.

"The child has a respiratory infection: bronchitis. Heat the room and give her medicine regularly."

He said a few more words and picked up his hat, which had been lying on the floor.

The woman reached into her pocket and silently offered him her hand with money in it. Once more the doctor glanced quickly around and did not extend his hand.

"No need," he said as he reached the threshold. "No need! The child is weak and worn out. The illness will be long and she will need a good deal of medicine. I will come tomorrow."

He left. The widow fell on her knees in front of the pallet and held her child close.

"Oh, my child! My only child!" she whispered. "Forgive your mother! Forgive me! I could not warm you, I could not feed you! I let you fall victim to cold and hunger! You are weak and tired. You are ill! Oh, my child . . ."

She moved blindly from the pallet, beat her forehead on the floor and buried her hands in her hair.

"Oh, I have sunk so low! I am so worthless, so miserable!"

An hour later, medicine brought from town stood next to the ailing child, and at dawn, when the grocery shops opened, a large, hot fire burned in the fireplace, filling the room with refreshing warmth.

The doctor's prediction was fulfilled. Jasia's illness lasted for a long time. The doctor visited every day. When he arrived for the tenth time, the child still had a high fever; her hoarse, labored breathing could be heard from the floor like the scraping of a saw.

Again Marta stood mute and motionless at the foot of the pallet. The doctor turned to her.

"Do not lose hope, madame," he said gently. "Your child can recover her health, but now, especially today and tomorrow, she needs exceptionally diligent care. It is too cold in here again. The temperature should be at least six degrees higher. Bring the medicine I prescribed as soon as possible and give it to the child throughout the night without missing a dose. It may be a little too expensive, but it is the only remedy."

He left. Marta stood in the middle of the room with her arms crossed on her chest, staring at the floor.

Raise the temperature of the room! With what? Buy medicine! With what?

She did not have a penny in her pocket. On the first day of her child's illness she had had four rubles and a few złotys; that treasure had burned up in the hearth, where a fire blazed every day, and in the retort at the apothecary's shop, to which she ran several times a day.

She did not pull her hair any longer; she did not fall on the floor or beat her chest in self-abasement. She was hardly even a shadow of the old Marta. She had grown haggard and her yellowed face was filled with the suffering that had become the normal state of her soul. That suffering, having penetrated the most delicate fibers of her body, boiled in her chest and head dully and silently, but unceasingly. Her blue lips were tightly set, like those of a person who is accustomed to clench her teeth to stop her moans and cries. Her eyes were faded and glassy as she glanced around the room.

Perhaps there was something to sell?

No—there was nothing besides the pillow under the head of the sick child, the woolen cover under which the child breathed heavily, and two shirts and some old dresses of the child's for which no one would give even enough to buy a bundle of wood.

The woman let her hands fall helplessly.

"What will I do?" she whispered with her head bowed. "What can I do? Let her die? I will lie next to her and die with her!"

At that moment the child moved on the pallet and emitted a weak cry. A joyful laugh and an inarticulate moan of sorrow were mingled in it.

"Papa!" she cried, reaching into the air with her thin, hot hands. "Papa! Papa!"

Oh, heartbreak! The murderous fever had brought the image of her father before her. She was smiling at him, moaning to him, calling for help.

Marta lifted her head. Suddenly her eyes, which until then had been dry and without luster, were flooded with tears. She wrung her hands and looked at her child as if through a curtain of glass.

"You are calling your father!" she whispered with her chest heaving. "He could certainly have brought you help! He would have worked and given you a warm room and food, and now medicine."

She stood silent for a moment. Suddenly she rushed toward the pallet and stood in front of it.

"Ah!" she cried. "I will not leave you without help, either! Your father would have worked for you. Your mother—will go and beg!"

A red flush covered her sallow face and her eyes burned with passionate resolve. She threw her black scarf onto her head and ran down to the concierge's apartment. There, in front of a fire where food was cooking, sat a woman in a big cap and thick shoes.

Marta stopped in front of her, breathless from running.

"Madame!" she cried. "For pity's sake . . . for charity's sake . . ."

"You want money, no doubt!" the woman replied huffily. "I have none. I have none. Where would I get—"

"No, no! Not money! I will go to town for that! Meanwhile, sit with my sick child!"

The woman frowned, though not so angrily as at first.

"Do I have the time to watch my ladybird's sick child . . ."

Marta leaned over, grasped the woman's large, thick, hard hand, and put it to her lips.

"Have pity, madame! Be charitable and sit with her. She wants to drink constantly. She thrashes about and cannot lie still. I cannot leave her alone today."

She kissed the hand which not so long ago had beaten her child.

"Well, well, never mind. I will go, I will go and sit with her, but do not be too long, because in an hour my child will return from school and must be fed!"

The dark figure of a woman could be seen running in the deep shadow near the arched gate of the building.

"I will go. I will reach out. I will beg," Marta whispered to herself.

She ran into the street, stopped, thought for a moment and hurried toward Świętojerska. The flaming wings of fear and anguish carried her again with astonishing speed. Blind, deaf, paying no attention to the jostling of passersby or their looks or sneers, she cut through the crowd like lightning and sped along the sidewalk toward one of the places in which she had encountered a compassionate hand.

At last she stopped before the gate through which she had entered joyfully once, with hope and pride. She took a deep breath and went quickly up the lighted stairs. With a trembling hand she touched the handle of the electric doorbell. The door opened; a young, nimble, smartly dressed maid stood on the threshold. A wave of light struck Marta's eyes while a wave of noise—the din of people's voices—assailed her ears. The hallway was brightly lit, and behind the door to the drawing room a dozen, perhaps several dozen voices buzzed, chatted, and laughed.

"What does madame wish?" the servant asked.

"I have business with Madame Rudzińska."

"Oh! Then come tomorrow, please. Tonight there is the weekly soiree; the guests are just gathering. Madame cannot leave the drawing room."

Marta stepped back onto the stairway. The servant closed the door behind her. Behind that door lived a truly kind, sincerely compassionate woman, but her merciful hand could not open to Marta at that moment. And that is a very normal thing.

There is a cruel uncertainty about compassionate hands. Even the best man cannot devote every minute of his life to good deeds. Not only pressing difficulties and personal concerns, but otherwise blameless, obligatory and even socially responsible occupations turn the compassionate hand to other goals and actions, so that it is not a reliable support for those in misery.

Marta walked, or rather ran, toward Krakowskie Przemieście. She was certainly thinking of the kind bookseller. But she had hardly stopped in front of the bookshop and looked through the window when she stepped back onto the sidewalk. In the bookshop she saw several people, a few fashionably dressed ladies and two men with cheerful faces, who were selecting and buying books.

||

It was between seven and eight in the evening, the time when the great city boils inside and out with traffic moving at dizzying speeds, and is decked out in its most dazzling garb. The sights and sounds of civilization are multiplied almost to infinity, inside buildings, along the streets, and through wide spaces full of bright light, music, crowds, talk. Night life is half of life, perhaps more for those living in a city where the sun shines only a few hours a day through long months.

The weather was fine, and Krakowskie Przedmieście seethed with wheel and foot traffic, life, and hurry. A little March snow fell on the frozen ground and cleared the sky of white clouds. Now the blue tent of night unfolded over the town, deep, dark, and starry.

Wheels rattling constantly like endless thunder ran through the middle of the street. Thousands of human heads moved in waves along the sidewalks. It was almost as bright as day there because the gaslights and the multitude of store windows flooded the wide space with light.

The main streets of Warsaw are never so crowded as at that time—crowded with hardworking people and with idlers. The working people hurry to their rest or some entertainment. The idle bask in their favorite elements: the noise, to which they listen mindlessly, the varied sights, at which they gape as the glare caresses their sense of sight, perhaps the mysterious evening twilight itself. In this rushing, racing, chattering crowd there are no doubt many compassionate souls, but they are occupied with something other than pity. They are caught in the whirlpool of the world, and the end of the day has summoned them to join the rush. Amusements, business matters, emotions at this hour capture the imagination, engage the thoughts, and give the hurrying steps their goal.

And by the artificial light the furrows on the faces of the suffering appear less clearly than by daylight; the beams of the lamps reflected in faded eyes imitate the lights of health and life; the rattle and the noise deafen the voices from exhausted lungs. The compassionate souls and hands stop most often and longest where the skeleton of a poor person rings loudest with its bare bones, and stares most terrifyingly with its corpse's eyes.

Marta had been on Krakowskie Przedmieście for a quarter of an hour.

A quarter of an hour? A year, a century, since the beginning of time!

She did not run now. She walked slowly. Stiff, mute, with her own face inert and her eyes vacant, she glanced at the faces of those who passed her.

The flaming wings that she had had an hour ago had fallen away and she was overwhelmed by exhaustion, but she walked on, over the streaks of light on the pavement. In the twilight before her, over her, and around her, between the stars in the sky and the faces of people moving on the earth, floated the face of her child, staring at her with a silent lament. She walked on, for at the sight of people an accusation formed itself clearly in her mind for the first time. Resentment toward them simmered in her heart with all the tears that had clotted there and slowly turned to a boiling cauldron.

For the first time it occurred to her that people were to blame for her endless misery—that they should carry the heavy load of her life and her child's. At this moment the feeling of personal responsibility died out in her completely. She felt weak as a child, helpless and exhausted as a dying person.

"These powerful, knowledgeable, fortunate people," she thought, "should share what the world gives them with me, to whom it saw fit to give nothing."

However, she had not yet held out her hand even once.

Every time she passed a graceful, well-dressed woman walking with a light step, she took her hand from the folds of her thick scarf, but she did not hold it out. She opened her mouth, but said nothing. Her feeble voice was silenced by fear amid the noise of the street, in which it would undoubtedly have drowned, unheard by anyone. An invisible force struck her hand and threw it down.

Was it the force of shame?

The poor, sick child of an impoverished woman was writhing on a hard pallet, mumbling through lips parched with fever. With a rasping voice and weakening lungs, she was moaning and calling her dead father!

Two ladies in velvet coats walked hurriedly by, arm in arm, talking cheerfully. One was young and beautiful as an angel.

Marta stood in their way.

"Madame!" she said. "Madame!"

Her voice was soft, but she was not whining. She did not know how to tune it; perhaps she had not thought about how to speak in the pleading tone of a beggar. So the ladies did not understand her cry for help. They quickly passed her by, but then they stopped and one asked, turning her head:

"What is it, my dear? Have we lost something?"

There was no answer because Marta turned in the opposite direction and walked on quickly, as if she wanted to run away from the women and from the place where she had accosted them.

She slowed down. Blood-red flushes appeared on her sallow, faded, sunken cheeks—signs of the fever that burned in her heart. Keen, piercing lights flashed in her otherwise dull eyes, reflecting the conflagration of dark thoughts that was raging in her mind.

She moved on even more slowly and stopped again. A man was walking along the sidewalk, bent a little under the weight of his elegant fur coat, which was evidently heavy for him. Marta looked keenly into his face. It was good-natured, gentle, and garnished with a thick mustache as white as milk.

She took her hand from the thick folds of her scarf again, but did not reach out with it. She did say more loudly than before:

"Sir! Sir!"

The man was about to pass her, but suddenly he stopped. He looked into the face of the woman on whom lamplight fell from a wide window, and he understood what she wanted. He reached into the pocket of his coat and took out a small purse. He seemed to be searching for something among the coins there; he found what he was looking for, put a little money into her hand, and walked away. Marta looked at the offering and gave a hollow laugh. For her begging she had received tenpence.

The gray, stooped passerby had a compassionate hand. But could he know what she needed, this woman who called to him for help? If he had known, would he have wanted to help her, and could he have helped her sufficiently? How many times must a begging woman hold out her hand before such gifts add up to what for her are the greatest riches: enough to buy a bundle of wood and a bottle of medicine?

She walked on, stiff, silent, with a coin in her clenched hand. She stopped again. She did not look at the passersby now; she gazed into a wide window that was transparent as crystal and blazing with light. It was the window of a shop that by artificial light looked like an enchanted palace.

In the shop, rich purple curtains hung in rolls between marble columns. Patterned rugs on the walls pampered the eye with the colors of roses and the green of grass, forming a background for white sculpted busts. From bronze bases the branching arms of candelabra extended, gleaming with gold. Silver vases and goblets rose there, and porcelain baskets and crystal bells concealing groups of marble figurines. But the smoldering black eyes that stared from the street into the interior of the store were not trained on all that beauty and wealth.

In front of a long rosewood table, festooned with strips of fluffy patterned carpet like garlands of gigantic flowers, stood two men. One was selling, the other buying. They were carrying on a spirited conversation. The seller's face glowed; the buyer's was pensive and a little grieved at having to choose between objects that were masterpieces of craftsmanship and taste.

The glass door opened slowly and a woman entered the opulent store. She wore a black dress with a wide white band at the bottom. A large black scarf covered her head and fell with its ends crossing on her chest. Her yellow, wrinkled forehead was half covered by her disheveled hair, which was escaping from under her scarf. Her face was covered with a dark flush; her lips were colorless as paper.

The two men heard the door opening and looked toward the woman. She stopped in the doorway near a console with a marble top that stood under a large mirror. She had slipped into this sanctuary of wealth like a phantom, and like a phantom she stood motionless and silent by the wall.

"What would you like, madame?" asked the merchant, inclining his head slightly as he looked at the still, dark figure from behind a bouquet of artificial flowers.

But she did not look at him. She fixed her eyes on the buyer, who had an expensive fur coat thrown casually over his shoulders and one white hand resting on a decorative rug. He looked at her absently.

"What would you like, madame?" the merchant repeated. He gave her a long look, scrutinizing her black-clad figure from head to foot, and added more sharply, "Why do you not answer, madame?"

She went on staring at the man in the expensive fur coat.

It was as if she had a cruel, rending hand in her chest and a fire in her head, because her breath came shorter and faster and dark purple covered her cheeks and forehead. Suddenly she took her hand from the folds of her scarf and held it out. Her quivering blue lips opened and closed several times.

"Sir!" she said at last. "Kind sir! For medicine for my sick child!"

Her thin, cold hand trembled like an aspen leaf. Her voice rang with the long, mournful whine of the beggar.

The man in the fur coat looked at her for a moment and shrugged slightly.

"My dear lady!" he said dryly. "Are you not ashamed to beg? You are young and healthy. You can work!"

He turned back to the rosewood table covered with carpets and silver baskets. With a smile the merchant unfolded yet another carpet. The men resumed the conversation the woman had interrupted.

The woman in black still stood at the door as if some ominous, irresistible power had cast a spell over her. Her face and figure looked ominous at that moment. The words she had heard were like a drop that caused the goblet of poison she had been drinking for a long time to overflow. That drop fell deep into her heart with the force of a narcotic, straining her nerves, blinding her mind, dulling her conscience.

"You can work!" Could the man who said these words begin to imagine how sarcastic, how uncharitable they seemed to this woman who had exhausted her spirit and wasted her physical strength in useless attempts to work? Who had lost respect for herself, seen her self-esteem scatter into worthless dust because she could not work?

This man could not know that. His behavior toward her could not serve as evidence of a lack of kindness and pity in his heart. Very likely he was a compassionate man; very likely he would open a generous hand to a helpless cripple, or someone grown decrepit with age or reduced by illness. But this woman who had put out her hand to beg from him was young, not touched by any physical handicap. Her outward appearance carried no visible sign of illness.

He did not know about the moral disability that had brought her where she was, or about the devouring fever that for some time had burned in her heart, changing her finer human feelings into dust and ashes by degrees, filling her mind with ever more dense and suffocating dark smoke, and poisoning her thoughts. He did not know, so he said: "You are young and healthy. You can work!"

As a general rule, he would have been justified in saying that. Yet he had unwittingly perpetrated a cruel injustice.

A few months ago, perhaps a few weeks ago, Marta would have understood everything that was true and right in what he had said to her. But if she had been standing before him then, she would have asked for work—nothing more, only work. Now she was begging for alms, and now she heard nothing in his words but sneering injustice.

The red blushes that had covered her cheeks and forehead when she put out her hand had vanished without a trace. Amid the deadly whiteness that covered her face, her sunken eyes, deep and black as caves, burned with volcanic fire. A volcano was also erupting in her heaving chest, a volcano of anger, envy, and—covetousness.

Anger, envy, covetousness? Could it be that Marta, this child from a quiet, charming country house; this once respected married woman, this happy mother, this virtuous being who would not have carried on with work she was not capable of doing to save her life; this energetic worker who had searched, in the sweat of her brow and the pain of her heart, by every road in the world for an honest piece of bread; this proud soul who had stretched out her hands to God with a plea to save her from the lot of a beggar; could she fall prey to these cruel, infernal feelings that lead to a hell of evil desires and actions?

Yes, it could be so—unfortunately! Unfortunately! Not only could it be so, it had to be so. It was made so by the inflexible, eternal logic of human nature, which cannot be swayed by anything in the world. Marta was not a bodiless angel; she was not an airy ideal untouched and unbattered by earthly winds, because there is no such thing. She was a human being, and if in human nature there are lofty heights on which intellect, heroism, and the virtues of devotion develop, there are also deep chasms in which vipers lurk silently in the form of perilous temptations and dark instincts. It is not acceptable to exhaust a human being so profoundly, or shake her so violently, as to stir this mysterious abyss of silent, latent vice.

In human nature there are enormous powers, but there are also measureless impossibilities. Each human being should be endowed with appropriate rights and tools for survival, appropriate obligations and responsibilities. Otherwise she will not amount to anything, she will not endure, and she will not be able to hold her own against those who do.

A poisonous bitterness that for a long time had gathered drop by drop in Marta's heart now rose in an enormous wave. With it came long-dormant, then gradually awakening, now furiously rampaging vipers of temptation and serpents of passion.

The young man in the expensive fur coat was choosing carpets, silver baskets, china vases, and marble statuettes. He bought many; no doubt he wanted to furnish a beautiful house to which he planned to bring a young wife. He and the merchant were absorbed in what they were doing and forgot about the woman who stood by the wall in stony immobility, silent as the grave. But she did not take her eyes off the buyer's hand, which held a large, thick purse filled with money.

"Why does he have so much while I have nothing?" she thought. "What right did he have to refuse alms to me? To me, when my child is dying in the cold without help, while he holds in his hand such great wealth? He lied when he said that I am young and healthy! I am more than old because I have outlived myself. Do I know what became of the old Marta? I am terribly ill because I am helpless as a child . . . Why do people demand that I live by my own power, since they gave me no power? Why did they not give me power, if now they demand that I live by it? He is one of my oppressors; he owes me something! He should give me something!"

The woman's thoughts were terrible—mindlessly unjustified—but in her case they were inevitable and understandable. They originated from the same injuries, the same turns of fate, the same powerlessness on the one hand and need and responsibility on the other, that give rise to all the wild doctrines that from time to time erupt in the world in conflagration and murder—all the raging passions that arise because of a lack of justice, lose the sense of justice, and, born of injury, inflict injury.

"Well," said the buyer, "three hundred złotys for the rug and five hundred for these baskets, two hundred for the china vase, and . . ."

He was taking out his money to pay the merchant, but he stopped suddenly.

"Ah!" he exclaimed. "I almost forgot! You were supposed to give me this bronze group and that one over there . . ."

The merchant stepped quickly in the direction of those items, smiling and eager to please.

"This one?" he asked.

"No, that one. Niobe with her children."

"Niobe? It seems to me that you wanted Cupid with Venus."

"Perhaps. I must look at them again."

With a careless hand that was obviously accustomed to spend money freely, he threw his purse onto the marble top of the console and followed the merchant farther into the store, where groups of figurines depicting mythological characters, cast in bronze or sculpted in marble, stood on rosewood shelves under crystal bells. The purse so casually thrown down opened wider, and a few banknotes of various denominations fell out of it onto the marble slab.

The woman standing by the wall stared at the banknotes with deep, burning dark eyes. As certain species of snakes mesmerize birds, the multi-colored notes cast a riveting spell on her.

What thoughts revolved in her mind while she was staring that way at someone else's wealth? It is difficult to enumerate them and still more diffi-cult to extract a coherent theme. These were not thoughts, but chaos born in a feverish body and intensified by the storm in her soul. After staring at the money for two seconds, Marta began to tremble all over. She lowered her eyelids and raised them again; she took her hand out of the folds of her scarf and then tucked it back in.

She struggled, but unfortunately there was no hope of winning. There was no hope because there was not enough strength left in her to resist the shameful temptation; because she no longer had the clarity of mind to un-derstand that temptation; because she no longer had any conscience, for it had drowned in the sea of bitterness accrued in her heart; and because she had no shame, for it was pushed out by contempt for herself, by the long series of humiliations she had endured and alms she had accepted. Finally, she had no hope of winning because she was not fully conscious. Her body was burning with fever from hunger, cold, sleeplessness, tears, and despair. Dark furies born deep within her troubled soul had seized her spirit and become entangled with it.

All at once her hand made a quick motion. One of the banknotes van-ished from the marble slab, and the glass door opened and slammed shut.

The two men farther inside the store who had been so preoccupied with the choice of figurines heard a loud, unexpected noise and turned their heads.

"What was that?" asked the buyer.

The merchant rushed to the middle of the store.

"That woman ran out so suddenly!" he exclaimed. "She probably stole something!"

The young man turned toward the door.

"As a matter of fact," he said with a smile, looking at the marble slab, "she stole a three-ruble note from me. I only had one, and now it is gone."

"Ah, the wicked beggar!" cried the merchant. "How is it possible? A theft at my store? Under my eyes? Ah! Brazen!"

He bounded to the door and opened it halfway.

"Police!" he cried at the top of his voice, standing on the threshold. "Police!"

"How can I help you?" replied a voice from the street.

A yellow brass badge flashed on the chest of a man who stood on the sidewalk in the stream of light from the store.

"There!" said the merchant, panting with anger and pointing a finger toward the street. "A woman just stole three rubles in my store and ran out there!"

"Which way did she run?"

"That way," said a passerby who had heard the merchant's words and stopped in front of the store. He pointed toward Nowy Świat Street. "I met her. She is dressed all in black. She flew like a madwoman without seeing anything in front of her. I thought she was a lunatic!"

"You must catch her!" said the merchant to the policeman.

"Of course, sir!" cried the man with the yellow badge. He leaped forward and called loudly:

"People: attention! A thief is running toward Nowy Świat! Catch her!"

The door of the shop closed. Within seconds, even as the young man was apologizing to the merchant for causing so much trouble over such a small loss, a noisy, crowded scene took shape on the street.

Like lightning cutting through clouds, the woman in black ran among the throngs of pedestrians, racing blindly toward Nowy Świat. Probably she did not know which way she was running or which way she should run. She was not in possession of herself; she was half mad. At this moment she may have regretted having committed a shameful act, but she had committed it, and she was nearly out of her mind with terror. Driven by her survival instinct, she ran from people, but they were in front of her, behind her, around her. It seemed to her that by running swiftly, blindly, desperately, she could escape them.

Pedestrians she jostled looked after her with expressions of surprise and fear. They moved out of her way, assuming that she had lost her mind, or that she was hurrying because of some urgent need. But soon the cry sounded along the street:

"Catch her!"

Then a new one rang out:

"Thief!"

The words were not spoken by one voice. They came from the direction she had run from, and were tossed from mouth to mouth, growing like fireballs thrown by a powerful hand and rolling along the street with a rising roar. She was running more slowly now and stopped for a second because her strength was flagging. She heard the threatening shouts behind her.

The shouts and the trampling of people running along the sidewalk grew louder and louder. She shook from head to foot with terrible tremors and ran faster, as if she had wings. Indeed, she had them now—not wings of pain, but wings of fear.

Suddenly she felt that she could not run, not because she had lost her strength—her wings of fear almost lifted her off the ground—but because the people walking in the opposite direction began to block her way. They reached out and snatched at her dress. Her wings became not only swift but elastic, carrying her in various directions. With astonishingly nimble, light movements she avoided the outstretched hands, brushing against them but escaping.

Then, however, a few steps away, she saw not single figures but a crowd of people that filled the entire width of the sidewalk. It was impossible to pass them; if she confronted them, she would be caught.

She jumped from the sidewalk into the middle of the street, where there were many wheels and horses' hooves, but almost no people.

She ran in the street, passing the wheels and horses' hooves with the same agility she had shown in eluding the people on the sidewalk. But the moment she ran into the middle of the street, a dark mass of pursuers followed her. Who were they? In front of the moving throng gleamed yellow brass; behind them, shouting and laughing, ran street gawkers who were always ready to join in any lively scene. Behind them, idlers moved more slowly, looking for entertainment wherever they saw a crowd.

Cabs and private carriages began to dwindle in number. The woman stopped in the middle of the street and looked behind her.

There were only a few dozen steps between her and a black mass of figures shouting with human voices. She stood still for a few seconds, then once more ran straight ahead. A moving black mass appeared before her, like the one following her but different in shape; oblong and tall, with the great burning eye of a purple lantern at its top. A bright silver bell gave a long, piercing, warning ring, and the purple eye moved rapidly forward. Heavy wheels turned with a hollow rattle and horses' hooves made metallic sounds as they struck the iron bars that lay on the ground, bars on which the wheels moved.

It was an enormous omnibus on rails, pulled by four large, stalwart horses. It was full of people and weighed down with heavy loads.

The woman was still running down the middle of the street. Behind and in front of her two black masses came rushing, one shouting and laughing, the other ringing, rattling dully and glaring with a huge purple eye. Both were moving straight toward the fleeing woman. If she did not leap aside, one of the masses would swallow her. She swerved from her straight course, stopped, and looked around.

Her pursuers were hardly a dozen steps behind her. The same distance separated her from the large, steadily moving omnibus. But the crowd ran more slowly than the omnibus, which moved very fast.

She did not run any further. Perhaps she lacked the strength; perhaps she had decided to put an end to this terrible chase. She stood with her body turned toward the oncoming omnibus but with her face to the people who were running, running. Now the light of conscious thought shone in her eyes. It seemed that she was making a choice. What kind of choice? In one direction she saw shame, derision, prison, long, perhaps endless suffering, and from the other, death—terrible death, but sudden as a thunderbolt.

Yet her survival instinct did not leave her completely. Death must have seemed more terrible to her than people, because a moment before she had swerved from the straight line over which salvation was rushing toward her.

Yes—but now she began to move back to that line. The man with the yellow badge passed the gawkers who were running behind him. He reached out and touched the edge of her scarf. She jumped away; she stopped on one of the iron rails. With her face raised to the dark sky, she reached up with both hands. Her mouth opened in a vague cry.

Did she hurl toward the starry heavens a mournful complaint, a word of forgiveness, or the name of her child? No one heard. The man with the brass badge, taken off guard by the woman's sudden leap, found himself next to her and pulled at her scarf. Quick as lightning she threw off the scarf, leaving it in the policeman's hand, and dropped to the ground.

"Stop! Stop!" A terrible shriek ran through the crowd.

But the purple eye did not want to hear. It flew on through the air, and horses' hooves rang on the iron rails.

"Stop! Stop!" the crowd shouted ceaselessly, frantically. The driver moved abruptly in his seat, stood up, gathered up the long reins, and in a voice hoarse with terror screamed to his horses to stop.

They stopped, but only when the heavy wheels had moved with a light clacking sound off the chest of the woman who lay stretched out on the street.

The crowd stood quiet as the grave in the middle of the elegant avenue. Faces pale with horror and bodies breathing heavily with fear bent over the dark figure that lay still as a stain on the white snow.

The wheel of a great omnibus had crushed Marta's chest and taken her life. Her face was untouched; she stared with glassy eyes at the starry sky.

Anna Gąsienica Byrcyn is a translator of Polish poetry and prose in English. She has been teaching Polish language and Polish literature for many years at various American universities, among them the University of Illinois, Indiana University, the University of Pittsburgh, Loyola University, and Saint Xavier University.

Stephanie Kraft holds a PhD in English literature from the University of Rochester with a specialty in nineteenth-century literature. She is the translator of *Stone Tablets* by Wojciech Żukrowski.

Grażyna J. Kozaczka is a distinguished professor of English and the director of the All College Honors Program at Cazenovia College. She is the author of *William Dean Howells and John Cheever: The Failure of the American Dream* and *Writing the Polish American Woman in Postwar Ethnic Fiction*. She has also authored *Old World Stitchery* and articles on Polish folk dress and adornment.